"You weren't going to tell me about the baby, is that it?"

Lori heard the anger in Cord's voice and flinched. "I was just waiting for the right time."

"The right time." He swore, turning away from her.

"I didn't want to upset you before the rodeo finals," she said quietly.

"To hell with the finals." With another muttered oath, he faced her again. "We'll get married right away," he said, his voice rough with emotion. "We can be in Reno by tomorrow night. We'll get married the next day."

Lori felt a lump forming in her throat. They were the words she wanted so badly to hear, yet they'd been spoken for all the wrong reasons. "I'm not going to marry you," she said evenly.

"The hell you're not." He pulled off his hat and laid it on the table. "I'm not going to argue with you, Lori. We *are* getting married, and that's it."

Dear Reader,

Spring always seems like a good time to start something new, so this month it's Marilyn Pappano's wonderful new Western miniseries, HEARTBREAK CANYON. *Cattleman's Promise* is a terrific introduction to the men of Heartbreak, Oklahoma—not to mention the women who change their lives. So settle in for the story of this rugged loner and the single mom who teaches him the joys of family life.

Unfortunately, all good things must end someday, and this month we bid farewell to Justine Davis's TRINITY STREET WEST. But what a finale! Clay Yeager has been an unseen presence in all the books in this miniseries, and at last here he is in the flesh, hero of his own story in *Clay Yeager's Redemption*. And, as befits the conclusion to such a fabulous group of novels, you'll get one last look at the lives and loves of all your favorite characters before the book is through. And in more miniseries news, Doreen Roberts continues RODEO MEN with *A Forever Kind of Cowboy*, a runaway bride story you'll fall in love with. *The Tough Guy and the Toddler* is the newest from Diane Pershing, and it's our MEN IN BLUE title, with a great cop hero. Christine Scott makes the move to Intimate Moments with *Her Second Chance Family*, an emotional and memorable FAMILIES ARE FOREVER title. Finally, welcome new writer Claire King, whose *Knight in a White Stetson* is both our WAY OUT WEST title and a fun and unforgettable debut.

As always, we hope you enjoy all our books—and that you'll come back next month, when Silhouette Intimate Moments brings you six more examples of the most exciting romance reading around.

Yours,

Leslie J. Wainger
Executive Senior Editor

Please address questions and book requests to:
Silhouette Reader Service
U.S.: 3010 Walden Ave., P.O. Box 1325, Buffalo, NY 14269
Canadian: P.O. Box 609, Fort Erie, Ont. L2A 5X3

A FOREVER KIND OF COWBOY

DOREEN ROBERTS

Silhouette®
INTIMATE™MOMENTS®

Published by Silhouette Books

America's Publisher of Contemporary Romance

SILHOUETTE BOOKS

ISBN 0-373-07927-3

A FOREVER KIND OF COWBOY

Copyright © 1999 by Doreen Roberts

Look us up on-line at: http://www.romance.net

Printed in U.S.A.

Books by Doreen Roberts

Silhouette Intimate Moments

Gambler's Gold #215
Willing Accomplice #239
Forbidden Jade #266
Threat of Exposure #295
Desert Heat #319
In the Line of Duty #379
Broken Wings #422
Road to Freedom #442
In a Stranger's Eyes #475
Only a Dream Away #513
Where There's Smoke #567
So Little Time #653
A Cowboy's Heart #705
Every Waking Moment #783
The Mercenary and the
  Marriage Vow #861
*Home Is Where the Cowboy Is #909
*A Forever Kind of Cowboy #927

* Rodeo Men

Silhouette Romance

Home for the Holidays #765
A Mom for Christmas #1195
In Love with the Boss #1271

DOREEN ROBERTS

lives with her husband, who is also her manager and her biggest fan, in the beautiful city of Portland, Oregon. She believes that everyone should have a little adventure now and again to add interest to their lives. She believes in taking risks and has been known to embark on an adventure or two of her own. She is happiest, however, when she is creating stories about the biggest adventure of all—falling in love and learning to live happily ever after.

To Bill,
for being a forever kind of man.
I love you.

Prologue

It was like walking in a minefield. Thick branches of towering evergreens blocked out the light from the moon and closed her inside the cool, damp darkness of the forest. Every step she took seemed to put obstacles in her path—exposed roots, sudden deep ruts and tangled tendrils of undergrowth that threatened to send her sprawling facedown in the dirt.

Although it was still early September, it got cold in the Oregon mountains at night. Her sweatshirt wasn't much protection against the night wind. She shivered, and hugged herself in an attempt to keep warm.

She'd never been alone in a forest before. She couldn't remember the last time she'd been alone in the dark...except for the comforting security of her bedroom. For a second or two the treacherous longing to be back in that white-and-lavender haven was almost unbearable.

Fiercely she reminded herself of the reasons she'd left Seattle. The reasons that had seemed overwhelming at the time…but right now were beginning to appear less intimidating in light of her present predicament.

She had no idea where she was or where she was going. The trails she followed led nowhere, and all around her the night creatures whispered and snuffled, creeping ever closer to this stranger in their midst. Any minute now she expected to hear the menacing growl of a bear or the padding footsteps of a mountain lion.

She was a city girl, and couldn't tell the difference between the scuffling of a harmless squirrel and the shifting of a cougar above her head. Did they sleep at night? Or were they prowling the forest, just waiting for some unsuspecting human to wander into their territory?

A sudden rustling off to her left, too loud to be anything smaller than a cat, sent chills racing down her back. The urge to run was almost too potent too ignore, but she made herself stand motionless, aware that in this environment she would be at the mercy of a predator. She shivered, feeling the clammy night air through her torn clothing.

Gradually the rustling died away, and she forced her taut muscles to relax. If only she could see. If only she could know for certain that she was heading toward the road, instead of deeper into the forest. Bracing herself, she stepped out again…into nothing.

It was as if the ground had opened up in front of her. She toppled forward, hands outstretched to break her fall. She hit the ground hard with her shoulder, but before she could take a breath she was rolling down a steep incline. Brambles and sharp twigs tore at her exposed skin and clawed at her face. She felt a tug on her sleeve, which slowed her descent for a second or two before whatever she'd gotten caught on ripped away from her shirt. On down she tumbled, her head spinning, her hands scrabbling for a hold.

At long last she jolted to a halt, checked by the wide trunk of a fir. The impact knocked the breath out of her and she lay there for a moment, determinedly holding back tears. She couldn't give in now. Not after all she'd been through. She had to keep going.

Wearily she struggled to her feet and brushed the dirt and brush from her clothes as best she could. She'd never felt this exhausted in her entire twenty-two years, she thought, doing her best to pluck the twigs from her matted hair. She must look terrible. If Richard could see her now he wouldn't recognize her. The thought gave her a little twist of satisfaction.

Deciding it would be easier to keep going down than to climb back up to the trail, she cautiously began a more sedate descent. A soft sound from just a few feet below brought her to a halt again. The faint trickling of water raised her hopes. She was close to a stream. Maybe if she followed it down, she'd find civilization somewhere along the way.

She found it a few minutes later...a narrow gully that disappeared into the darkness ahead. But here the trees weren't quite so thick, and there was enough light to see where she trod. Her feet hurt, her knees felt weak and her back ached, but she struggled on, preferring the pain of moving to sitting uselessly under a tree. At least she was making an effort to improve the situation. In fact, now that she had a definite goal she was beginning to feel more optimistic.

She came upon the cabin without warning. She froze at the sight of it, aware that she hadn't prepared a story to explain why she was wandering around the forest alone at night. There were no lights on inside. The occupants would be fast asleep by now.

She hesitated, torn between the urgent need to rest her

aching body and the necessity of accounting for her presence. Then it dawned on her. There was no car. If people were there, surely they would have had to use some kind of transportation to get there. She strained her ears but could hear no traffic that would indicate a road nearby. All she could hear was the wind sighing in the trees and the never-ending scuffles of the animal nightlife.

Feeling a little less apprehensive, she crept closer, her nerves tensed to react at the slightest movement. It was probably a vacation cabin, stuck all the way out here in the woods, she assured herself. No one would possibly want to live in these primitive surroundings.

She reached a window and peeked in. She could see nothing through the dusty panes of glass. Treading silently, she stole around the entire cabin. It wasn't big enough to be a real house. And nowhere could she see anything that resembled transportation.

The need to lie down was becoming imperative. Her entire body shook from exhaustion. The effects of what she'd been through were beginning to make themselves felt, and she knew she had to rest or she'd collapse right where she stood. Taking a deep breath, she curled her hand into a fist and rapped on the door.

Chapter 1

"**C**ord McVane, ladies and gentlemen!"

Poised above the skittish horse in the chute, Cord nodded briefly at the sparse crowd in the arena. Rain pelted down, kicking up little spurts of dust and saturating the ground which had been bone-dry only moments ago. The sudden shower had taken everyone by surprise, sending a portion of the onlookers hunting for cover.

Cord grimaced as he looked down at the slick back fidgeting beneath him. That was the problem with riding bareback—the rain made things that much more difficult. He settled his hat firmly over his forehead, then dropped onto the horse.

The door of the chute crashed open and he rode through. Mud spattered up from the thrashing hooves as the horse twisted and bucked. Grimly Cord hung on, his feet thrust out in front of him and his left hand flailing in the air.

He figured he had no more than two seconds to go until the buzzer sounded...and then it happened. The horse slipped in the mud, twisting its body violently to keep it upright. The next thing Cord knew he was lying in the dirt, wincing at the white-hot pain in his shoulder.

Turk, the pickup man, leaned over him, his bearded face creased in concern. "Hey, buddy, you okay?"

Cord nodded and tried to get up. Pain slashed at him again and he grunted. "Damn shoulder. I think it's broke."

"Can you get up?"

"Yeah, I think so." Using his good arm, he levered himself onto his knees, then onto his feet, amid cheers from the anxious crowd. Nursing his right arm, he strode back to the gate, where Jed Cullen stood waiting.

"You took a while to get up, pardner." Jed squinted his golden eyes. "You okay?"

Cord shrugged, and caught his breath at the agonizing reminder of his injury. "Busted my shoulder, I reckon."

"I keep telling you you're getting too old for this game. You'd better get the doc to check that out. Wanna ride to the hospital?"

Cord scowled. "The hell I'm too old, and I'm not gonna go to no hospital."

"The hell you are," Jed assured him cheerfully, "because I'm gonna make you. And right now you're in no damn position to argue. I don't want you ending up like poor old Denver. The doctors say he'll never ride rodeo again."

Cord grunted. They both knew full well that their travel partner, Denver Briggs, was considering quitting rodeo because he'd wanted to, not because he was being forced into it. Right then, however, Cord's shoulder was giving him too much pain for him to waste time discussing it. He wanted a painkiller, and fast. "Okay, if you're so all-fired anxious to get me to a hospital, let's get it over with." He set off for the parking lot, doing his best not to jog his injured shoulder.

Two hours later he emerged from the cubicle in the emergency room, feeling a lot more shaken than he was willing to admit to Jed.

"Well?" Jed asked anxiously. "Is it broken?"

Cord shook his head. "Just a bad sprain. I gotta take a couple of days out to let it rest, then I'll be back as good as new. I need a favor, though."

Jed smiled his relief. "Sure. Anything."

"I need to borrow the truck. I'm going to the cabin."

Jed's smile faded. "Tonight? It will be two in the morning before you get there. How are you gonna drive with a bum shoulder?"

Cord remembered just in time not to shrug. "I'll manage."

Jed looked unconvinced. "You can't drive that far tonight. The cabin's in the middle of nowhere, Cord. You can't go up there alone. How are you going to get help if you're buried in the middle of the forest in the mountains?"

"I won't need help." Aware that he sounded surly, Cord made an effort to soften his tone. "I'll be just fine, J.C. I've got a phone, and I'm not that far from folk. I just need to be on my own for a while, okay?"

"Then I'll take you up there and drop you off. You can call me when you want to come back."

"It'll take all of three hours."

"Not the way I drive. Let's go."

Cord gave him a halfhearted argument, but Jed wouldn't take no for an answer. "I don't know why you're so hell-bent on going up there all by yourself," he muttered, as he pulled out onto the highway. "You could rest just as easy in the camper and you'd have me and Denver to take care of you."

Cord uttered a humorless laugh. "No offense, pal, but if I had to stay put in that camper for more than one day I'd be climbing the walls. In any case, it isn't just my body that needs a rest. I reckon I lost my concentration today. That tells me I'm getting tired. Maybe I'm getting too old for this line of work. I need time to think about that, and there's nowhere on this good earth I can think better than up there in the mountains all on my lonesome."

To his relief, Jed accepted that, and gave him no more hassle on the subject.

Jed was right about the driving; he made it to the cabin in just under two and half hours. The old place had been in Cord's family for as long as he could remember. He'd inherited it a few years back when his father died, and had escaped to it whenever he'd felt the need to step off the world for a while.

Jed helped him carry the supplies they'd picked up into the sparsely furnished building. He stacked them for him in the cupboard above the rickety, stained sink but declined Cord's offer to stay for the night. "Gotta get back," he said, pausing at the door to look at his friend. "I've got a ride tomorrow. That bum shoulder's going to slow you down a lot. You sure you're gonna be okay?"

Cord nodded. The painkillers had dulled his senses and all he could think about right then was crashing on the bed.

"You'll call if you need help?" Jed asked, obviously uncomfortable with the thought of leaving his partner alone.

Cord decided it was time to get tough. "For God's sake get outta here," he growled. "It's been a good many years since I needed a nursemaid to hold my hand."

Jed grinned. "Oh, I don't know. I reckon a couple of those nurses down at the hospital might change your mind.

Not that I'd want to leave a helpless female here alone with a bear like you. She'd be in dead trouble from the start."

"So will you be if you don't get outta here." Cord took a threatening step forward and Jed raised his hands.

"Okay, I'm leaving. Just make sure you call if you need someone."

"I'll call, I'll call, okay? And hey…thanks, pardner. I owe you one."

"Sure." Jed gave him one last searching look and disappeared out the door.

Cord waited until the roar of the pickup's engine had died away before letting out a sigh of relief. Jed meant well. Denver's recent injury still played on both their minds. Denver had hurt his back in a fall from a bull, and for a while it seemed as if he would disobey his doctor's orders and risk permanent injury by staying on the circuit. Luckily his future wife had changed his mind about that.

Cord scowled as he crossed the room to the dilapidated cupboards that clung precariously to the wall. It would take more than a female to get him to give up the rodeo. There wasn't one damn thing he'd give up for a woman. Not one. Not anymore. He'd learned that particular lesson a long time ago.

He reached in the cupboard and grabbed a can of soda from the six-pack. Tomorrow he'd take the rest and stick them in the stream to stay cool, along with the beer he'd brought. Right now he'd settle for warm soda. As he raised the can to his mouth, he paused. Ever since he'd walked into the place something about it had been bugging him. An odd feeling that something was out of place. That same sense of something being wrong disturbed him again now.

He looked around, his gaze taking in the bookcase with its well-thumbed books; the woodstove stocked, ready to light; the shabby armchairs on either side…. Even the faded curtains at the window looked the same. He frowned, and stared at the electric stove. The scarred surface, the grungy rings, the burn marks on the Formica counter—everything seemed just as he'd left it the last time.

Deciding that it was the painkillers playing tricks with his mind, Cord prowled across the threadbare carpet to the bedroom. The door squeaked as he opened it, and he made a mental note to put some oil on the hinges. The fact that he'd been promising himself to do that ever since he'd taken possession of the place a few years back didn't worry him at all. He'd get to it when he was good and ready.

He headed for the bed and slumped on the edge of it. The springs rattled and groaned in protest. He tipped a couple more mouthfuls of soda down his throat and set the can down on the scratched bedside table. Leaning over his knees, he reached down to pull off his boots. It was then that it hit him.

His nose was attuned to the musty smell of wood smoke and damp cedar inside the cabin. But now he could smell something else. Perfume. He could smell perfume. Not the cheap stuff, either. He'd been around enough to know the difference. This was a light, flowery scent that made him think of warm, sun-drenched islands in the Caribbean.

Very slowly he leaned across to the pillows and took a deep breath. The scent was subtle, but it was there. Someone had been sleeping in his bed. Recently.

He buried his head in his hands and tried to sort out his tangled thoughts. Denver had spent a couple of days here a month ago. Maybe April, his fiancée, had visited him here. But that was a month ago. Did the smell of perfume hang around that long? He didn't think so.

The painkillers were turning his brain to mush. Damn, he couldn't think straight. He had to get some sleep...give the medication time to wear off.

Wearily he pulled off his boots, then tugged his jeans down over his ankles and kicked them across the room. Without bothering to undo the buttons, he dragged his shirt over his head, fell on the bed, and thankfully gave himself up to the fog that filled his mind.

What could only be moments later, he jolted awake again, grunting in surprise as the bed seemed to jostle beneath him. His first thought was that someone had stuck a hot knife into his shoulder. His second was the realization that he wasn't alone.

His head felt as though it were stuffed with cotton, and he had to force his eyelids open. It was dark in the room, but not too dark to prevent him from seeing the shadowy form slipping through the doorway.

For a big man, he was light on his feet. In spite of the daze that befuddled his brain he bounded into the living room and flung himself at the trespasser, who had just reached the outside door. He grabbed a handful of soft flesh and heard a very feminine squeak, then the two of them crashed to the floor. He landed right on top of his intruder. She uttered one strangled gasp, then lay still.

The agony in his shoulder and neck almost immobilized him. In all the excitement he'd temporarily forgotten about his injury. Obviously the painkillers weren't strong enough to mask the new soreness his swift movements had caused. The thought that he might have done even greater damage to himself infuriated him all the more. Gritting his teeth, he snarled, "I'm not getting up until you tell me who the hell you are and what you're doing in my cabin."

He kept to himself the fact that, in any case, right then he couldn't have moved if his life was at stake. The pain was now reverberating in his head, thumping like a piston at full blast and turning his limbs to jelly.

The body under him still didn't move—a warm soft pillow of humanity. For a minute he thought he'd stunned her. "Hey," he said sharply, "did you hear me?"

"The entire forest can hear you bellowing," her breathy voice said plaintively.

"I'm gonna do a lot more than bellow if you don't start answering some questions. Pronto." Given her precarious position, she'd sounded pretty calm, Cord thought, seething with resentment.

"You're lying on my stomach," the breathless voice stated. "It's a little hard to talk."

It suddenly occurred to Cord that he was lying full length on top of a woman, and he was dressed only in his shorts. Sweat broke out on his brow. He swung his hips away from her and shifted his weight to the floor beside her. Holding her down with his good arm, he said grimly, "Don't try anything stupid. I don't want to have to hurt you."

She didn't answer right away, and he lay there for a moment or two, considering his next move. He wasn't all that sure he could get to his feet and still hang on to her. From what he could tell, judging by her slender figure, she was young, and probably fast on her feet. He wasn't about to give her the opportunity to slip out of his grasp. Not until he found out what she was doing in his cabin. In his present condition, he had no illusions about his ability to give chase.

"I think we'd both be a good deal more comfortable if we sat in a chair," the woman said, breaking the prolonged silence.

Cord heartily agreed. He couldn't afford to let her know that he didn't have full possession of his capabilities, however. On the other hand, they could hardly spend the night on the floor, waiting for the effects of the damn painkillers to wear off.

"All right," he said at last. "Just get up slowly and

carefully, and wait for me to turn on the light. Make the wrong move and I'll pin you down so fast you'll wonder what day it is."

"I won't run." He saw her shadowy figure sit up. "I have nowhere to run to."

That should have reassured him, but it didn't. All he knew was that he was alone in the cabin with a woman. In his shorts. It might have been better if he'd let her escape. For a second or two he half hoped she'd make a run for it, but she rose easily to her feet and stood waiting for him to get up.

"Do you need some help?"

The tentative question galvanized him into action. Gritting his teeth, he shoved himself upright, disguising his sharp intake of breath as a cough. He raised his good arm and felt along the wall for the switch. Finding it, he flicked it on.

He wasn't quite sure what he'd expected. Certainly not this ragged kid with ugly scratches all over her face and arms. Her dark-brown hair tumbled to her shoulders in a tangled mess. Her grimy jeans were ripped and the baggy yellow sweatshirt she wore reached halfway down her thighs and had one sleeve missing. She looked as if she'd been in a fight with a bunch of raccoons. And lost.

Relieved that he wasn't dealing with a full-grown woman after all, Cord let out his breath. "What's your name?" he demanded abruptly.

The kid was obviously making a deliberate effort not to look below the level of his bare chest. She flicked a wary glance across his face, down to his shoulder, then snatched her gaze back to his face. The expression in her dark-brown eyes was guarded as she muttered, "Lori."

"Lori who?"

"Just Lori."

"Where did you come from?"

"Nowhere."

Cord sighed. "I'm beginning to lose patience. Maybe you'd better tell me where your family is, before I lose it altogether and haul you off to the nearest sheriff's office."

Her eyes widened at that. "I have no family," she said, a note of defiance creeping into her voice.

"You must have come from somewhere."

She shook her head. "It doesn't matter where I come from."

"It does to me." He figured that behind the mask of rebellion she could be hiding a fair dose of fear. He was bigger, older and a lot tougher than she was. Although he had to admit, his lack of clothes took away some of his authority. On the other hand, he wasn't about to be taken in by her fragility. "I don't want to be hauled into jail for harboring a criminal," he added deliberately.

Her chin came up smartly, and a blaze of indignation lit up her eyes. "I'm not a criminal."

"No? Where I come from breaking and entering is a pretty serious offense. Maybe you'd better explain to me what the hell you were doing hiding under my bed."

Her thin face turned a dull red. "I got lost in the forest and came on this place by accident. It was empty and I was tired... I didn't think anyone would mind if I spent the night."

"If it was all that innocent, why didn't you holler when you heard us come in?"

"I woke up and heard you talking." She sent a hunted look around the room as if searching for a way to escape. "I was shocked.... I didn't know what to do. I acted out of pure instinct. Self-preservation. I thought I'd hide until I got the chance to slip out of here unnoticed."

"So that you wouldn't have to mess with the sheriff, right?"

Again the alarm flashed in her eyes. "I have my own reasons for not wanting to talk to the police. Private reasons. I've taken nothing from you except some stale crackers. I thought this was an abandoned cabin."

Her look of disgust as she glanced around the room offended him. "So what did you expect in the middle of the forest?" he said testily. "A five-star hotel?"

She gave him a pitying look that did nothing to soothe his irritation. "I'm sorry I intruded on your privacy. I'd like to leave now."

"You're not going anywhere until I say so." He narrowed his eyes, trying to figure out what to do. He was convinced that she was an underage runaway. Came from a good family, too, judging by the way she talked. Been well educated, that was for sure. Clearly his duty was to take her to the sheriff's office. They'd know how to handle it. The last thing in the world he wanted was to be saddled with any complications. And the bedraggled kid standing in front of him was definitely a complication.

On the other hand, since he had no truck, he'd have to call the cops to come and get her. He didn't want to have to wait up half the night for them to get there. He rubbed the back of his neck with his good hand. The pain had faded to a dull ache. Apparently the painkillers had gotten the upper hand again. Now he was so tired he could hardly stay on his feet.

He glared at the kid, wishing like hell she hadn't chosen his cabin to take refuge in. Still, he could hardly turn her out to take her chances in the forest in the middle of the night. "You might as well stay here the rest of the night," he muttered. "I'll figure out what to do in the morning."

She studied him for a moment. "Where would you sleep? There's only one bed."

Cord sighed. "I'm gonna be sleeping in my bed." He watched her eye the chair with obvious dismay. The pills had to be addling his brain. He heard himself add, "You can take your chances in there with me if you want."

She frowned. "I don't think that would be a good idea. How do I know I can trust you to behave like a gentleman?"

He almost laughed, and would have done if he hadn't been too damn tuckered. "For God's sake, kid, I'm in no shape to bat an eye, let alone make a move. Even if I were, you'd be safe. I'm no damn cradle snatcher."

She opened her mouth to say something else, but he'd had enough. Holding up his hand to silence her, he said harshly, "Look, kid...Lori...whatever your name is...it's up to you, okay? You wanna sleep out here, fine. You wanna share the bed, that's okay, too, as long as you stay on your half and don't jostle my shoulder. Or, if you wanna take your chances with the bears and the wolves, you're free to leave. I'm too cold and too damn tired to argue anymore."

He turned and headed for the bedroom, hoping she wouldn't call his bluff. He didn't want to fight her, but right now he felt responsible for her. He wasn't too thrilled at the idea of having to chase after her out there in the dark. Gingerly nursing his shoulder, he settled himself on the bed and pulled the covers over him. Before he could start worrying about what she was doing, he was asleep.

Lori sat in the moth-eaten armchair and evaluated the situation. She was alone in a cabin, miles from nowhere, with a man she didn't know. Things seemed to be going from bad to worse. She should have realized the cabin belonged to someone. She should never have broken in. Now she'd broken the law.

When she'd received no answer to her knock, she'd checked the windows. Since they didn't appear to have locks, it had been easy enough to shove one up and climb in. She'd searched the rickety cupboards in the kitchen and all she'd found was a box of stale crackers. She'd emptied the box, then—too tired even to undress—she'd fallen onto the bed and gone straight to sleep.

She'd woken up to hear voices in the living room. She should have owned up to her presence right away, but two things had held her back. One, she didn't know what they might do to her if they found her there, and two, she didn't want to have to explain why she was there.

After she'd hidden herself, she'd listened to the two men talking long enough to realize that one of them intended to stay awhile. She'd been horrified when he'd crashed down on the bed. She'd waited until she figured he was asleep, then had tried to slip out. Her shoulder had hit the edge of the bed as she was getting to her feet, and woken him up.

Under the circumstances, she could see why he was such a grump. Still, he hadn't called the cops, so maybe he wasn't too mad at her. The last thing she needed was to be arrested for breaking and entering.

Now at least she had a little breathing space to decide what she wanted to do next. She really hadn't given much thought to the long-term logistics of her impulsive decision to leave town. Her parents were probably worrying about her. Her brothers were no doubt searching for her by now. And Richard.... Her stomach gave a little flip of remorse. Richard would be devastated.

Maybe she should have thought it through. She wasn't used to making her own decisions; that was the trouble. All her life her family had dictated the directions she should go. They'd made all the important choices for her, and she'd gone blindly along, accepting that they knew better than she did what was good for her. Until Richard.

The more plans that were made and the closer the date of the wedding, the more confused and afraid she'd felt. Something was missing in her feelings for Richard. Something vital. She wasn't sure what it was; she just knew it wasn't there. She'd tried to tell him, but he'd laughed away her doubts. Her parents thought it was wedding nerves.

When she'd tentatively suggested postponing the wedding until she was more sure of her feelings, her brothers had warned her that they'd physically carry her to the church. Her father had threatened to disown her and her mother had cried and told her she would ruin the family's reputation. Finally, after being unable to sleep for over a week, she'd panicked. She didn't know what she wanted to do. She only knew that she didn't want to marry Richard. She'd packed a suitcase, left a long letter of explanation and had driven out of town without even knowing where she was headed.

She yawned, and stretched her aching arms above her head. Now she was stuck in a cabin in the middle of nowhere with a grump. And she was hungry. The crackers hadn't been much of a dinner. She got up, wincing as pain sliced through her shoulder. She'd bruised it when she'd fallen down the steep slope. Her benefactor had hurt his shoulder, too. She'd heard his friend mention it, and it was obvious from the way he'd acted that it was hurting him pretty badly. That was probably why he was so grouchy. She wondered how he'd injured it.

She walked softly in her sneakers across the carpet to the cupboards and opened one of them. More cans and some packaged food had been stacked on the shelves, and a couple of six packs of beer sat on another. In the other cupboard she found two loaves of sliced wheat bread, a bag of apples and some packages of instant potatoes, as well as some cans of soda.

Lori sighed. Not exactly gourmet dining. She took one of the apples and a package of cookies and carried them back to the chair. Biting into the crisp apple, she concentrated once more on her dilemma. She was taking a chance by staying.

She knew nothing about this man, other than he had a friend who worried about him. He could still have her arrested in the morning and he certainly wasn't too sociable. In fact, he was intimidating. Even his being half-undressed hadn't seemed to bother him. Not half as much as it had embarrassed her, anyway. Yet something told her he wouldn't hurt her. He'd acted as if she were a little kid. She wondered how old he was.

One thing she was certain of, staying in this run-down shack was infinitely preferable to taking her chances with the bears and the wolves in the forest. She had no doubt the grump was serious about that. She wondered why he was staying here all by himself, nursing an injured shoulder, when he had people who really cared about him. She knew his friend cared about him; she'd heard it in his voice.

She took another bite of her apple. Maybe tomorrow she'd find out the answers. Just as long as she didn't have to answer any of *his* questions. She couldn't go back now. She absolutely refused to go back now. She'd finally made the break and nothing would convince her to give up her freedom. The problem was, she had no visible means of support.

If only she'd checked the car for gas when she'd left, she wouldn't have run out in the middle of the freeway. Then she wouldn't have had to accept a ride from a strange man, and she wouldn't have been robbed and forced to run for her life. But then again, when had she really had to fend for herself before? Her family had always come to her rescue. Now she was alone.

With a sigh she finished the apple and started on the cookies. She had no clothes, other than what she wore, and no money. She'd left her credit cards at home. Not that she could have used them. Her brothers would have had no trouble tracking her down. What she needed was a job. How she was going to find one without clothes to wear or the means to get to an interview she didn't know.

She dropped the package of cookies on the floor and yawned. Now she was tired. She needed sleep if she was going to face the grump in the morning. She looked at her watch. Almost two-thirty. Stifling another yawn she curled up on the chair.

For a long time sleep eluded her, in spite of her weariness. Worries and doubts about her immediate future swirled around in her head, and to make matters worse, the dilapidated chair obviously had not been designed for use as a makeshift bed. It was as hard as the ground she'd rolled on last night.

She'd also discovered that jeans were not the most comfortable attire for sleeping in. After squirming around for what seemed like hours, she reluctantly slipped off her shoes and slid out of the offending jeans. Curling her knees under her chin for warmth, she willed the troubling thoughts from her mind.

Much to her surprise, she opened her eyes again to find the sun streaming in through the dusty windowpanes. She sent a swift glance around the silent room, expecting to see the grump glowering at her with his black-eyed gaze. To her relief she saw that she was alone, and there was no sign of movement from beyond the closed door of the bedroom.

Now she had a decision to make, and quickly, before her reluctant host reappeared and insisted on taking her to the sheriff.

Chapter 2

Lori's first instinct was to grab the opportunity to run. The door was right there, beckoning her with a promise of freedom. All she had to do was grab her shoes and pants and climb out. By the time the grump realized what was happening she'd be long gone.

In the next instant she realized how impractical that was. First, she had no idea where she was or how to get back to the road. Second, even if she did, where could she go without money or decent clothes? What she needed was time. Time to figure out how to find a job. Time to decide where she was going to live.

She frowned, turning over her options. There weren't that many. In fact, she could come up with only one, and that was by no means certain. Maybe she could make a deal with the grump. Maybe she could convince him she meant no harm and persuade him not to turn her in to the cops.

Obviously he was having trouble using one of his arms.

Maybe if she offered to take care of things around the house, maybe clean up a bit, he might let her stay for a day or two, long enough for her to get things sorted out.

Instinct told her she could trust him, up to a point. As long as he didn't ask too many questions, he could be the answer to her problem. She could stay until he was ready to leave, then ask him for a ride into whatever town he passed through. He might even be willing to lend her some money. She could always pay him back when she got her job.

It all seemed so simple now. Her spirits rising, she bounced out of the chair. This was an adventure, and she might as well enjoy it. She'd worry about the future when it arrived.

She padded across to the bathroom in her bare feet and listened. The silence reassured her and she nudged open the door. An electric razor sat on the back of the sink, next to a hairbrush. She picked up the brush and pulled it through her hair, wincing as the bristles tugged at the tangles.

Leaning forward, she peered at her face in the mirror. A couple of the scratches still looked angry, but the rest were beginning to fade. A few days and there'd be no trace of her flight through the woods. She gazed longingly at the ancient shower hanging over the stained bathtub. Remembering how cold the water was, she gave up on that idea. She turned on the faucet, instead, and sluiced her face. Icy droplets splashed down her neck and she shivered. She'd wash properly later, she decided. Once she could heat some water.

When she buried her face in the towel it smelled of soap, the kind only a man would use. The thought gave her a tingle of excitement, though she couldn't imagine why. Right now she preferred to be as far away from male companionship as possible.

Her sweatshirt was a mess, and she brushed at the mud stains. She should wash it—or what was left of it. Her underwear as well. But she'd need something to wear in the meantime. Maybe the grump would lend her a shirt while she waited for her clothes to dry. Her hair needed washing, too. She gathered the loose strands in her hands and twisted them into a makeshift braid. That would have to do for now.

The slamming of a door made her start. She heard heavy footsteps cross the living room, and instinctively reached for the lock on the bathroom door. She froze when she saw there wasn't one. A series of thuds was followed by a clatter. Plucking up her courage, she pulled the door open and looked out.

The grump squatted in front of the woodstove. Fallen logs were scattered around him, and he was holding a lit match to the papers piled inside the stove. He looked up when she advanced warily into the room.

"Oh, so you're awake."

She caught her breath. When she'd last seen him the night before he'd badly needed a shave, his eyes were red-rimmed and his face was white and drawn. Either he'd been in awful pain or her memory had played tricks on her. Whatever it was, this morning he seemed utterly different.

His firm jaw was now clean shaven, and he wore a black cowboy hat pulled down on his forehead. Beneath the wide brim his eyes glinted like black coals. The long sleeves of his dark-blue shirt had pearl buttons at the wrist, and the same buttons marched down the front to the huge silver buckle at his waist. Black jeans hugged his hips, and the hems rose at the ankles to reveal a gleaming pair of black boots. Fully dressed, he looked even more intimidating than he had the night before.

He wasn't a handsome man by movie star standards. His

nose was too big and his mouth a little too hard. But there
was a rugged quality to his uneven features that appealed
to her. And an expression in his dark eyes that unsettled
her.

Aware that she was staring, Lori said hastily, "Good
morning."

He didn't answer. He continued to study her, until she
felt compelled to ask, "What's the matter?"

"How old are you?"

His harsh voice startled her. "Twenty-two," she answered, before she'd had time to consider that it was none
of his business how old she was.

"Holy sh—" He closed the flap on the woodstove, got
to his feet and brushed wood chips from his jeans with his
left hand. The other he kept tucked close to his side, with
the thumb in his belt. "Why didn't you tell me that last
night?"

She raised her chin. "You didn't ask."

"I thought you were a kid."

"You were mistaken."

"So I notice." He swept his gaze over her body, down
her bare legs to her feet. "I must have been really doped
up last night."

Her skin tingled under the insolent scrutiny. "I don't see
what difference it makes."

"I wouldn't have invited you into my bed, for one
thing." He brushed past her and strode over to the sink.
Water gushed from the faucet when he turned it on, and he
stuck his hands into the cold spray.

"Is that coffee I smell?" She was determined to be
pleasant. She needed this man's help and she had to find a
way to disarm him. He wasn't making it very easy.

"It was. You can make some more if you want."

Right at that moment she would have killed for a cup of

coffee. The saucepan sat on top of the stove and she walked over to pick it up, then waited for him to finish washing his hands. She needed an opening if she was going to ask him to let her stay. She watched him dry his hands carefully on a kitchen towel, then asked, "How did you hurt your shoulder?"

"I fell off a horse."

That intrigued her. She'd never met a real cowboy before. "You work on a ranch?"

"Nope." He opened the cupboard above the sink and pulled out a box of cereal.

She tried again. "You were horse riding?"

"That's usually where you have to be to fall off one."

She bit back her resentment. "I meant taking a horse for a ride. You know, for pleasure."

He tipped some of the cereal into his hand and shoved it into his mouth.

She watched him crunch on the dry grain, wondering how anyone could eat cereal without milk. "So what do you do?"

He wiped his mouth with the back of his hand. "Rodeo," he said briefly, and tipped some more cereal into his palm.

Her eyes widened. "You're a rodeo rider? I've never seen a rodeo. Where do you ride? Do you ride bulls?"

He put the box down on the counter with a thump. "You ask way too many questions for someone who doesn't want to answer any."

She turned away and held the pan under the faucet. Watching the water gush into it, she said carefully, "There isn't much to tell."

"Where's your home?"

She hesitated. "I don't have one. I'm in between homes. Looking for a new one."

"You must have kin somewhere."

She turned off the faucet and set the pan on the stove. "No, I don't."

"Where did you stash your bags? I didn't see any lying around here.

"I don't have any bags."

He pursed his lips, his gaze narrowing. "What kind of trouble are you in?"

"I haven't broken any laws, if that's what you mean. Not until last night, anyway, and that was unintended. I'm not wanted by the police or anything."

"Women like you don't run around the woods all by themselves for the fun of it. Who are you running from?"

She shrugged. "Myself, mostly."

"That's no answer, lady."

She met his gaze defiantly. "It's the only one I'm prepared to give."

For a moment she thought he was going to demand she provide him with a better one, but after frowning at her for a moment or two, he asked, "Just where were you planning on running to?"

"I don't know. That depends on you, I guess."

"Me?" He took a step backward, holding up his hand as if to ward her off. "Hey. Now, just hold on. I don't know what you've got in mind, but you'd better forget it real quick. I'm not looking for any woman. 'Specially one who won't tell me where she came from."

She would have laughed if she hadn't felt quite so desperate. "I didn't mean it that way. I need some time to…figure out what I'm going to do next. I just thought…since you've hurt your shoulder, maybe you could use some help around here. I could clean up, make the bed, whatever needs doing."

"No way, lady. What I can't do doesn't get done. I don't

need anyone keeping house for me.'' He moved over to the sink and turned on the faucet. He stuck his hands under the water in a gesture that said he'd reached the end of the subject.

She was up against a brick wall. She'd have to tell him at least part of the truth. ''I really do need someplace to stay for a while. I was robbed. I don't have any money. I need time to figure out where to go from here.''

''Who robbed you?''

''I didn't stop to ask his name.''

He scowled at her. ''If the police are not looking for you, as you keep saying, then why aren't you down there talking to them, instead of bugging me?''

''I told you. I prefer not to have to deal with the police right now.''

He went on washing his hands in silence, and she held her breath, wondering what on earth she'd do if he insisted on turning her out. Finally, he sighed, and reached for the kitchen towel on the counter.

''Can you cook?''

''Of course.'' She didn't tell him that her knowledge of cooking was limited to heating up a frozen dinner now and again. Marietta, the family housekeeper, had done most of the cooking. Other than that, Lori's meals were either catered or she ate out at a restaurant.

He dried his hands, his face creased in concentration. ''I really don't think—'' he began at last, but she interrupted him before he could turn her down.

''I know your shoulder hurts when you try to do things. It will heal that much faster if you don't have to use it. I'm stronger than I look...and I promise I won't get in your way. There's a lot I could do around here to help out.'' Once more she held her breath, while he continued to stare at her for several nerve-racking moments. Then, when she could stand his silence no longer, she added softly, "Please? We could help each other."

She let out her breath on a sigh of relief when, after another lengthy pause, he gave her a curt nod.

"All right. I'll more'n likely live to regret this, but...okay. Just for a couple of days until I get rid of this bum shoulder."

"All right." She beamed at him. "So, what's your name?'

"McVane. My friends call me 'Cord.' What's yours?"

She dropped her gaze and pretended to be busy looking for the instant coffee in the cupboard. "I told you. It's Lori."

"Lori who?"

"Just Lori." She grabbed the package of coffee and took it down. "It's all you need to know."

He let out his breath in an explosive sigh. "All right, but I'm warning you. You bring trouble down on my head and I'll see you pay for it. Understood?"

"Understood. Where are the mugs?"

He pointed to the one standing by the sink. "Right there."

She picked it up, wrinkling her nose when she saw the coffee dregs in the bottom. "This is it? You don't have any more?"

"I wasn't exactly expecting company."

"What about if people come to call? Don't you offer them a cup of coffee?"

He snorted. "The only callers I get are the kind who drink beer out of a bottle. I don't have no use for anything fancier than that." His expression changed to a sly look. "Not like you're used to, I reckon."

The water in the pan began to bubble, and she poured it into the mug, breathing in the aroma of the coffee. It had never smelled so good. "How do you know what I'm used to?" she asked lightly.

Cord tipped back his hat on his forehead with his thumb. "I can tell. I've been around enough women to know when one's been mollycoddled, I reckon. And you've got 'pampered' stamped all over you. You sure you want this job?"

"I'm sure." She lifted the mug to her eager lips. The coffee tasted as wonderful as it smelled. She was pretty confident she could handle anything he wanted her to do. How hard could it be? This wasn't exactly a mansion to take care of, and as for the cooking…all he had were cans in the cupboard. It was just a matter of heating things up. Any fool could do that.

Cord seemed satisfied with her answer. He offered her the box of cereal. "Want some breakfast?"

She took the box and peered at the dry flakes of corn. "Do you have any cream?"

"Might be a can of milk in the cupboard."

She pulled a face. "Evaporated milk?"

"Not much else, seeing as how there's no fridge."

She looked around in alarm. "No fridge?" She hadn't even thought about it yesterday. "How do you keep things cold?"

"I stick 'em in the river out there. Which is what I'm gonna do right now with this beer and soda." He reached over her head to retrieve a couple of six-packs from the cupboard. "While I'm gone you can take a shower. The water should be hot by now."

She stared at him in surprise. "We've got hot water?"

"Now that the fire's lit we do." He hoisted the beer under his good arm, clutched the soda in his hand and headed for the door. "There's a clean shirt and jeans in that bag over there, if you need something to wear." He gestured at a travel bag lying in the corner. "You might want to wash out the shower first. I usually take my baths in the river.''

The door banged behind him and she scowled at it. Of course. Where else. Mr. Macho wouldn't even flinch at plunging into the icy water.

Still, it was nice of him to light the stove for her, she acknowledged later, as she stood under the healing warmth of the water. The heat felt good on her scratches. Already her bruises were turning purple. A deep scrape on her arm stung when the water hit it, but otherwise she seemed to have survived her ordeal.

All things considered, she'd done pretty well after all, she decided. She'd managed to turn a disaster into a triumph. She was assured of food and shelter, at least for a little while, and there was small chance of her brothers finding her in this isolated neck of the woods. Cord McVane seemed to have given up with the questions, at least temporarily, and for the first time since she'd flung herself into the car yesterday, she felt safe and deliciously free.

She sobered for a moment when she thought about her family, then hardened her heart. They had brought this upset on themselves with their scheming and manipulation. All they thought about was what was good for them, for the family image. Never about what was good for her. For once she was thinking for herself, and she liked it. She was doing what she wanted to do, without having to worry about approval from everyone.

She felt adventurous, daring and incredibly sophisticated. Not at all the amenable, obedient wimp who'd accepted everything handed out to her. She'd left that Lori behind in the family mansion. This was a new Lori… And she was going to make it on her own.

Striking a pose, she flung out her arms in a gesture of welcome. Let the new life begin.

Cord stomped across the uneven ground, pushing his way through the undergrowth with an impatient kick of his boot. His mind whirled with doubts. He had to be nuts…inviting a young woman to stay in the cabin with him. Those painkillers had sure as hell addled his brain. He could just imagine what Jed would say if he knew what his friend was doing.

No one understood better than Jed Cullen how Cord felt about women. Except for Denver. All three of them had started out the same way—he, Jed and Denver Briggs. They'd met up at the Barstow Stampede seven years ago. He and Jed had just bought the camper together and were looking for a third partner. The first time they shared a beer with Denver, Cord knew the bull rider would fit right in. For one thing, Denver was no direct competition with the other two men. Jed rode saddle bronc and Cord rode bareback, so each did his own thing.

Except for the all-around championship, that was. None of them had ever won the big prize. The best of the best. They'd bet on it, though, and a couple of times each had come close. This was the year they reckoned one of them would win it. Each had his reasons for wanting it bad enough, and each had done real well in the standings so far. The rivalry between them was always fierce and friendly, and Cord thrived on it.

They had all agreed on one thing, though. Women were trouble. For seven years the three men had looked out for one another, making sure that they didn't weaken. Not that they'd sworn off women altogether. They'd just made sure that none of them did anything stupid, like get in too deep with a woman. There were plenty of women around the circuit willing to spend a few hours with a rodeo man. There was never any need to get serious beyond that.

Cord reached the tumbling river and squatted at the edge of a small overhang. He laid down the fishing pole he'd brought along, then leaned down to wedge the six-pack securely in the hollow where the cool water would wash over it without dislodging it.

The rodeo had been a good life so far, he reflected, sitting back on his haunches. Only, now it was all changing. He took off his hat and ran a hand through his hair before settling the hat back on his head. Denver's tangle with a bad-tempered bull would probably cost him his chance at the championship. Not only that, he was planning on getting married at the end of the year. And Jed was talking about some fool idea of taking a fake wife back to his hometown to impress some folks who thought he was a no-good bum.

Cord heaved a long sigh. Things just weren't the same anymore. At least with the other two. As far as Cord was concerned, he hadn't changed none, nor was he likely to, especially where women were concerned. He'd been bitten once and there wasn't a woman alive who would ever get the chance to make fool of him again. Not one.

A mental image of the runaway popped into his mind and he frowned. She'd given him quite a start that morning, when he'd realized he was looking at a full-grown woman. A good-looking one at that, in a kind of fresh, untouched way.

If he'd known she wasn't a young kid last night, he might have called the cops just to get rid of her. On the other hand, he had to admit, she had him curious. She seemed pretty intelligent, and spoke real nice. He couldn't tell much from her ripped clothes, but he was willing to bet she'd come from a family with money. Lots of money.

Which made him real curious about why she was on the run.

He wondered what kind of situation she'd been in to get robbed. If she was even telling the truth about that. More likely she took off without the time to grab anything. If someone had done something to her to make her run away, he'd like to know what it was. She was too young and too smart to be wandering around in the woods on her own, with no money and nowhere to go. Something was real wrong with that picture.

He might be done with women, as far as living with them went, but he never could abide to see one in trouble. And that little lady was obviously in need of help. She was hiding from someone or something, and he wanted to know what it was. In any case, he could use the help around the cabin, he assured himself. Just long enough so he could give his shoulder a rest.

As for her being a woman, well he reckoned he was pretty safe on that score. She was so far removed from his world it was a joke. He just figured on letting her stay around for a day or two until he found out what kind of trouble she was in, and maybe he could help. If not, he'd find someone who could. Then he could go on his way without having to feel guilty about abandoning her. Having reassured himself, he picked up the pole with his left hand and awkwardly threw out his line.

Lori tightened her belt around her waist and wished she had a full-length mirror. The jeans were way too long, and much too big in the waist. She'd found a blue-and-white bandanna in Cord's bag and used it to tie back her hair. The shirt she'd picked out was a light cream color, with a gold trim above the pockets and along the edge of the collar and cuffs. She rolled the sleeves back to her elbows, enjoying the feel of the cool, soft cotton. Cord McVane had good taste in clothes, at least.

She sent a scathing glance around the living room. Too bad that didn't apply to his cabin. Obviously he couldn't afford both clothes and furniture. Since he was in the public eye she supposed he'd have to spend whatever pittance he made on his appearance.

She walked over to the chair and bent down to retrieve the bag of cookies she'd dropped there the night before. She wasn't used to picking up after herself, but if she was going to earn her keep, she decided, she'd better learn.

She made the bed and hung up the towels in the bathroom, added logs to the woodstove and rinsed out the coffee mug. When there was still no sign of Cord, she ventured outside to look for him, wary of going too far in case she got lost again.

She was sorting through the cans in the cupboard, trying to decide what to heat up for lunch, when the front door flew open and Cord walked in. He was carrying something big and slimy that smelled awful.

He stopped short when he saw her and looked her over with that same look that had unsettled her earlier. "I see you found something to wear," he said.

His husky drawl sent little shivers of excitement chasing over her body. Before she could decide just why he had that weird effect on her, he brushed past her and threw the disgusting thing he was carrying into the sink.

"Here, I brought you lunch."

She stared in horror at the shiny eye that seemed to glare back at her from the head of the dead fish. "What in heaven's name is that thing?"

"That thing is a trout, and it cost me an hour to catch the damn thing. Could have done it in half the time if I'd had two good hands."

How he could sound so pleased with such a revolting achievement she had no idea. "What am I supposed to do with it?"

He sighed. "You saying you never cleaned a fish before?"

"I'm telling you I wouldn't touch that thing with a ten-foot pole."

He stared at her for a moment as if he thought she might be joking. Then he shook his head. "All right, I'll clean it. You can watch and learn."

She shuddered. "No, thank you. I'll wait outside while you finish playing with it."

He scowled at her and pulled off his hat. With his left hand he threw it across the room, apparently aiming it at the armchair. It hit the back of the chair and fell to the floor. Mumbling something, he bent over and tugged at the cuff of his jeans until it rose over his boot. When he stood up, she saw a wicked-looking knife in his hand.

"If you're going to cook for me you need to know how to gut a fish. You'll be doing a lot of it over the next few days."

"Not unless you want me to puke all over you."

His black eyes glittered at her. "Lady, suit yourself. There's the door, if the job's too much for you."

For a moment the urge to do just that was almost too strong to ignore. Then she reminded herself of what might be waiting out there for her if she got lost again. Maybe if she closed her eyes and held her breath she could get through it, she told herself.

"Well? What's it gonna be?"

Gritting her teeth, she muttered, "You know, you remind me of someone."

"Yeah? The husband you're running away from?"

She couldn't prevent the start his words gave her. She

managed to cover it up with an exaggerated shrug. "I'm not married."

"The hell you're not." He eyed her suspiciously. "I sure hit a button there, didn't I?"

"You're so wrong." She waved her left hand at him. "See? No ring."

"You could have taken it off."

She thought about the engagement ring she'd left on the bedside table in her luxurious bedroom. The longer she was away from all that comfort, the more she missed it, she thought gloomily.

"Well, I reckon it will come out eventually." Cord turned to the sink and turned on the faucet. "Now, here's where you start."

She immediately closed her eyes, then snapped them open again when she felt strong fingers closing over her hand. To her horror he stuck the knife handle in her palm and nudged her over to the sink. "I can't do it," she said faintly.

"Sure you can. It's easy." He stood close behind her and grasped her right hand with his. "Now, don't fight me on this or you'll jog my shoulder. I'm not a real nice man to know when I'm in pain."

Personally she was beginning to think he was not a nice man, period. He was way too bossy, for a start—a huge shortcoming in his character as far as she was concerned. If there was one thing she couldn't stand, it was someone professing to know better than she did what was good for her.

She tensed when he snaked his other hand around her and grasped her left hand in his. His chest nudged her back, and his mouth was so close to her neck she could feel his warm breath. "Now," he said, tightening his grip on her fingers, "you hold it like this with this hand, take the knife and slice down here."

"Ugh!" She drew back sharply but was prevented from going too far by the solid length of his body. She jerked forward again and heard him catch his breath.

"Damn!"

Immediately she dropped the knife and twisted her head to look at him. "Oh, gosh, I'm sorry. Did I hurt your shoulder?"

She was so close to him, her wrists still captured in his grasp. His mouth was just a few inches away, and for a moment his black gaze seemed to burn right through to her soul. Her heart thumped, her stomach quivered and she couldn't think of a thing to say.

His mouth tightened. He dropped his hands and backed away from her. "Forget it'" he said brusquely. "I guess I can manage the cleaning. You just worry about the cooking."

Surprised to discover that her legs felt as fragile as spun glass, Lori backed away, then escaped across the living room. His hat still lay on the floor and she stooped to pick it up. Her mind whirled with confusion as she struggled to justify her reaction to him.

He was older than Richard by at least ten years, probably more. She wasn't used to being alone with older men. That had to be the reason he affected her so. The only men over thirty she'd had any contact with were her father's friends, and they were all married.

A thought struck her and she glanced over at Cord, who now stood with his back to her while he worked on the fish. Was he married? It was hard to imagine a man like him reaching that age without some woman getting him to the altar. He was not unattractive, and there had to be a certain glamour about his profession.

Not that she would find it glamorous, she assured herself. Rolling around in the dirt under horses' hooves wasn't her idea of a good way to make a living. Still, there had to be some women out there who thought a rugged, good-looking rodeo rider would make a great husband and lover.

"Okay, I reckon you can start cooking it now."

She jumped violently, disturbed by her thoughts. Cord McVane's love life was was none of her business. She opened her mouth to tell him he was crazy if he thought she could cook a trout, then she shut it again. She'd made a deal with him. She'd told him she could cook.

How tough could it be, anyway? People cooked fish over the campfire all the time. All she had to do was heat the thing long enough to cook it. Although she wasn't sure she could eat anything that looked and smelled that bad. It certainly didn't resemble any of the trout she'd had in restaurants.

Cord squatted in front of the oven and pulled down the door. He reached in and dragged out a large frying pan that appeared to have spent time buried under a woodpile. Her spirits sank. The adventure was beginning to lose some of its appeal. She wished Marietta were here to take over.

In the next second she chided herself. She'd gone through a lot to gain her independence, and she wasn't going to cave in the first time she met with a setback. She eyed Cord warily. "Do you have any butter?"

"Nope." He waved the pan at her. "You'll have to manage without. There's cooking oil in the cupboard."

She thought about the numerous menus she'd studied in her favorite restaurants. None of them had mentioned pan-fried in cooking oil. Somehow pan-fried in butter sounded so much more appetizing. Determined to show this cantankerous cowboy that she could cook as well as any woman, she advanced on him and held out her hand.

"I don't suppose you have wine to cook it in." She had no idea what to do with it, but chefs always seemed to be cooking in wine.

She was happy to note that Cord was beginning to look impressed. "No wine, but I guess you could use beer."

She shuddered. "I don't think so. I'll manage without."

She took the pan from him and tried her best to appear as if she knew what she was doing. She found the cooking oil, unscrewed the cap and poured a generous amount into the pan.

"Isn't that a little heavy-handed?"

She glanced up at him. Unnerved by his concern, she said impatiently, "I'm sure there's something you could be doing while you're waiting."

"What are you going to serve with it?"

She stared at him blankly. She hadn't thought about that. She tried to remember what came with the fish entrées she'd ordered. "Rice?" she ventured. "Asparagus?"

His eyebrows shot up. "Sorry to disappoint you, ma'am, but we're plumb out of asparagus. Might be a can of peas in the cupboard."

"Oh, right." She found a spatula in the drawer and waved it at him. "Now, leave me alone. I get nervous when people watch me cook."

"I'm beginning to get a little jittery myself." He eyed the pan of oil, which had begun to spit in the midst of a blue haze. "Maybe you'd better turn that down a smidgen."

"I was just about to," she said haughtily. "I do wish you'd quit giving me orders."

He held up his hands. "Okay, I know when I'm not wanted." With a last worried look at the spitting pan, he walked over to the door and disappeared through it.

Once alone, Lori studied the fish. Cord had left it on the

counter, draining on a wad of paper towel. Although the smell still bothered her, she had to admit the trout did look a little more like the fish she was used to seeing on her plate. He'd cut off the head and tail, taken out the bones and left the insides nice and clean. Without the poor thing's eye glaring at her, she felt a lot more confident about touching it.

Steeling herself, she picked it up and slid it into the pan. A series of minor eruptions punctuated the loud sizzling of the hot oil. Globs of it sprayed down the sides of the stove and splattered on the front of her shirt. A bright-yellow flame licked up the side of the pan and disappeared. Lori jumped back with a little yelp. She reached out to turn down the heat, and more of the burning fat spit onto her hand. This time her yelp closely resembled a scream.

Cord must have been standing right outside the door. In less than a half-dozen strides he was at her side, reaching for her burned hand. Quickly he shoved her fingers under the faucet and turned on the frigid water full blast. Lori whimpered when the water hit, then relaxed as the pain faded.

"Feel better?"

She nodded.

"Hold it there while I take care of this."

She watched him snatch the pan off the stove and wave his hand in the cloud of smoke billowing up from it. After a moment or two the pan stopped spitting, and he set it down on a cold ring.

"Why didn't you tell me you don't know how to cook fish?" he muttered, lifting the trout out of the pan with the spatula.

Lori winced when she saw its scorched skin. "I didn't think it was that difficult," she mumbled.

"It's not." He narrowed his eyes. "Just how much experience have you had in cooking?"

She shrugged. "Not much."

"*How* much?" he insisted grimly.

She stared miserably at the water gushing over her hand. "Hardly any."

"That's what I figured."

"I'm sorry."

"Not nearly as much as I am. It took me most of the morning to catch that fish."

She was beginning to feel indignant about his attitude. After all, she hadn't asked him to catch the stupid fish. "I suppose you want me to leave."

She'd more or less said it in the heat of the moment, and immediately regretted the words. She held her breath while he appeared to think it over.

Finally, he replied caustically, "That's not going to solve anything. If you want to make it out there on your own, you're gonna have to at least know how to take care of yourself. And that includes cooking for yourself."

She let out her breath slowly. He understood more than she'd realized. Either she hadn't been too successful at hiding her background or he was an exceptionally perceptive man. She suspected it was a little of both. She looked up to find him watching her.

"I'll make another deal with you," he said. "I'll teach you what you need to know, and you tell me who you are and where you came from."

She hesitated. That was something she couldn't afford to do. Yet she had a strong feeling that if she didn't accept the offer, Cord would lose patience with her and send her on her way. Much against her better judgment she heard herself say, "It's a deal."

Chapter 3

Cord decided the best way to learn what he needed to know about Lori was not to pressure her. Fairly certain that she would keep her end of the bargain eventually, he figured he'd concentrate on teaching her the rudiments of simple cooking and leave the confession until later. He managed to rescue the fish by cutting off the worst of the burned end and cooking what was left. Luckily the trout was big enough to supply them both with a good-sized lunch.

Lori's hand, though sore, had only a minor burn, and she followed his directions with the packaged rice and peas without further mishap. They shared the meal seated in the armchairs, with plastic plates balanced on their knees.

A couple of times Cord tried to steer the conversation toward Lori's background, but each time she managed to forestall him by asking questions of her own. In the end he gave up, deciding that for now the information could wait. Sooner or later she'd trust him with the truth.

"Tell me about the rodeo," she urged, when the plates were clean. "It must really be an interesting life."

He settled back in his armchair and eased his shoulder into a more comfortable position. He'd promised himself he'd stay off the medication until he was ready to sleep. Right now the ache was pressuring him to change his mind.

He wasn't much one for talking, preferring to keep his thoughts to himself. If it helped to keep his mind off his aches and pains, though, he was willing to make an exception. He looked at Lori curled up in the other armchair. It gave him an odd feeling to see her dressed up in his clothes.

It had been a long time since he'd been this cozy with a woman. Too long. There was something about his unwelcome houseguest that made him remember just how long.

"Is anything the matter?"

Her voice jerked him off that dangerous path. He stared at her, realizing that he'd forgotten, for the moment, what it was she'd asked him.

"Is it your shoulder?"

In an effort to reassure her, he shook his head. "I was just wondering how my partners were doing back at the arena."

"Where is the arena?"

"When I left them we were in Pendleton. When I catch up with them again they'll be in Yakima."

"You must do an awful lot of traveling."

"More than I want to think about," he said wryly. "I reckon a rodeo man is always on the road. It's up to us how far we go."

"It must make it tough on the wives."

"Depends on the man, I guess. Some manage it—some don't."

She wriggled around to get more comfortable. Watching her had just the opposite effect on him, he noticed.

"What about you?" she demanded. "Are you married?"

"Nope."

"Never?"

He narrowed his eyes. Talking about it was something he didn't want to do. "Once. Enough to know I wasn't cut out for married life. There's no woman out there worth giving up my freedom for."

"Don't you ever get lonely?"

He shifted his shoulder and grunted as a stab of pain reminded him he wasn't healed yet. "Depends what you mean by 'lonely.' I like being on my own better than being with someone else. If I do have a hankering for company, I've got a couple of partners who travel the road with me. They're as much company as I want." *And the occasional woman to satisfy my needs,* his mind added. He decided not to dwell on that particular thought.

She leaned forward, her face alight with interest. "Tell me about them. Where do you all live? What do you do in the rodeo? What's it like being on the road all the time?"

He couldn't help noticing that she was a good-looking woman. Though he wouldn't exactly call her "beautiful," her skin was as smooth and clear as a mountain lake, and she had the kind of mouth that could make a man forget the kind of trouble he was heading into. He fancied he could see a touch of red in her dark-brown hair...hair that was so thick, so shiny, he itched to run his hands through it.

Too bad she wasn't more experienced—and something about her told him she wasn't. He might have considered spending a little time in bed with her. The treacherous idea jolted him back to his senses.

Up until now he hadn't given much thought to the sleeping arrangements. Last night he hadn't paid much attention to her, figuring she wasn't more than a young kid. Now that he knew better, it put things in a different light. Especially given the fact that his thoughts kept straying where they didn't ought to be.

Realizing that he'd let the silence go on too long again, he said abruptly, "It isn't as much fun as you might think. Though I reckon it does have its moments." Pushing his worries aside for time being, he concentrated on answering her questions.

"For the last seven years or so I've shared a trailer with a couple of travel partners," he began. "Jed rides saddle bronc in the rodeo, and Denver rides bulls. Or he did do, until he fell a few weeks ago and busted up his back. Now I reckon he's about ready to quit rodeo and settle down with his new wife come next year."

"Really? Where'd he meet her? Does she ride in the rodeo, too?"

"No. She was married to his brother. But then his brother got killed, and I guess Denver kind of stepped in."

Lori got a real dreamy look on her face that unsettled him. "Oh, how romantic."

He quickly changed the subject, and switched to recounting the hardships of travel on the road. He talked for a long time, intent on losing himself in memories to escape the distractions. He described the rodeo, and talked about his adventures, all the time uncomfortably aware of her fascinated gaze fixed on his face, her slender hands propping up her chin, and the way the shirt she wore parted enough for him to know that she wasn't wearing a bra.

He'd seen her underwear hanging from the shower rail to dry, but he hadn't really thought about the significance of it until now. He couldn't remember ever chattering on so much, yet his mind refused to give up the erotic images that kept popping up to torment him.

Finally, he'd had enough. He needed air. He needed

space. What he needed most of all was to get away from her eager gaze and supple body. "Guess it's time I went looking for supper," he said, pushing himself lazily to his feet.

She sent him a look of alarm. "You're not going to catch another fish, are you?"

"Not until tomorrow. Thought I might get me a rabbit or maybe a deer."

Her eyes widened. "You're going to kill a deer?"

He had no plans to hunt a deer. He was just using that as an excuse to get out of the cabin for a while. The way her voice had risen, however, put him on the defensive. "You got something against hunting?"

"Everything." She shuddered. "I think it's a barbaric and inhumane sport, and I despise the thought of it."

"You might change your mind if you were starving in the wilderness with no grocery store in sight."

"I still couldn't kill a helpless animal."

"Who knows what we're capable of doing when we're pushed?"

She lifted her chin. "Well, we're not pushed now. You have food in the cupboard, and you're not exactly starving. I don't think it's necessary to take the life of an innocent animal."

"What about the trout you gobbled down for lunch? I didn't hear you complaining about its innocent life."

She opened her mouth, shut it again…then looked helplessly at him. "That's different. I don't know why—it just is."

He stared at her for a long moment, then shook his head. "Lady, you got one hell of a lot to learn about survival. I just hope you never come face-to-face with a bear. I don't reckon it'll care much about your innocent life when it makes a meal of you."

When he saw her stricken expression he felt bad for being so blunt. He couldn't expect her to understand. If his instincts were right, she came from a fancy city neighborhood with a grocery store on every corner, where in her mind a package of steaks or a pork chop had nothing to do with an innocent cow or a pig. From the looks of it, she probably had little to do with meat anyway until it was cooked and on her plate. No wonder she didn't understand.

What did she know about sleeping in barns and killing chickens with bare hands? What did she know about riding a snow-covered range, herding cows to their winter quarters with your butt freezing off and icicles sticking your eyelashes shut? What could she possibly know about the long, empty, dusty roads; the noisy taverns choked with tobacco smoke; the ugly, vicious brawls; the women who loved too much and the men who cared too little?

Nothing. He'd talked about all those things, but he could see that she viewed them all the way she would a big movie extravaganza. She couldn't understand how it really was. She might as well have come from another planet. One more good reason to stay the hell away from her. He grabbed up his hat and jammed it on his head.

He didn't know why he was angry. He just knew he had to get out of there. Not trusting himself to speak, he headed for the door and the cool green peace of the forest.

Lori sat for a long time after he'd gone, thinking about what he'd told her. His life sounded so tough, so dangerous, yet so exciting. He was a strange man. She sensed a lot of bitterness behind his words, a lot of hidden anger, and she couldn't help wondering what made him so mad at the world. He was a loner, preferring his own company, yet underneath it all she detected a melancholy that told her he wasn't a happy man.

In some ways, he reminded her of her family, telling her what to do and how to do it. He liked to be in charge, and that was all right with her as long as he didn't think he had the right to order her about. She could learn a lot from him, but she had an idea that given the opportunity, he would try to dictate to her...and that was something she couldn't tolerate. It was the reason she was there. The reason she'd left everything and everyone familiar to her and charged out into the world without any clear idea of what she wanted.

She stared across the room at the chair that now sat vacant. Just a little while ago he'd sat there, filling her mind with exciting pictures of a strange, restless life on the road. The room seemed empty now that he was gone.

Her pulse quickened as she remembered the feelings he'd aroused in her when they'd stood so close at the sink. She'd never felt that kind of shivery excitement before. Certainly never with Richard.

Maybe that was what she needed. Maybe that was what she'd sensed was missing in her feelings for Richard...that slow, burning excitement that promised unknown and unimaginable pleasures. She closed her eyes for a moment, envisioning Richard as she'd last seen him.

He'd brought her home from a dinner date, their last before they were due to be married. He'd worn his dark-blue suit, white shirt and the silk tie she'd bought him for his birthday. Richard was a nice-looking man, with thick light-brown hair trimmed neatly above his ears, a square-cut face and an easy grin that she'd once thought so engaging. Lately, though, Richard's grin had become just a tad patronizing at times. Cord could be patronizing, too, but in a different way, somehow. Cord's caustic attitude was the complete opposite of Richard's subtle put-downs.

Lori opened her eyes and smiled fondly at the empty

chair. She'd never seen Cord smile once, yet she'd rather see that scowl on his face than Richard's condescending grin. A man like Cord McVane would know how to make a woman's heart beat faster. He'd certainly sped up hers now and then.

The unbidden thoughts seeped into her mind, though she did her best to ignore them. It would be exciting to be loved by a man like Cord. The notion seemed to grow in her mind, expanding and reaching, until her entire body seemed to hum with a weird expectancy. She could feel the tingling awareness way deep in her belly, heating, pulsing, making her feel weak yet powerful all at the same time.

She shook her head and massaged her upper arms in an effort to expel the unfamiliar sensations. They frightened and confused her, yet something deep inside her urged her to explore the strange yearning that tormented her.

She'd never felt this way about Richard. She'd actually been nervous about her wedding night. When he'd mentioned it, that last night they were together, he'd told her how much he was looking forward to making her a fulfilled woman. All she'd felt was an odd reluctance even to think about it.

Now she knew why. Richard didn't excite her the way Cord did. That's what was missing. Making love with someone like Cord would be an adventure, full of excitement, energy and a more than a dash of danger. Lori hugged herself. How her mother would hate it if her only daughter gave up her virginity to a man like Cord McVane. Just the thought of defying her parents that way made the possibility seem all the more exhilarating. It made her feel powerful, in charge of her destiny. It was a heady sensation.

Her heart was drumming now, and her whole body felt alive, vibrating with an intense current of longing and anticipation. If Cord had walked in at that moment she wasn't

sure what she would have done. She knew only that she
was afraid of her tumultuous feelings...afraid and incredibly reckless. It was a terrifying, wonderful feeling.

Cord sat at the water's edge, listening to the water
splashing over the rocks, and tried to clear his mind of all
thought and reason. He concentrated, instead, on the
screech of the blue jays and the cawing of the crows. He
watched the wind sway the branches of the majestic firs,
and the sunlight dapple shadows across the tumbling
stream. He sat there for a long time, until the crows were
quiet and the sparkling sunbeams had faded, then he
climbed to his feet and headed into the dense thicket of the
forest.

He trudged down the narrow trail between the thick
trunks of pines, skirting fallen logs and gnarled roots until
he reached a small clearing. Daisies bobbed in the evening
breeze, covering the sloping meadow in a thick, white carpet of blossom. Cord stood in the midst of them, his face
tilted to the sky.

His anger had long since evaporated, leaving only the
heartache inside him that had been his constant companion
for too many years. It followed him everywhere, sometimes
only a dull ache, at others a torment that would not fade.
It had been so long he had forgotten how bad it had felt
back then, nor did he want to remember. He had forced the
memory from his mind. Yet the remnants of his shattered
life had scarred him forever, and he would never escape
from the scars they had left behind.

For a little while this afternoon, though, he *had* forgotten.
The memories had faded in the glow of a young woman's
face; she had been mesmerized by his stories, her chin resting on her hands and excitement gleaming in her expressive
dark eyes.

He had to admit—he'd enjoyed her rapt attention to his words. She'd made him feel proud of his achievements and had given him a sense of being whole again. Until he'd remembered all the reasons he couldn't afford to let down his defenses. He was playing with fire, and he knew it. There was no way he was ever going to allow himself to get burned again.

After a while he felt calmer, and hunger drove him back to the cabin. To his surprise he saw smoke curling from the chimney. He'd let the fire out in the stove that morning. Lori must have lit it again. Inexplicably the knowledge gave him a warm feeling, thawing some of the cold edges of his heart.

She sat in front of the stove when he walked in, and didn't even turn her head when he asked gruffly, "You eaten yet?"

She shook her head but still didn't speak.

A little knot formed in the pit of his stomach. "What's wrong? Did something happen?"

"I thought you weren't coming back."

Her subdued voice made him feel guilty. He didn't wear a watch, but he knew by the sun that it was later than he should have stayed away. Relieved that it wasn't worse than that, though he wasn't sure what he'd been worried about, he said brusquely, "We'll get supper, then we have to talk."

"I'm not hungry."

A note of rebellion had crept into her voice, and he felt better. This was the Lori he knew. "You gotta eat."

"I'm not going to eat Bambi, nor am I going to cook him for you."

A reluctant grin tugged at his mouth. "Relax, sweetheart. I didn't do any hunting. If you'd paid attention you'd see I didn't take my rifle with me."

"I'm not your sweetheart."

"Okay, no need to get uppity. How about rustling up some supper? You'll feel better."

"Rustle it up yourself."

"Hey, I thought we had a deal."

She sighed and turned around to face him. That was when he noticed the nasty-looking swelling on her forehead. It hadn't been there when he'd left.

"What have you been up to?"

His concern had sharpened his voice and she frowned. "I'm not a kid. I'm twenty-two, remember?"

"Obviously you're gonna see to it that I remember," he said grimly. "So what did you do?"

"I was getting cold and I wanted to light the fire. I found the logs outside, but when I pulled one out of the pile a bunch of them came down on me."

He sighed. "I don't suppose you thought to take them from the top of the pile."

She glared at him. "I'm not stupid. I couldn't reach the top of the pile. I couldn't find anything to stand on, and I didn't want to have to drag a chair out there. So I thought I'd just ease one out from the side. I picked the wrong one. It was bigger than I thought and the pile shifted..."

Her voice trailed off and he looked at her in alarm. "You're not going to cry, are you?"

"No," she said stiffly. "I'm not going to cry."

"Good. I can't abide a woman crying. You'd better get some cold water on that swelling."

"I'm fine."

"No, you're not. Come here." He grabbed her arm and led her to the sink. "Now, stand still and let me put a cold pack on that."

He opened a drawer and pulled out a clean kitchen cloth. He ran the water until it was ice-cold, then soaked the cloth and wrung it out. All the time she stood there, her back as stiff as a fence post, looking as if she were poised to bolt like a scared rabbit the second he touched her.

"This shouldn't hurt a bit," he murmured, as he took hold of her arm and turned her to face him. Carefully he pressed the folded cloth to her forehead.

She winced, then said in a stiff little voice that seemed to tie knots in his stomach, "I do wish you wouldn't treat me like a child. I am an adult, you know. A grown-up woman, in case you haven't noticed."

"I noticed," he said dryly.

There must have been something else in his voice, because her eyes widened, and she parted her lips as if she were shocked by his answer.

She stood close enough for him to see the curve of her breasts in the deep neckline of the shirt she wore. He watched the soft mounds rise and fall for a moment. The sight was seductive, and his response was predictable. Inwardly cursing his active imagination, he dragged his gaze back to her face.

Her eyes were dark, velvety brown, with tiny gold flecks that seemed to beckon to him like stars in an endless sky. His hand stilled as he felt himself drawn closer, held captive by their spellbinding depths.

He felt strange, a weird sense that the world had suddenly stopped revolving. Somewhere outside a squirrel chattered in the branches of the pine trees...a cloud drifted across the sun...the wind fluttered the leaves of the aspens, while inside the cabin the still silence vibrated with a breathless anticipation.

He could smell his soap on her. The fragrance seemed a hundred times more exotic than he remembered. He was aware of so many things. The thick, dark lashes that framed those incredible eyes. The delicate curve of her eyebrows.

The faint flush that had stolen across her smooth cheeks, and the soft whisper of her uneven breathing.

He was having trouble breathing himself. Abruptly he stepped back, and turned away to drop the cloth on the counter. "That should help," he said, hoping his voice wouldn't betray his rattled nerves. "I've got aspirin if you have a headache."

"I feel fine. Thank you."

She'd sounded breathless, and he wondered if she'd been affected by the same erotic sensations that still coursed through his hungry body. Unnerved, he forced himself to look at her.

If she had shared that momentary encounter, she'd recovered faster than he had. She was looking at him with a faintly injured expression. "You were gone so long. Where were you?"

Normally he would have told her it was his own business where he'd been, but he was still feeling the effects of his reaction to her. In an effort to regain some sense of balance he said lightly, "You weren't worrying about me, by any chance?"

"Of course not." She'd said it just a tad too quickly, and he felt a twinge of satisfaction.

She opened the cupboard door and studied the contents. "I was just wondering if you were coming back, that's all. Because if not, I planned on leaving myself."

"How did you plan on doing that without a truck?"

"I have two good legs."

He shook his head. "It's close to four miles to the nearest road."

"I walked in from the road—I can walk out again."

He seized the opening at once. "Was that where you were robbed? You were hitching a ride? Don't you know how dangerous that is for a woman alone?"

She looked over at him, and the dispirited expression on her face tugged at his heart. How could she seem so vulnerable and innocent one minute and so damn womanly the next?

"I ran out of gas," she said wearily. "What was I supposed to do?"

"When someone stops to pick you up you don't get in his car—you ask him to call the cops for you—" He broke off and snapped his fingers. "Of course, I forgot. You don't want to talk to the cops...for private reasons."

A faint flush stained her cheeks. "You don't have to get sarcastic with me. I know it was a stupid thing to do... I just had no choice."

"So a guy picked you up, right?"

She nodded miserably.

"And tried to make a move on you."

Again she nodded.

"And when you fought him off he threw you out of the car without your stuff."

"Not exactly. He chased me. I think he was going to..." She shuddered, and took down a can of beans from the cupboard.

Cord felt a white-hot anger uncoil inside him. "So you ran."

"Yes." She reached up into the cupboard again and pushed a few cans around. "I ran into the trees because I thought it would be easier to hide from him. It was dark. I was afraid to run down the road. After a while I lost him, but then I was lost myself. I just kept walking, and that's when I found the cabin."

Right then Cord would have given a lot to get his hands on the bastard who had done this to her. He walked over to the armchair and sat down. "Why didn't you tell me all this when you first got up this morning? We could have had someone pick up your car.''

''There's no gas in it.''

''So I'd have told them to take a couple of gallons.''

She sent a wary look at him across the room. ''The police have probably found it by now.''

All his instincts jumped to attention. ''And you don't want them to find you. I think it's time you told me why, Lori. If you want to stay here, I gotta know.''

She stopped hunting through the cans in the cupboard and closed the door. Beside him, logs crackled and popped in the woodstove, spreading a warmth that radiated around the room. ''All right,'' she said quietly. ''I'll tell you.''

His nerves tightened, and he wasn't at all sure in that moment that he wanted to know. He knew only one thing right then. If she was in deep trouble, he would have to do his best to help her.

She walked back across the room and sank onto the other armchair. ''My parents are not dead,'' she said, her words coming out in a rush. ''I left home because I didn't want to marry Richard.''

It was such an anticlimax that all he could do for several moments was sit and stare at her. He didn't know what he'd been expecting—an abusive husband or parent, trouble with the law, a political refugee—anything but this. When he thought about how he'd agonized over what he should do about her, he felt like taking her by her slender shoulders and shaking her. What he did, instead, was something he rarely did. He threw back his head and laughed. Deep belly laughs that echoed from the walls and the ceiling rafters.

Lori stared at him, and when he finally paused for breath, she said icily, ''I can assure you, it's not a laughing matter. Right now my fiancé is probably nursing a broken heart, my brothers are more than likely organizing a search party for me, and knowing my family, I'm sure they have notified the police.''

His humor vanished as quickly as it had arisen. ''You got that one right, lady. This is not a laughing matter. You are going to call your folks this very minute and tell them you're all right. It's none of my business why you ran away from your own wedding, but I won't be a party to causing people unnecessary grief and worry.''

She pushed herself up from the chair, resentment burning in her face. ''You don't understand,'' she said furiously. ''No one understands. I've known Richard all my life. Early this year he proposed, and ever since then my parents have been pressuring me into marrying him. All I've heard for the past six months is what a great catch he is, how incredibly stupid I'd be to let him go, how lucky I am that a man like Richard wants to marry me, on and on and on until I'm sick of it.''

He gave her one his narrow-eyed stares, then held up his hand. ''Okay, calm down. Every bride gets nerves before the wedding—it goes with the territory. That's no reason to run away.''

She let out an explosive grunt of exasperation. ''I did not run away—I left. There's a huge difference. If only they'd listened, I wouldn't have had to leave like that. I tried to explain to them how I felt…that I was rushing into a marriage with a man I didn't love. They ignored everything I said. At the time, leaving seemed the only solution. And now you sound just as bad as them. It isn't nerves, as I kept telling them. I don't love Richard. I don't want to marry him. Is that so hard to understand?''

''Not to me. Sounds as though you've made up your mind pretty good.''

''Well, yes.'' She seemed appeased by his acceptance, and continued a little more calmly, ''Anyway, they wouldn't listen to me. I couldn't stop them all from making the plans. My mother and Richard's mother are best friends. They were having such a good time planning the wedding they wouldn't accept the fact that I didn't want to be married. And my father has always thought that he knows better than I do what I want and need. As for my brothers—"

"How many brothers?"

Stopped in the middle of her tirade, she stared at him. "Three of them."

He nodded slowly. "They're all older than you, right?"

"Yes. How did you know?"

"Lucky guess." He leaned back in his chair and closed his eyes. "Your brothers—they wouldn't all be over six feet tall with muscles of steel, would they?"

"Well, Mike works out, and Dennis used to wrestle in school, but he's only five-eleven. What's that got to do with anything?"

Cord groaned and rubbed a hand over his face. "I'm in more trouble than I thought."

As if finally realizing what he meant, she hurried to reassure him. "Oh, they wouldn't blame you. Even if they found me here, and I doubt very much that they would, I'd explain everything to them."

He opened one eye and looked at her. "You'd explain what? That you ran away from your future husband and ended up in a shack in the woods with a rodeo man? 'Shack' being the operative word, if you get my meaning."

Heat washed over her face. "Oh, they wouldn't. I mean I wouldn't...no, I'd tell them—"

Cord leaned forward again. "Sweetheart, look around you. There's only one bedroom and one bed. What else are they gonna think?"

She lifted her chin. "They can think what they like. I don't care."

"Maybe you don't care, lady, but I do. The sooner I get you on a bus back to town the better. By the way, which town is it?"

She stared at him mutinously in silence.

Cord sighed. "Okay, don't tell me. But you are going to make that call. Now."

Looking for all the world like the rebellious kid she kept insisting she wasn't, she dug her fists into her hips. "Don't you dare tell me what to do. I'm sick of being ordered around. From now on I make my own decisions, and I'll call when I'm ready to call. Not one second before."

Cord got slowly to his feet. He managed to sound calm when he spoke, but he warned her with his eyes that she was on thin ice. "I reckon I'm as patient as the next guy, but I have to tell you, when I'm pushed I've got a mean temper. It might be better if you trusted me on that. So, either you make that call now, or I call the sheriff's office and you can talk to them."

"I'm not going back. I'm over twenty-one and you can't make me go where I don't want to go."

"Neither can they," he said, gentling his voice. "All I'm asking is that you tell them you're okay. You don't even have to tell them where you are if you don't want to. Just put their minds at ease, that's all. If the cops have picked up your car they'll want to know why it was abandoned and what happened to you. You are supposed to report a crime, you know."

"I don't want to tell them about the robbery. Then I'll have to make a statement, and my brothers will find me and take me back."

"Then tell them you don't want to go back."

"You don't understand." Her obvious frustration made her voice rise. "They won't listen to reason. They never do. They'll just ignore everything I say."

"Not if you sound as if you really mean it. After all, I reckon you did a pretty good job of standing up to me once or twice."

She shook her head. "But I don't know you," she wailed. "You're not my brother."

Feeling like a heel, Cord moved closer and patted her awkwardly on the shoulder. All he was trying to do was what he felt was best for her. He hadn't meant to make her cry. "Aw, come on, sweetheart," he mumbled. "It'll all work out all right, you'll see."

"No, it won't. You don't know them."

She was obviously doing her best not to cry, but she looked as if she was losing the battle. He dropped his hand. "All right. You don't have to report the robbery if you're that dead set against it. Just tell your folks that you ran out of gas and hitched a ride. Tell them you're fine, and you'll be in touch with them soon. If they start asking too many questions, just tell them you have to go and hang up."

After a moment, she nodded. "You're right, of course. I'm sorry. I guess I overreacted."

He watched her, finding it hard to understand how anyone could be so intimidated by her family. When she finally looked at him, he said softly, "They must be some strong opposition."

"You don't know the half of it." She glanced around the room. "Where's the phone?"

"In my jacket. It's a cell phone. I'll get it."

He crossed the room to where his leather jacket hung from the wall on a pegboard.

"What if they trace the call? They have caller ID," Lori said anxiously behind him.

"The number's unlisted. It will show up as a blocked call." He unhooked the jacket and took the phone from one of the pockets. "Here you go. Want some privacy?"

She shook her head. She seemed to have calmed down now, apparently satisfied that he was on her side. He watched her dial the number and hoped like hell he was doing the right thing.

If she really had good reason to be afraid of her family, he wasn't doing her any favors by exposing her to the risk that they might track her down. Apart from anything else, after seeing how she reacted to his insistence that she call, he wasn't too eager to see her being taken back home by her bullying brothers.

On the other hand, he didn't need three angry young men and the cops coming looking for him, either. All he could do was hope that her family would be satisfied with her call and drop whatever measures they'd taken to find their missing daughter. If not, Lori wouldn't be the only one who could end up in deep trouble.

Chapter 4

Lori dialed the number and waited, her throat dry, for someone to answer. There was a click, then a familiar voice stated, ''Ashford residence. This is the housekeeper speaking.''

''Marietta?'' Lori paused, trying to erase the tremble from her voice. ''Is my mother there?''

''Lori?'' Marietta's cry echoed down the line. ''Are you all right? We've all been so worried.''

Guilt swamped her for a moment, and she struggled to regain the convictions that had set her on this devastating path. ''Yes, I'm fine, thank you, Marietta. Could you please put me through to my mother.''

''Right away, Lori. She'll be so happy you called. That poor Richard has been out of his mind. Just a minute.''

Lori glanced at Cord. He gave her a nod of encouragement, then winked at her.

She smiled back, then gripped the phone as her mother's plaintive voice came on the line.

"Lori? What were you thinking of? Your brothers have been going crazy and poor Richard—"

Everyone, it seemed, was more concerned about Richard's feelings than hers, Lori thought with a flash of irritation. "Mom, I'm sorry, but I honestly thought I was doing the best thing. Did you read my letter? I explained everything—"

"Of course I read it. Everyone's read it and no one can make any sense of it. Do you realize how heartbroken Richard is? And all that money for the wedding…having to cancel everything at the last minute…it was such an embarrassment. We'll never live it down, you know."

Lori closed her eyes. "I'm sorry, Mom. I just couldn't go through with it, that's all."

"Well, we'll talk about it when you get home. When are you coming home? Richard will be so happy to see you. Maybe we can reschedule the wedding for next month—"

Lori gritted her teeth. "I'm sorry, Mom. I have to go. I just wanted you to know that I'm perfectly well and happy. I'll call soon."

"Lori, wait a minute. Where are you? When are you coming home?"

"I don't know… I'll have to let you know. Not for a while yet anyway."

"But Lori…wait…speak to your father. Maybe he can talk some sense into you. Hold on, he's right here."

Lori pulled the phone away from her ear and hit the End button. She handed the phone back to Cord, who took it from her, his expression unreadable.

"You didn't tell her goodbye," he said lightly.

"She wanted me to speak to my father." Lori drew a trembling breath. "I didn't want to speak to him. Not yet."

"You look beat. Why don't we heat up some of that canned stew? You'll feel better when you've eaten."

No, she wouldn't, Lori thought, heading over to the cupboards. The call had intensified her guilt. If she wasn't very careful, she could find herself weakening in her resolve to stay away. One thing she was sure of. No more phone calls. Not for a long time.

She opened the can of stew with the can opener she found in the drawer and dumped the contents in the pan. Her mind still on the call, she stood the pan on the stove and turned on the ring.

"You've got that too high," Cord said a moment later, startling her out of her thoughts. "It'll burn if you don't turn it down."

"I wish you'd quit telling me what to do," she snapped irritably. "I'm quite capable of thinking for myself. How many times do I have to remind everyone of that?"

"Whoa!" He held up both hands in mock surrender. "Take it easy. I'm not the enemy."

"Sorry." She turned down the heat. "I guess I'm still steamed at my mother."

"Want to talk about it?"

Lori shrugged. "My mother still thinks I'm going to marry Richard. She wants to reschedule the wedding. She didn't understand anything I said in my letter."

"Have you told Richard you don't love him?"

She lifted her head sharply, but he'd turned away and she couldn't see his face. "I've told him I'm not ready to marry him," she said warily.

Cord nodded. "Not exactly the same thing, was it?"

"No." She sighed. "I didn't want to hurt his feelings."

"How much do you reckon he's hurting now?"

She stared at him, wishing he would turn round so she could read his expression. "I know what you're saying. It would have been kinder to tell him the truth."

"I guess that's what I'm saying. It's always better to get

the truth out, because sooner or later, if you don't, it'll backfire on you. Believe me, I know. I've been there.''

She searched in the drawer for a wooden spoon. Sticking it in the stew, she gave it a vicious twirl. ''Is that why your marriage broke up?''

He didn't answer her at first. She glanced up, unnerved by his silence. Then he turned his head, and the pain in his face shocked her.

''Something like that,'' he said quietly.

She wanted to go to him—to put her arms around him. She wanted more than anything to erase that awful torment she saw in his eyes. All she could do was stand there, helplessly wondering who had hurt this man and bitterly regretting her thoughtless question.

It seemed a long time until Cord spoke again. Then he said gruffly, ''I reckon that stew is about ready.''

Keeping her anxious thoughts to herself, Lori turned back to the pot and gave the contents another stir, then reached for the plastic plates she'd washed earlier. The enticing fragrance of cooked beef and onions, laced with a spicy herb gravy, made her stomach roll. She hadn't realized she was hungry again until that moment.

She dished up a generous portion for Cord and a smaller helping for herself. Cord found a packet of crackers in the cupboard, grabbed a couple of forks out of the drawer and took them over to his armchair, while she followed, carefully carrying the steaming plates.

He took the plate from her with a nod of thanks and offered her the crackers. She helped herself to a handful, then settled down on the other armchair with the plate balanced on her knees. After capturing a plump slice of carrot on her fork, she stuck it in her mouth.

''Not quite what you're used to, I reckon,'' Cord said, with an odd note in his voice.

She looked up and met his dark eyes. Something in their black depths stirred that quivery feeling in her stomach again. "Maybe not, but I can't remember food ever tasting this good."

"That's probably because you fixed it."

"I just had to heat it up."

"Maybe. But you didn't burn it. That's a big plus with me." To her astonishment and delight, he smiled at her.

The effect was startling. He seemed younger, and infinitely more approachable. A faint dimple flashed in his cheek, then was gone as he bent his head to take another mouthful of the stew. Even so, in that brief moment, she'd detected something in his face she hadn't seen until now—the warmth of compassion, caring and understanding. Cord McVane was human after all.

The knowledge seemed to spread a comforting blanket around her, and for the first time since she'd left her home, she felt a sense of security. This man would not let anything bad happen to her. She was sure of that now.

Reassured by that glimpse of benevolence, she wondered if she dared venture to find out more about his personal life. So far he'd told her about the rodeo and his travels with Jed and Denver, but she wanted to know more. Up until now he'd avoided any conversation about his earlier life.

She waited until he'd cleared his plate, then asked him, "Were you born in Oregon?"

"Idaho." He wiped the edge of a cracker around the edge of his plate and popped it in his mouth.

"What made you decide to become a rodeo rider?"

He shrugged, then winced when the movement apparently caused him pain. "I'd grown up with horses. Seemed like a good idea at the time."

"How old where you when you started riding for the rodeo?"

For a minute she thought he wasn't going to answer, then he sighed.

"What is this? An inquest on my background?"

She met his gaze squarely. "You know all about mine. I was just curious about yours, that's all. I was wondering if you had family. You never mention them."

He leaned forward and set the plate on the floor at his feet, then leaned back, a brooding expression shadowing his face. "There's not much to mention. My pa's dead. My mother's living with my sister back East."

"Do you see them very often?"

"Nope. Not since my marriage broke up."

She felt a cold stab of dismay. "I'm sorry."

He nodded. "So am I."

She remembered his insistence that she call her parents to let them know where she was. It seemed odd that he hadn't kept in touch with his mother. Unless... "Did they blame you for the breakup of your marriage?" she asked tentatively.

Her stab in the dark had been on target. His face closed up. "Maybe."

She hesitated, wary of treading on forbidden ground. "Sometimes it helps to talk about things that bother us," she said quietly. "It always helps me. You must know I wouldn't repeat anything to anyone else."

He stared at her, his dark eyes glinting in the glow of the lamp at his side. Then he startled her by pushing himself to his feet. She watched him reach for a log, open the flap of the woodstove and shove the thick piece of wood inside. The acrid smell of wood smoke filled the room. Sparks spat and jumped, and a small yellow flame licked around the edge of the timber. He threw two more logs into the glowing embers and stood for a moment staring into the crackling, leaping flames.

Then he closed the flap and returned to his chair. "I don't talk much about what happened," he said quietly. "But I reckon you're right. Maybe I should."

She waited, hardly daring to breathe, while a warm feeling of pleasure washed over her at the thought of him sharing his most private thoughts with her.

He leaned back, closed his eyes and laced his fingers across his chest. "I was twenty when I got married. Ellie was eighteen. She was pregnant, and I wanted to do the right thing by her. I didn't know much about having babies in those days, so I didn't think too much about it when Ellie had the baby two months earlier than she'd told me it was due. I believed her when she told me the baby was premature."

He paused, and his voice was dry when he continued. "Toby was eight months old when I found out he wasn't mine at all. Ellie's old boyfriend had gotten her pregnant before she started going out with me, and wouldn't admit the baby was his. So Ellie figured on giving her baby a father by leading me on and then lying about when she got pregnant."

Lori uttered a cry of dismay. "Oh, Cord, I'm sorry. That must have been a terrible shock for you."

"Yep, you could say that." He sat up and thrust his hands between his knees. "What made it worse was the reason Ellie had told me. It seems the boyfriend had a change of heart. He wanted Ellie back, as well as his son."

Lori stared at him in horror, too choked to speak. He'd lost his wife and the child he'd cared for as his own at the same time, through no fault of his own. No wonder he was bitter about women.

"I let them go," Cord said, his voice still devoid of

emotion, "but I had too much pride to tell my folks the reason. I let them blame me, instead. I left town and joined the rodeo. End of story."

"It's such a sad story," Lori said brokenly. What was even sadder was the things he'd left out. How lonely, how betrayed, he must have felt. She wished desperately she could think of something to say to ease the pain she saw in his eyes. But there was nothing, she knew, that would ever take away that kind of heartache.

For a long time they sat in silence, while the logs hissed and spat in the woodstove and outside the night owls hooted in the darkened forest. Finally, Cord stretched out his feet in front of him. "I reckon it's time I took some more of those painkillers and tried to get some shut-eye."

A shaft of excitement streaked through Lori's body, taking her breath away. She struggled to sound natural when she asked, "Would you rather I sleep out here?"

He paused and looked down at her. "No, I'll take the chair. You can have the bed."

She phrased the words carefully in her head before she spoke them. "The chair isn't very comfortable. I tried it last night, and with your bad shoulder—"

"I'll be fine." He crossed to the sink and opened the cupboard above it. "These pills would put an elephant down."

She stood up, her heart thumping so hard she was sure he could hear it. "I really don't mind if you want to share the bed."

For just a second or two she saw his hand pause, then he took down a bottle of beer and twisted off the cap. "You were right last night. It isn't such a good idea."

"I trust you."

Slowly he took a small bottle out of the cupboard and

opened it. He looked at her then, and his dark eyes gleamed in the shadows. "Maybe you shouldn't."

Without taking his eyes off her, he tipped a couple of the pills into his palm and tossed them into his mouth. Then he poured himself some water from the faucet and lifted the glass to his lips. "You play with fire, sweetheart, you're likely to get burned." Throwing back his head, he took a deep drink.

"I don't think you'd do anything I didn't want you to do."

"That kind of thinking is likely to get us both in trouble."

"With someone else, maybe. But I have a feeling that with you, it's the truth."

He set the glass down with a thump, as if he were tired of arguing. "Any other time I might give you an argument on that. Right now I'd say you're probably right. What with the pills and this damn shoulder, I'm not much of a threat. I won't get much sleep in that chair, and I'll more'n likely keep you awake with my fidgeting. So if you're all that sure it's all right with you, I guess I will take half of the bed."

She smiled at him. "It's all right with me."

"Good." He gave her a weary nod. "Then I guess it's lights-out time."

She left him in the kitchen while she used the bathroom. Her stomach felt as if there were kittens leaping around inside. She'd meant what she said about trusting him. And because he'd been so kind to her, she couldn't bear the thought of him losing a good night's sleep on her account. Still, the thought of sleeping with him tonight gave her a sense of shivery anticipation.

The tragedy of his earlier life had affected her deeply. She longed to do something, anything, to erase those dreadful memories, yet she knew that nothing she could do could possibly make up for losing a wife and child in that cruel way.

She slipped out of her borrowed jeans and shirt. After a moment's hesitation she untied the bandanna and shook her hair free. Maybe he wouldn't mind if she borrowed the comb again, she thought, picking it up. She coaxed out the tangles, then laid down the comb and reached for the oversized T-shirt Cord had loaned her and pulled it on.

She opened the door of the bathroom and peeked into the living room. Cord must have already gone to bed, she thought, advancing into the room. She couldn't seem to stop the tingles of fear and excitement chasing up and down her body. And she didn't need to analyze and wonder about why she felt the way she did.

What was it he'd said? *You play with fire, sweetheart, you're likely to get burned.* Well, she was beginning to like the idea of playing with fire. Especially with Cord. There'd never been any man in her life except Richard, and compared with Cord, her fiancé was totally dull. Cord was all man, all brimstone and fire. It was a new experience, and a little frightening, but that was what made it exciting. She felt more alive than she'd ever felt before, and more of a woman than she ever dreamed possible.

Trembling with suppressed emotions she wasn't fully sure she understood, she opened the door of the bedroom. Surprisingly, disappointment knifed through her when she saw the empty bed. The lamp had been turned on, but Cord had apparently left the cabin for some reason. Hoping she would be fast asleep before he returned, she slipped between the sheets and lay there, every nerve in her body tense.

Outside the cabin, Cord paced up and down in the darkness. He'd decided to give himself some time for the pills to start working before he risked joining Lori in the bed.

She had a lot more faith in his willpower than he did, which was probably the only thing that would keep him on his side of the bed...her trust in him. He just wished he had that same trust in himself.

He couldn't quite shake the memory of that moment when he'd tried to show her how to clean the trout. Standing that close to her, his nose practically buried in her clean shiny hair, he'd forgotten that she was a young woman on the run, with a secret past that more than likely spelled trouble. All he remembered was how long it had been since he'd been with a woman.

Then she'd jolted his shoulder. He'd stared into those dark-brown eyes and seen compassion there, tenderness and something else that had stirred his body and quickened his pulse. All he'd had to do was lean forward an inch or two and that tempting mouth of hers would have been his.

He'd felt again that urge to kiss her when he'd attended to her bruised forehead. His body stirred at the memory. A sudden image of himself lying on top of her body dressed only in his shorts heated his mind. Damn, he had to stop thinking this way. He couldn't afford to let his lack of female companionship lead him down a path to certain destruction. As far as he was concerned, she was way off-limits. She was too vulnerable—not the kind of woman he could seduce and forget about.

There was no doubt in his mind; the longer he was around her the more he wanted her. She was so different from the women he knew around the rodeo. She had more class, more guts and more sex appeal than any woman he'd ever met. There was an innocence about her that made him want to protect every breath she took, yet at times she was so damn seductive it was all he could do not to grab her and kiss her senseless.

She didn't play games like the other women he knew. She was straightforward and wholesome, honest and sincere...and that's what made her so appealing...she didn't know what she was doing to him. She didn't realize that every time she walked across the room, swaying those gorgeous hips of hers, he longed to haul her into his arms.

She didn't seem to understand that whenever she stood close to him and gazed into his face, he wanted in the worst way to touch her hair or run a finger down her smooth cheek. She couldn't know that the sound of her breathless voice twisted his gut or her smile melted his soul. She was angel and enchantress, innocence and temptation, and the combination was dynamite. Never in his life could he remember being this agitated by a woman.

Jed and Denver would sure get a laugh out of this one. Cord, the woman hater, at the mercy of a naive young woman who hadn't the slightest idea she was driving a man out of his mind.

Impatient with himself and his rampaging needs, Cord stomped over to the woodpile and began stacking the fallen logs with his good arm. He needed to tire himself out so that the moment he hit the bed he fell asleep. He should have insisted on taking the chair, he thought fiercely. Although he knew he wouldn't sleep at all if he did. He needed his rest if he wanted to stay on guard against his rampant animal instincts.

The pills hit him without warning, making him sway on his feet. It was time to get to bed. He stumbled into the cabin and locked the door, then switched off the lamp in the living room before heading across the room to the bedroom.

He opened the door slowly, hoping she'd be asleep. She stirred as he crept around the foot of the bed.

"Cord? Are you all right?"

"Yeah, I was just out getting some air. Go back to sleep."

She mumbled something he didn't quite catch, and he waited a moment or two before reaching out to turn off the lamp. The room plunged into darkness, and thankful he couldn't see her now, he dragged off his boots one by one, then his jeans, and lastly his shirt. Usually he slept in his shorts, but tonight he wished he kept a pair of sweats at the cabin. Then again, he hadn't thought he would be sharing his bed.

The sheets felt cold when he slid in, though the air outside had seemed heavy and still. He pulled the covers over his shoulder, and then froze as Lori murmured something at his side. He waited, but after a moment, all he could hear was her soft, rhythmic breathing.

Weariness and the medication had made him drowsy, and he closed his eyes, expecting to go to sleep straight away. Instead, he felt restless, his muscles refusing to relax. He was painfully aware of the warmth of Lori's body, just inches away. He found himself wondering what she was wearing, and managed to fight off the urge to find out. His body ached with wanting her, and he cursed the forces of nature that could allow the medication to deaden his mind and destroy his resolve, yet leave a pertinent part of his body as lively as a bunch of tree frogs.

Tomorrow, he promised himself, he would talk to Lori and find out what she had in mind to do. She couldn't stay there in the cabin forever. He was due back to the rodeo in a couple of days, and he couldn't leave her alone in the cabin to fend for herself. He hadn't mentioned it to her, but as the summer heat waned in the mountains, the bears and coyotes would be coming down to hunt for food. Not to mention the hunters who roamed the woods with rifles and shotguns.

It just wasn't safe for her to be there alone. It was luck that had sent him back to the cabin as it was. Luck, or fate, he thought grimly. He didn't want to feel responsible for her. He didn't want to worry about her, to care what happened to her. His life had been uncomplicated for so long; he had no wish to mess things up now. What he should do was talk her into going back to her kin. That was where she belonged. She just had to learn to stand up to them, that was all.

He lay for a long time staring at the darkened ceiling. He'd miss her being around, he finally admitted. But she would be better off with her folks, and his conscience would be clear. That was the best thing he could do for her.

Having decided that, he finally fell asleep. When he woke up again, it was to find Lori's head on his shoulder, her knees curled into his side and her long, silky hair spread over his pillow.

He shoved himself away from her so suddenly she woke up with a little yelp of surprise. Without looking at her, he climbed out of bed and grabbed his pants. "I'm gonna light the fire," he mumbled, and fled from the room as if all the witches in hell were after him.

Lori lay there for a while, until she heard the front door slam. She frowned, wondering what had put Cord in such a bad mood. Maybe his shoulder was hurting him, she thought, as she slipped her feet out of bed. He must have had a bad night.

The floor felt cold beneath her feet as she padded across to the window and peeked out. A fine mist hung between the firs, and she could see the dew clinging to the spider webs in the lacy branches. Chattering squirrels darted along the boughs, which bent beneath their weight, then sprang back as the tiny animals leaped into space.

Lori saw a shadow move in the trees, and realized it was Cord. He was leaning against a thick trunk, his hands thrust into the pockets of his leather jacket, his booted feet crossed. He seemed to be staring at the ground, but she couldn't see what held his attention. She watched him, waiting for him to move, while the squirrels played unnoticed above his head. Minutes ticked by, and still he remained motionless, almost as if he were part of the forest, until at last, he uncrossed his feet and shoved himself away from the tree.

Lori backed away from the window, reluctant to let him know she'd been watching him. She felt unsettled, as if she'd witnessed an intimate moment that she wasn't supposed to see. Quickly she crossed the bedroom and hurried into the living room. She headed for the sink, where she busied herself filling the pot with cold water.

She didn't turn her head when she heard him come through the door. She felt unsure of herself, on edge, though she wasn't sure why. For some reason, Cord seemed like a stranger again, unsettling and unfamiliar. She wasn't sure if he had put the distance between them, or if she had engineered it in her mind. All she knew was that the glimpse of him alone in the forest, when he thought he was unobserved, had made her more aware of how close she had become to the inscrutable and complex stranger who had given her shelter.

She had never shared this kind of relationship with Richard. They had been constant companions since childhood, yet looking back, Lori knew now she hadn't really known him at all. She had met Cord just a few days ago, yet it seemed as if she had known him forever and had just been waiting for him to walk into her life. It was a strange sensation. It scared her and excited her at the same time.

"The water should be hot enough for your shower soon," Cord said, his voice sounding a little strained.

She nodded, not trusting herself to look at him just yet. Something warned her not to let him see how vulnerable he made her feel. He must never know how she felt about him. She couldn't explain her feelings, anyway. Not even to herself. She just knew she'd never truly understood before the power of a woman's yearnings.

"I'm making some coffee." She stuck the pot on the stove and turned on the ring. "You want some?"

"Sure."

Out of the corner of her eye she saw him cross the room to the woodstove. He'd taken off his jacket and he wore a black sweatshirt with his jeans. He needed a shave, and his hair was mussed. He looked primitive, and wholly masculine. He leaned over to pick up a log, then opened the flap of the stove and shoved the wood inside. She watched the fluid movements, struck by the agility of this strong, rugged cowboy.

She'd love to watch him ride, she thought. From the little she'd seen about the rodeo, it was a tough way to make a living. Yet there was something almost graceful about the way he moved, in the long swing of his stride, the way he held himself, even when he was angry, as he'd been that first night.

The memory of him standing half-naked in front of her sent a sudden heat throughout her body, and she turned away, flustered by her reaction. "Is it cold out there?" She'd asked the question in a vain effort to break the tension inside her. It was almost a shock when he answered.

"Nope. As a matter of fact, it feels muggy. Wouldn't be

surprised if we don't get some lightning before the day's out.''

"I hope not." Thunderstorms were rare over the city. Even so, she hated to be caught in one. She didn't think she wanted to be in the mountains when a thunderstorm hit.

"Probably won't be much, I reckon."

She glanced at him. He seemed as uncomfortable as she felt. She had an ache of regret when she remembered how relaxed they'd been with each other last night. He'd even admitted that he didn't usually talk about his breakup with his wife. Maybe that was what was bothering him. He could be regretting having told her so much about his personal life. The thought filled her with dismay.

In an attempt to find out the cause for his tension, she asked lightly, "Is your shoulder hurting? Did you have a bad night?''

His glance touched her face, then slid away. "No on both counts. The shoulder feels a lot better this morning. Reckon I'll be going back to the circuit any day now.''

She stared at the water boiling furiously in the pot. It was as if the bottom had just dropped out of her world. She deliberately hadn't thought about leaving the cabin. She'd known that she would have to eventually, but whenever the prospect had arisen in her mind, she'd simply pushed it away. It had been enough just to enjoy the peace and quiet of the cabin, the tranquillity of the forest and the stimulating company of Cord McVane.

She didn't want to think about leaving. There were too many unanswered questions...too many unknown consequences. She jumped when Cord spoke again.

"Have you given any thought to what you're going to do when you leave here?''

She shrugged and did her best to sound indifferent. "Get a job, I guess."

"What kind of job?"

She dropped a coffee bag into the mug. "I don't know."

"Where did you work before?"

Carefully she lifted the pot and poured the boiling water into the mug. "I didn't."

"You've never worked?"

She heard the disbelief in his voice and winced. "No, I haven't."

"You just got out of college, then."

"I didn't go to college. My father thought it was a waste of time to send a girl through college."

"So what did you do?"

"Helped my mother, mostly."

He muttered something. "How in blazes do you think you're going to support yourself if you've never had a job?"

She dumped the pot back on the stove. "I'll find a way."

"That settles it." He strode over to the sink and turned on the faucet. "You're going back home. You're not safe to be out in the world on your own, and that's a fact. No wonder your family is so worried about you."

She whirled on him, furious at this unexpected reversal. "I'm not going back. Nothing in this world will make me go back. I'll get a job. It can't be that hard. I can type. I can answer the phone. I can do lots of things. I'll be all right, you wait and see."

"No, *you'll* see." He snatched his hands from under the running water and grabbed the kitchen towel. "You wouldn't last five minutes out there. Where are you going to live? Dammit, Lori, I can't let you wander the streets all alone, and I can't play nursemaid forever. I've got a championship to worry about. I don't have time for this. You're going home, and that's final."

She was so angry and hurt she was shaking. Her voice trembled when she answered him, and she fought to hold back tears. "I'm not asking you to be my nursemaid. You don't have to be responsible for me. I'm quite capable of taking care of myself."

"Oh, yeah?" He advanced on her, his eyes blazing fire. "Just how are you going to do that, Miss Ashford, without any experience, let alone money, credit cards or social security?"

Cold with shock, she stared at him. "How did you find out my last name?"

"I redialed the number on the cell phone. Your housekeeper answered."

She couldn't believe it. She shook her head, while resentment poured into every fiber of her being. "Damn you, Cord, how could you? Didn't you hear anything I said? I don't want my family to know where I am. I'm twenty-two years old. I'm not a child. I'm a responsible adult and I need to take charge of my own life. I was never allowed to do that at home. And you're not going to stop me now. Not you, not them, not even the police. I don't need your protection. I don't need your advice. And I certainly don't need you butting into my life and telling me what to do. I'll leave. Right now. Then you won't have to worry about me anymore."

Fury and desperation propelled her across the room. Before she could reach the door, however, Cord sprinted ahead of her. Planting his feet apart, he barred her way out. "You go through that door, sweetheart, and I'll call your parents and tell them where to find you."

"I'll be long gone before they get here."

"Not if I have you picked up for breaking and entering."

She glared at him. "You wouldn't."

"Try me."

Her temper got the better of her and she lunged at him, intent on shoving him out of the way. Instead, he neatly sidestepped and wrapped his arms around her, trapping her hands at her sides. She shoved her heel into his shin and he yelped. Immediately she felt guilty.

"I'm sorry. Please let me go." She didn't tell him that being clamped to his chest like that had suddenly wiped out all her anger.

"Only if you swear you won't run away."

She could feel his heart beating against her shoulder. Why couldn't she stay mad at him? It was the only way she could fight him. "I won't run away."

"And you'll talk about this quietly?"

"As long as you promise not to call my parents." A thought struck her and she looked up at him anxiously. "You didn't tell them where I was, did you?"

He looked down at her. His stubbled jaw was just inches from her face. Her heart skipped a beat when he didn't answer right away. His eyes burned into hers, and a tiny muscle moved at the corner of his mouth. "No," he said softly. "I didn't tell them. I didn't speak a word. When the housekeeper answered I hung up."

She nodded, potently aware of his arms clamped around her, his hard body crushed against hers. "Promise you won't."

"Won't what?"

"Tell them where to find me."

"Oh."

He started to lower his head and her pulse leaped. She felt winded, as if she'd been running hard for a long time. She tilted back her head and parted her lips. Her heart thudded against her ribs, and her legs trembled as she waited, quivering with anticipation.

She heard him draw in a sharp breath, and for a second or two he tightened his arms as his mouth hovered just above hers. Then, with an explosive curse, he shoved her away from him.

"Dammit, Lori. What the hell are you doing to me?" With a savage twist of his body, he spun on his heel and jerked open the door.

Shaken by his anger, she cried, "Where are you going?"

"I'm gonna take a long swim in a cold river." He grabbed his hat from the pegboard and then the door slammed shut behind him, leaving her alone in the cabin. Alone and feeling every bit as frustrated as he had looked.

Chapter 5

Cord clenched his teeth as he strode swiftly through the trees to where the chilled mountain water waited for him. His whole body felt as if it were on fire. The minute he'd grabbed hold of Lori he'd realized she was wearing next to nothing under the T-shirt. He'd come so close...so damn close to kissing her. He'd never wanted anything quite as much as he wanted her. Except maybe the all-around championship. Even that seemed to pale into insignificance compared with the raging hunger inside him. God, how he wanted her.

He wanted her in his bed. He wanted her under him, on top of him, all over him. He wanted to cover her slender, smooth body with hot, smoldering kisses, from her tantalizing mouth to her belly button to her ankles. He wanted to be inside her and feel her body clamp around him, holding him there. He wanted to drive her wild, the way she drove him crazy. God, what he wanted *was* crazy. He had to be plumb out of his mind.

He reached the water's edge, threw down his hat, then pulled off his boots. His jeans came next, then his shirt and finally his shorts. Pausing for a moment on the bank, he braced himself for the cold shock of the water, then waded in. He submerged his head and came up gasping. It wasn't a deep swimming hole, but it was wide enough to take a dozen swift strokes or more to cross to the other bank.

By the time he reached the other side the icy water had cooled the fires that had blazed in his body. He turned and stroked back across the river, satisfied that he had everything under control again. He was getting used to the water now, but he knew he wouldn't be able to stay in there too long. He scrubbed himself with his hands, as if trying to erase the memory of his craving, then he pulled himself out of the water.

He dressed quickly, enjoying the warm comfort of his clothes after the chill of the river. The cool air was abnormally still, and felt clammy. He stared up at the hazy sky. In the distance he could see the thick white mushrooms of cloud forming over the mountains. Thunderheads. He'd been right about a storm brewing. Maybe that was why his head was so crazy.

He had to do something about that. His shoulder was healing fast now...there was no reason he shouldn't go back to the circuit. The longer he was around Lori, the worse he was going to feel. He'd have to call Jed and ask him to come pick him up tomorrow. One more night with his houseguest was about as much as he could stand. Now he had to decide what he was going to do about her.

She was right—he couldn't make her go back to her parents, much as he felt it was the best solution. She was bound and determined to strike out on her own, and she'd find a way to do it, with or without him. It looked as if it would have to be with him. He couldn't just abandon her, especially now that he knew how inexperienced she was.

He took his time walking back to the cabin, turning things over in his mind. It was bound to get complicated. She needed clothes, money… He'd have to find her somewhere to live. She could hardly bunk with him and his partners. That was something else. Jed and Denver would have plenty to say about him taking charge of a woman.

He kicked at a root before stepping over it. He'd gotten himself into a real mess this time. He should have called the sheriff the minute he'd found her hiding under his bed. Now it was too late. Now he was compromised, and he didn't like it one bit.

Lori was outside, washing a window, when he got back to the cabin. She'd piled logs up and stood on them to reach the top panes. He paused in the shelter of the trees and watched her for a moment. She wore his jeans and one of his checkered shirts tied up at her middle. When she stretched up to clean the glass he could see an expanse of bare flesh above her waistband. She looked young, vibrant and maddeningly seductive.

He clamped down on his erotic thoughts before they could get the better of him again. The sooner he quit thinking about her that way, the better for both of them. Shoving his thumbs into the pockets of his jeans, he sauntered across the clearing toward her.

She looked round at him when he hailed her, a wary expression on her face. "Did you enjoy your swim?"

"Yep." He nodded at the sparkling window. "Nice job."

She smiled, turning his insides over. "Thanks. I couldn't see out of them too well, so I cleaned them."

He had to admit he was impressed. For someone who wasn't used to lifting a finger around the house, she was catching on real good. "I reckon that's the first time they've been cleaned any, at least since I've had the place."

She peered at the glass. "They were really dirty. I had to use the kitchen towel to clean them. I'll wash it out. I'd also like to wash some clothes. Do you have any detergent? I couldn't find any in the cupboards."

"Sorry. I usually drop everything off at the Laundromat when I get back to town. Speaking of which, I've decided to go back tomorrow."

She kept her back to him, appearing to be absorbed in her efforts to remove a smear from the windowpane.

When she didn't answer him, he said impatiently, "We have to talk about this, Lori."

"I'm not going back to my parents' house."

"Okay, I guess I'll have to go along with that. But we do have to figure out what to do with you."

Again the long pause. Her voice was cool when she finally answered. "I told you, I don't want you to feel responsible for me. I can take care of myself."

"No, you can't. At least not yet. You have to find a job, somewhere to live, buy some clothes—"

"I know what I have to do." She stepped down from the logs and faced him. "I've been thinking about it. I was wondering if you could loan me some money. It doesn't have to be much...just enough to get me one good outfit and a place to stay. Maybe a motel would be good until I can earn enough to get an apartment. I'll pay you back, with interest, just as soon as I can."

She wore a determined expression on her face, but he could see the fear and uncertainty in her eyes. He shook his head at her. "Lori, you have no idea what you're up against. I'll lend you the money, on condition that I find you a place to stay and help you find a job. You're gonna need help, so you might as well take mine. It's the only way you'll make it."

"I don't want to be a liability."

"You already are, sweetheart, so quit fighting me on this. Fate dumped you on my doorstep and I gotta see this through."

He could tell by her look of defiance that she didn't like it any better than he did. But he wasn't about to back down. She'd either have to do it his way or go back home.

No matter what had happened in the past, he couldn't change the way he was. He'd accepted responsibility for her when he'd agreed to let her stay on in the cabin. He'd never turned his back on what was clearly his duty before and he wasn't about to start now. It was the code he lived by and he couldn't ignore it.

He knew full well the risks he was taking. He'd opened his heart to a woman once, and had paid a bitter price. Even now, after all these years, he heard Toby's soft chuckle in his dreams, and smelled again the clean, warm smell of newly-bathed baby's skin. The memory of all he had lost would always haunt him, and although he had learned to live with his heartache, he had never fully escaped it.

He could never allow himself to trust like that again. No matter how much he craved a woman's body. So far he'd managed to satisfy his needs with women without losing his head over them. And that was the way things had to stay. As long as he remembered that, he'd be okay.

"All right," Lori said at last. "I accept. Just as long as you don't use it as an excuse to order me around and run my life. Is that understood?"

He held up his hands in a gesture of surrender. "Understood." He wasn't sure where she'd draw the line between helping her and ordering her about. He wasn't about to argue the point just then. He had an idea he'd have more than enough trouble just figuring out what to do with her...as well as the added problem of resisting all the things he'd like to do with her. One way or another, he thought gloomily, he was in for a lot of heartache. He just hoped he could pull it off without destroying everything he'd worked so hard for all these years.

"I don't know about you," he said, heading for the cabin door, "but I'm ready for some lunch."

Lori followed him inside, struggling with confusion. She wasn't sure what she felt—dismay at having to leave the security of the cabin, excitement at the prospect of starting her new life, guilt for having to be dependent on Cord and relief that he wasn't just walking out of her life...so many emotions, so many things to think about.

"I didn't have time to catch a fish this morning," Cord said, his face hidden by the door of the cupboard. "I reckon we'll have to find something in here to open. How about some canned corned beef?" He emerged holding a square-shaped can in his hand.

She glanced at it warily. "I've never eaten canned corned beef."

"Well, that figures. How about baked beans? I reckon you've eaten them before."

She stiffened at his note of sarcasm. "I'll heat them up for you." She took the can from him and opened the drawer to find the can opener.

"We'll have to get you a copy of your social security card so you can get a job," Cord said, taking down a bottle of beer from the cupboard.

"I can't do that." Carefully she fitted the can opener to the edge of the can and began turning the key.

"Why can't you do that?"

"Because my brothers will trace me." She finished

opening the can, then bent down to the cupboard to get the pot.

"How are they gonna do that?"

"Computers." She poured the beans into the pot and lit the ring, taking care to keep it on low. "Nowadays you can find anything or anyone on a computer. That's why I left my cards at home."

"You know how to work a computer?"

He'd sounded impressed, and she tried hard not to let him see her little spurt of satisfaction. "I know a bit. Gary has one in his bedroom. He lets me play around on it now and again."

"Gary one of your brothers?"

"Yes, the youngest. He's the only one at home. Dennis lives on his own and Mike is married."

Cord didn't answer. She glanced at him, but he seemed to be working something out in his mind. "You're not gonna get a job without a social security card," he said at last.

"Can't I get a new one with a different number?"

"I don't know. I guess we'll have to find out."

She found the wooden spoon and gave the beans a stir. The can of corned beef sat on the counter, and she picked it up and reached for the can opener.

"Not like that!" Cord took the can from her and peeled off a part of the label. He showed her the key that had been hidden underneath. "This is how you open it. How're you gonna make it out there on your own if you can't even open a can of corned beef, for Pete's sake?"

"I don't plan on living on corned beef," Lori said crossly. He'd sounded irritable again and she shot him a look of resentment. "Is your shoulder giving you trouble?"

"My shoulder is fine, which is why I'm going back tomorrow. In fact, I'm gonna call Jed right now and set it up. He'll have to come up here to get us.''

She felt a nervous twinge in her stomach. ''Does he know about me?''

Cord eyed her darkly. ''No, he sure as hell doesn't. That's gonna take a little explaining. Don't be surprised if he starts wondering about our…situation. He and I go back a long way and I know he'll be curious.''

She wasn't sure how she felt about being mistaken for one of Cord's ''women.'' ''Surely he wouldn't think we—'' She broke off, blushing furiously.

Cord's face looked as if it had been carved in stone. ''Well, now, you know that we haven't, and I know that we haven't, but Jed, well…he might see things differently.''

She met his gaze squarely. ''Then we'll just have to set him straight, won't we? I'm sure you're more than capable of doing that.'' This time the sarcasm was hers.

Cord's eyes darkened. ''I'm gonna call him,'' he muttered, and headed for his jacket hanging on the wall.

Lori stirred the beans once more, then sliced the corned beef. She arranged the slices on the plates, trying not to listen to Cord's conversation—an almost impossible feat, since they were in the same room.

''What time can you get up here?'' Cord was asking, as he paced back and forth across the room with the cell phone at his ear. He paused for a moment to listen. ''Yeah…that'll be good. Uh, Jed? There's just one thing. I'm gonna have company.''

Cord had his back to her, but Lori could hear the edge in his voice. She pulled a face at the back of his head. He was making it pretty obvious how much he regretted having to tell Jed about her.

''No,'' Cord said tightly. ''It's a woman.''

Lori's fingers closed on the wooden spoon. She concentrated on the beans, swirling the spoon slowly round and round the pot.

Cord made a guttural sound. "Drop it, J.C. It's not like that." He paused to listen again. "I'll tell you about it when I see you, okay? Just watch your mouth around her...no low-down cracks, okay? She's not used to roughnecks like you... No, she's not... No, she doesn't... J.C., I'm warning you... This is a real classy woman... I told you, it's not like that..." He swore under his breath. "I'll see you tomorrow. Yeah. Bye."

Lori kept her gaze on the beans. Obviously Jed was making waves. Cord thought she was a classy woman. She liked that.

"He'll be here around midday," Cord said, wiping his brow with the back of his hand.

"All right." She didn't want to look at him, afraid she might give away some of her apprehension in her face. Now that leaving the cabin was settled, her uncertain future loomed ahead of her like a dense fog on an endless ocean. "The beans are ready." She turned off the stove and spooned the beans onto the plates next to the corned beef.

He took his plate from her with a muttered, "Thanks," and she followed him across the room to her armchair.

"Will you be going back to the rodeo right away?" she asked, as she balanced the plate carefully on her knees.

"I reckon. I'm booked for a ride day after tomorrow."

She looked at him in concern. "Will your shoulder be healed by then?"

"As healed as it's gonna be." He filled his fork with beans and jammed it in his mouth.

She gazed at her plate, fighting her resentment at his curt tone. He was the one insisting on making her his personal problem. He didn't have to be so damn irritable about it.

"You're sure you wouldn't rather go back home?" Cord asked abruptly.

For a moment she wavered. But only for a moment. "I'm sure," she said quietly.

"Okay. Maybe I can find some work for you, though I don't know what it will be."

"I'm not sure what I could do."

"You can answer phones, you can type and you can use a computer. You should be able to do something around an office."

She thought about it. "All right, I guess I could handle it. I did a lot of stuff like that for my mother when she worked on her charities."

"Charities?"

She caught the note of interest in his voice. Pleased to have something constructive to say, she explained, "My mother volunteers a great deal of her time to charity. I used to help her organize everything—advertising, soliciting volunteers and contributions, that sort of thing."

He looked at her, his eyes crinkling at the edges. "Well, I'll be…" he said softly. "So that's what you meant about helping her."

She frowned. "What did you think I meant?"

He shrugged and didn't even wince, she noticed. He'd been telling the truth about his shoulder feeling better. "I dunno. I figured you helped her pick flowers and stick them in a vase, I guess…shop for clothes… I don't know what rich ladies do. I've never been around any."

Lori smiled. "Who says we're rich?"

"I guess I figured it out from what you've said. Well, aren't you?"

"I guess so. Anyway, most rich ladies work harder than anyone else. There's always someone wanting some of their time…and money."

He was looking at her thoughtfully, and didn't seem to hear what she said. After a moment or two she asked uneasily, "What is it?"

"I think I just might be able to find you a job after all. At the rodeo. In the producer's office. They're always looking for someone to help out. It will keep you out of trouble, anyway, until I have time to think of something better."

And under his thumb, she thought resentfully. Apparently he meant what he said about keeping an eye on her. Still, it might be fun to work at a rodeo, and much as she hated to admit it, she was really counting on seeing as much of Cord as possible. "What will I have to do?"

"Well, I don't know everything they do in there, but they handle advertising, promotion stunts, book the acts, supply the stock—" He suddenly slapped the arm of his chair, making her jump. "That's it!"

"What is?"

"Why didn't I think of it before? Kristi."

She felt some of her enthusiasm fade. "Who's Kristi?" One of the women in Cord's life? she wondered.

"Kristi is the daughter of the stock contractor who produces the local rodeos. She helps out with the animals and some of the acts. While she's on the circuit she lives in a trailer. A big trailer. I reckon she wouldn't mind having some company for a while."

In spite of her reservations, Lori felt a stab of excitement. "You think? What's she like?"

Cord waved a hand in the air. "Oh, you know, young and sassy, always trying to impress her pa. Thinks she can outride every cowboy out there if only they'd give her a chance. No one takes her seriously, least of all Jed. He's always needling her. But then, Jed enjoys agitating most folks."

"She doesn't mind?"

Cord finished the last bite of corned beef, then leaned down to put the empty plate on the floor. "Oh, she minds, more'n most. She's got it bad for Jed, but all he sees is a hell-raising, tough, ornery woman who thinks she's better'n any man. That's sure no way to get a man's attention."

Lori had to agree with him. "Why doesn't Jed tell her?"

Cord snorted. "Jed? He's got no interest in any woman. All he can think about is the all-around championship. He got into trouble in his hometown a while back, and they more or less ran him out. Even his own kin gave up on him. Rodeo's big in Jed's town, and he's got a burning notion to take that championship buckle back with him and show them he's the best there is. Not only that, he's looking for some fool woman to pretend to be his wife so he can appear respectable when he goes back."

Lori was intrigued. "A pretend wife? Why doesn't he find a real wife? Like Kristi, for instance."

Cord scowled at her. "'Cause Jed's like the rest of us. He knows what trouble a wife can be. He's not gonna tie himself down with no darn woman when he can pay one to pretend to be his wife for a day or two."

"You can't judge all women by what happened to you," Lori said quietly.

"The hell I can't." He stood up and walked across the room to where his hat hung on the wall. "Don't you go telling Jed what I told you. He'll have my hide for talking about him behind his back." He jammed his hat down on his head. "I don't know what it is about you, Lori Ashford, that makes me run off at the mouth like a gossiping housewife. Seems to me the sooner I get back to the circuit the better." For the second time that day the door slammed behind him.

Lori sat glowering at the door, wondering what had put a bee under Cord's bonnet. He was irritable about something, and she had a horrible feeling it was because he'd been forced into taking her with him. If she hadn't been so darn helpless without him, she thought fiercely, she'd leave right now and get out of his life.

She had no illusions, however, about how long she'd last with no money to buy food, clothes and shelter. It all came down to a matter of choice; either stick with Cord or go home. There was absolutely no doubt in her mind which scenario she preferred.

She needed the loan, and the job at the rodeo and the chance to share a trailer with this Kristi person seemed to be the perfect answer. It surely wouldn't take her that long to get on her feet, pay back Cord and finally be independent. She could do it, she thought, with a little spurt of excitement. For the first time since she'd crept out of the house with her suitcase in her hand, she really felt that she could make it on her own. She just needed time...and Cord's help. She was just sorry that he resented it so much.

Restless and unable to relax on her own, she ventured outside. It was cool enough that she could have used a jacket, but the clean air felt good after the smoky warmth of the cabin. She intended staying out only long enough to clear her lungs, but the glint of water through the trees drew her attention.

She'd followed the river down that first night without really seeing it. She had known it was growing wider and deeper by the sound of the water, but she hadn't been able to see the other bank in the darkness. Now she was curious to find out just how much it had expanded after the place where she'd first stumbled across it as a small stream.

She headed through the trees, following a narrow trail toward the water. The air was so still; not a whisper of breeze disturbed the feathery branches of the firs. Even the squirrels seemed to have deserted the forest, and only an occasional chirping from the birds broke the eerie silence. As she emerged into the open, the tumbling river seemed deafening after the quiet of the trees.

She looked up and saw the dark clouds beginning to boil over the mountains. She remembered what Cord had said about the storm brewing, and she shivered. Ever since she was a child she'd been nervous about thunderstorms. The father of one of her childhood friends had been killed on a golf course during a storm, and Lori had never forgotten the shock of discovering that lightning could kill. She'd hated it ever since.

She rubbed her forearms with her hands and glanced warily up at the towering trees. This was no place to be in a storm. She was about to turn away and hurry back to the security of the cabin, when something caught her eye. She moved closer and realized it was a pile of clothes lying on the bank. Cord's clothes.

Her insides clenched as she absorbed the significance of the sight. He had to be swimming in the river. Naked. Shaken by the thought, she backed away. She shouldn't be there, she thought frantically. He could climb out any minute and see her standing there.

Part of her wanted to run back to the cabin and pretend she had never noticed that pile of clothes lying there. Another part of her—the new, liberated, awakened part of her—yearned to stay.

While she was still struggling with indecision, Cord's head popped into view at the edge of the bank, just a few yards from where she stood. Horrified, she realized that he was about to climb out. All he had to do was turn his head and he'd spot her.

Somewhere in the back of her mind a little voice suggested that she'd made her way to the river mainly in the hope of seeing him. Maybe that was true, but she'd die if he thought she'd come to spy on him.

Very carefully, she moved back into the shadow of the firs, until she had put several thick trunks between her and the river. She could still see the pile of clothes, however, through the narrow space between the trees.

An insistent inner voice of rebellion kept her rooted to the spot, her heart pounding, while she waited for Cord to move into her view. She felt wicked, as if she were treading on forbidden ground, and wildly exhilarated by her own daring.

To her intense disappointment, most of him was hidden by the undergrowth when he finally appeared. He disappeared from view when he bent down to pick up his pants, and when he straightened again she could see him clearly only from the waist up. Abandoning her viewpoint, she fled back to the cabin, afraid now that he would discover her watching him.

He barely glanced at her when he came through the door a while later. Without uttering a word, he strode over to the cupboard and took out a bottle of beer. He twisted off the cap, then headed out the door again with a muttered, "I'll be back for supper."

Lori felt ridiculously like crying. What was the point of him offering to help her if he was going to resent it so much? She'd rather take her chances on her own, she assured herself. The last thing she wanted to be was a burden on someone. If only she hadn't lost all her cash in the robbery, she wouldn't be in this mess. She would never have stayed in the cabin, knowing how much Cord begrudged her being there.

Face it, she told herself miserably, as she threw a couple of logs on the dying fire in the wood stove. She was just in the way here. Cord was worried she'd prevent him from pursuing the championship and concerned about his friends' reactions to her having stayed with him. She was a liability, and the sooner she established her independence and got out of his life the better.

Cord seemed less grouchy when he came back an hour or so later. He was carrying another trout, and set about cleaning it without even suggesting that she help. Wary of saying something to set him off, she looked in the cupboard for something to serve with the fish.

She opened a can of corn and a can of new potatoes, all the time aware of Cord's silent presence behind her. Just when she thought she would have to spend the entire evening in silence, he made her jump by saying gruffly, "I'll fry those potatoes in with the fish, while you heat up the corn."

"I can fry the fish. I won't burn it this time." She didn't look at him, but she knew he was watching her.

"You don't have to cook dinner," he said finally.

"I know I don't have to. I want to." She reached down in the cupboard for the frying pan and placed it on the ring. Carefully she pulled the cap off the bottle of cooking oil and poured a little into the pan. All the time she was aware of his steady gaze on her.

"I know this isn't what you're used to," he said, as she turned to take the cleaned fish from him. "I reckon you're doing pretty well, all things considered."

Surprised by the compliment, she glanced up at his face. He wore his usual stoic expression, but the approval lurking in his eyes quickened her pulse. "Thanks," she murmured, unable to conceal her gratification. "I appreciate that."

His words warmed her as no amount of heat from the stove could have done. She cooked the fish and potatoes with great care, determined to show him that his faith in her efforts had been justified. She took a great deal of pride in serving up her meal, and if the fish tasted a little dry, Cord didn't comment on it. In fact, he cleaned his plate with obvious enjoyment. She'd had no idea that cooking a meal for a man could give her such a sense of achievement.

He'd said little throughout the meal, answering her questions about the rodeo with brief comments that did little to satisfy her curiosity. As she gathered up the empty plates, she felt a deep sense of sadness at the knowledge that this would be the last dinner they would share in the cabin. And their last night together.

She was disappointed when Cord announced that since they were leaving the next day he had things to take care of outside. She had hoped to spend their last evening together relaxing in the armchairs, while she tried to find out more about her future employment.

When it grew dark and he still hadn't come back, she busied herself washing out clothes as best she could with the bar soap, which was all she could find. She hung them up in the bathroom, where she hoped they would dry overnight. She waited, seated in front of the woodstove, and watched the flames die to embers, until at last she heard his footsteps outside.

He seemed surprised to see her sitting there when he walked in. "I figured you'd be in bed by now," he said gruffly, as he headed across the room to the cupboards. "I'm gonna have a beer before I turn in."

She felt a pang of dismay at his tone. He'd made it sound as if he'd hoped she'd be in bed. Apparently he wanted to be alone. "I was just thinking about going," she said stiffly.

She got up and headed for the bedroom, miserable at the thought of ending the evening on such a sour note. She would never again have the opportunity to be alone with him like this. The thought depressed her far more than she had anticipated.

She switched on the lamp by the bed, then closed the door behind her. The room felt stuffy and smelled of fried fish. She opened the window and stood for a moment, hoping for a breeze to dispel the odor. The damp, night air outside was as still as the air inside the cabin.

Sighing, she left the window open and quickly climbed out of her clothes and into a T-shirt. She slid into the bed and tucked the covers under her arm. She didn't know how she was going to fall asleep with the persistent ache under her ribs that wouldn't go away.

She didn't want to leave the cabin. She would miss the peace and quiet of the forest dreadfully. Here she had been content, with nothing to worry about except what to cook for the next meal. She didn't want the upheaval of starting a new life. Before she'd left home, she'd felt trapped, suffocated...and helpless. All she'd thought about was escaping, and it really didn't matter where or to what. Anything had seemed better than what she was facing then.

Now it was different. She'd been so happy at the cabin, so content. If only she could just stay there and never have to worry about finding a job, finding somewhere to live or making a living or any of the numerous problems that were bound to crop up in her new life.

Lori shifted onto her back and stared up at the shadowy ceiling. That was impossible, of course. She had to get on with her life and let Cord get on with his. Even if it hurt far worse than anything she had ever experienced before.

Cord sat in front of the cold woodstove, his beer long forgotten at his feet. He'd intended to spend the night in the chair, rather than put himself through the kind of agony he knew awaited him in the bedroom. But as the room grew colder and the chair became harder and more uncomfortable, he began to think longingly of the comfort of a warm soft bed.

He argued with himself for a while longer, before finally giving up. He was tired, his shoulder was aching again and he had to be rested for the trip back to town tomorrow. He had a lot of negotiating to do when he got there, and he needed a clear head.

He stretched his hands above his head and yawned. As he did so, a flash of lightning lit up the room. The storm had finally moved off the mountains and was heading this way. A faint rumble of thunder confirmed his prediction, and he rose quickly to his feet. If he was going to take his chances in that bed with Lori, he told himself, he'd better do it before the storm woke her up. His best defense was to fake a deep sleep, and he couldn't do that if she heard him get into bed.

He picked up the empty beer bottle and took it into the kitchen, then turned off the lamp before quietly opening the bedroom door. Another flash of lightning gave him a clear view of Lori lying on her side with her back to his half of the bed.

He got out of his clothes as quickly and silently as he could, then eased himself down beside her. She stirred, and he held his breath, then let it out when she was still once more.

Thunder rumbled again, closer this time. He dragged the covers over his ear and resolutely shut his eyes. He'd slept through plenty of storms in his life, and he wasn't about to let this one rob him of a night's rest. Within seconds the world faded.

Beside him, Lori opened her eyes, confused and still drugged with sleep. She'd been dreaming that she was in a bowling alley and was stuck in the space behind the pins with a huge bowling ball rolling toward her. Her heart still raced from the nightmare, and she was totally unprepared when a blinding flash exploded into the room, followed immediately by a deafening crack of thunder.

Her shriek was almost drowned out by the angry rumbling and growling that accompanied yet another flash of lightning. Thoroughly unnerved, Lori grabbed the closest thing to her, which happened to be Cord's bare arm. Another almighty crash sent her burrowing into his side, trying frantically to shut out the awful noise.

She barely heard his mumbled, "What the—?" before another thunderous roar split the sky open.

"It's so loud!" she wailed.

She felt his arms clamp around her, drawing her to his warm body. "Okay, just relax," he muttered close to her ear. "It's only a storm. Nothing to worry about."

Lightning flashed again, and a gust of wind hit the open windowpane, rattling the glass. "I've never heard one this bad." Lori scrambled closer to him as thunder ripped through the sky. "I hate thunderstorms. They're so dangerous."

"They're dangerous only if you're out in them. You're safe enough in here."

She heard the soothing note in his voice and did her best to relax. She concentrated, instead, on the warm, musky fragrance of his body, the soft fuzz of chest hair beneath her cheek, the pressure of his strong arms holding her near. She could hear his heart thudding next to her ear, and as she listened to the steady beat, she could swear she'd heard it speed up.

Her own heart jumped at the realization and began to keep time with his. Thoughts flooded her mind... tantalizing, tormenting thoughts. She remembered how she'd felt the last time she'd been in his arms. She remembered standing in the forest, hidden by the trees, aching to catch a glimpse of him as he climbed naked from the river.

She felt a sudden, sharp longing to feel Cord's hands on her body. The yearning was so strong it took her breath away. Her arm lay across his bare chest, and she tightened her hold, curling her fingers into his side.

His hiss of breath in her ear sent a thrill sizzling throughout her body. Vaguely she was aware of lightning lighting up the room again, but now it didn't seem to matter. All that mattered was Cord's chest cushioning her face, his hip nestled into her stomach and his thigh grazing her knees.

She moved against him, and again a thrill shot through her when she heard him softly groan. "Lori," he whispered hoarsely, "this is a real bad idea—"

She lifted her chin. Her heart jumped when she saw his profile highlighted by the flashing lightning. "What is?" she whispered back.

He turned his head, and in the second before the lightning died, she saw his eyes. It was as if the fire of the storm echoed in their black depths. "Damn you, Lori," he whispered fiercely. "You've got to stop this. You don't know what you're doing."

Chapter 6

Up until that moment Lori hadn't been entirely sure what she'd intended. Now she knew. Maybe she'd known all along and just hadn't had the courage to admit it, even to herself. She wanted to know what it was like to make love with Cord McVane. "Yes," she said deliberately. "I do know what I'm doing."

He seemed to hold his breath for the longest time, then let it out on another groan. He muttered something, something she didn't understand, and then he moved, so suddenly she was taken by surprise.

His mouth claimed hers, burning, bruising, probing in his savage surrender to his passion. Startled by the furor of his kiss, she tensed, prepared to draw back in the face of his aggressive onslaught, but he held her head, refusing to give up his fierce conquest.

Unnerved by what she had unleashed, she held back, refusing to open her lips when he nudged them with his tongue. He gently nipped her bottom lip with his teeth and she gasped. Immediately he took possession of her mouth again, and liquid fire ran through her veins as his tongue flirted with hers.

She forgot her doubts as the sweet, intense desire uncurled deep inside her. She felt hot and cold, excited and afraid, confused yet so sure. For years she'd thought about making love with a man. A few times she'd come close to it, but always she'd held back, determined not to experiment just to find out what all the fuss was about.

When it happened to her, she'd promised herself, it would be forever. It would be on her wedding night, with the one man in her life she could ever love. He would be her only love, her once in a lifetime. A forever kind of man. And she would be true to him for the rest of her life.

All those dreams and promises now seemed to fade in the yearning that gripped her. Nothing she had ever felt before came even close to this. For the first time in her life she didn't care that it wasn't her wedding night. She didn't care that he had promised her nothing but these brief moments. She didn't care that this wasn't the love of her life as she'd imagined it.

She only knew that this man could set her soul on fire. His gentle hands roamed her body, his caresses setting off tiny explosions of pleasure wherever he touched. His mouth traveled over her bare flesh, nudging the T-shirt out of his way until finally he drew it over her head.

She was drowning in his kiss again when he suddenly lifted his head. "Wait," he muttered urgently. "I don't have any protection. I wasn't figuring on this—"

She laid her fingers on his lips, determined not to let anything get in the way of her decision. "I don't care," she whispered.

He stared at her, his face just a shadow in the darkness,

and she heard the growl of thunder, farther away now. "Wait a minute—"

"No, it's all right. I promise."

Eagerly she drew his head down to hers, and was once more swept away in the fiery eruption of his kiss. Now he was building a storm of his own. New sensations coursed through her body, and her senses whirled as if she were on a massive roller coaster.

All the things she'd read about making love suddenly made perfect sense. There were no more questions in her mind. This new kind of hunger that engulfed her body was right, it was good, it was why she'd been born a woman.

She felt Cord reach for her hand and guide it down his body. She held him, tentatively at first, afraid of hurting him, until he closed his fingers over hers. Excitement exploded through her body and in her soul. She felt him touch her in the most intimate of places and tensed for a moment, but his kiss drove the uncertainty out of her mind.

He moved over her, his knee parting her thighs. This was the moment, she told herself, the moment when she would become a real woman and her life would never be the same again. Impatient for the discovery, she clung to him, her body desperate for the release from the fierce tension, the insatiable hunger gnawing and drawing deep in her belly.

Once more his mouth covered hers, and she gripped his shoulders, prepared for the pain that she knew was supposed to sever her from her innocence. She felt him enter her, and once more the pressure built, this time down there, where his body joined hers.

Now there was pain, and she welcomed it. She felt her muscles tense, and instantly he paused, bracing himself with his hands on either side of her hips. His voice was harsh and ragged when he spoke. "Dammit, Lori, why in hell didn't you tell me?"

Confused, she tried to draw him back again. "Tell you what?"

"That you've never... Hell, Lori, I didn't know you were a virgin."

"It doesn't matter." Impatient with him, she dragged him down on top of her once more. "Please, don't stop now."

"You don't know what you're doing...."

"Would you please stop saying that." She found his mouth, intent on proving that she knew exactly what she was doing.

He returned the kiss, savagely, as if punishing her for not telling him. "Damn you," he muttered again. "I've got to..."

"Then do." Instinctively she wound her legs around his hips again. "I want it to be you, Cord. It doesn't hurt that much—I swear it doesn't."

She felt a shudder ripple through his body, then the world exploded around her as he carefully entered her once more. It was different now, somehow. Somewhere in her mind she knew he was fighting his own driving passion. She sensed the tight leash he had on his desires while he strove to awaken hers. The pressure increased, but she was oblivious of the pain. Then it was gone, and she was drowning in a pleasure she'd never even imagined before.

Greedily she welcomed it, exulted in it, celebrating her journey to fulfillment with a joy and passion that overwhelmed her mind and inflamed her body. Higher she climbed, until the dizzying heights claimed all thought and reason. Nothing in the world mattered except the culmination of her driving need.

Shocked and awed by the depth of her feelings, she uttered a gasp of surprise when it finally happened. It was as if every tiny nerve in her body exploded with pleasure.

Nothing she had ever read or heard had prepared her for this. She felt herself soaring, then sliding, drifting, in an ethereal peace that transcended everything that had gone before.

She wasn't allowed to rest for long. She could hear Cord's labored breathing now, his harsh whisper penetrating her euphoria. "Are you all right?"

"I'm wonderful," she whispered back, smiling in the darkness.

"Then hold on, honey, 'cause now it's my turn."

He started moving again inside her, stoking the flames that had barely had time to fade. Now he drove faster, deeper, his unrelenting rhythm sending shock waves through her body. She felt the pressure build again and fought with him to reach that incredible pinnacle once more, joyfully launching herself into the vortex with him. This time, she drifted back to earth with him, rejoicing in the knowledge that he shared her contentment.

So this is what it was like to be fulfilled, she thought dreamily. If she'd realized it felt that good, she might have been tempted before this. As long as it was with Cord. She had chosen the right man for her initiation. He had met all her expectations. No, he had surpassed them.

She lay beneath the weight of his body, listening to his harsh breathing, until he finally uttered a shuddering sigh and shifted his body off hers.

She waited, wondering if she should say something and afraid of saying the wrong thing. She felt strange, as if she'd walked through a gate into a different world. She longed to know what he was thinking. Things were different between them now. She wondered what that meant for the future. Would he still see her as inexperienced and immature, or would he accept her now as a woman who was fully responsible for herself? If so, would he no longer feel obligated to take care of her?

She felt confused and uncertain about how to handle the situation. She need reassurance, some indication that she hadn't disappointed him. Hesitantly she laid her arm across his chest and curled up close to his side. Warmth engulfed her when he curled his arm around her and drew her closer.

It was going to be all right after all.

Cord lay awake for a long time after Lori's even breathing told him she was asleep. He felt stunned, unable to comprehend what had just happened. Never in his life had he experienced such a thundering response to a woman. His body still throbbed with the memory.

The whole experience had blown his mind. When he'd first realized she was a virgin, he'd tried to halt his raging needs, but it was too late. He'd already passed the point of no return. The driving force of his passion had swept him on, although he'd been terrified of hurting her. He'd gone through agonies trying to hold himself in check while he satisfied her craving.

It had seemed desperately important that it be right for her. It was her first time, and he was awed by the responsibility. And honored. Never in his life had a woman given up her innocence for him. Maybe that was why he'd experienced such a staggering sense of triumph, power and passion when he'd finally allowed himself to yield to the agonizing demands of his body.

Remembering again the crashing finale, he tightened his arms around her, as if trying to hold on to the memory. Somewhere in his mind he knew he'd have to pay the piper, but right now he wanted to enjoy the aftermath of what was for him the most complete, the most perfect, the most incredible lovemaking he'd ever known.

He awoke much later to hear the birds lustily greeting the morning. The room felt cool now that the storm had passed, and a chill breeze drifted in the open window, bringing a strong fragrance of pine and damp moss.

He turned his head as memory flooded back. He still had his arms locked around Lori, and realized he must have slept like that all night. Her face was tucked into his shoulder, and her eyes were closed. She looked so defenseless in her sleep.

With the full return of his senses came the blow of guilt that hit him like a sledgehammer. What in the hell was he thinking of? He'd taken her virginity, knowing full well that he had no right. She'd trusted him, and he'd betrayed her.

Panic gripped his gut as he tried to think what to do. He felt even more protective of her now, as if he were duty-bound to care for her, to make some sort of commitment to her. And that scared him.

But the more he thought about it, the less sense it made to him to feel bound by their night together. Why would someone like her tie herself down to a beat-up cowboy with nothing to offer her but miles of empty road and an uncertain future the older he got? She wouldn't, of course. She was young and had her whole life ahead of her. She was just starting out, with choices to make and so many paths opening up to her. He'd chosen his road a long time ago, and he couldn't expect her to give up her opportunities to travel it with him.

He wouldn't want that for her. Sooner or later she'd resent the ties, just as she did when she was under her family's thumb. He wouldn't want to hold anyone against her will just to ease his own guilt.

It would be better to forget what happened and let it go. She'd be all right. Once she had a job and was earning her own living, she'd do just fine. Until then, he'd keep an eye on her, help her out now and then, be there in case she needed a friend. To do all that, he must never, never get into bed with her again.

The thought of what he'd had and lost was like a physical blow. Very carefully he disentangled himself from Lori's grasp. He must never think about it again, because to do so would be the worst kind of torture. He had to put last night out of his mind, and hope like hell that he was never alone with her again.

He pulled on his shorts and was halfway across the room when she said sleepily, "Where are you going?"

"Bathroom," he said briefly, and escaped from the room before he was tempted to look at her. He was very much afraid that right then, if he took one good look at her lying naked in his bed, he'd forget all his good intentions and spend the morning reliving the intoxicating pleasures of last night.

Lori waited eagerly for him to come back. She had fallen asleep in his arms the night before, lulled by his whispered words of reassurance. She was disappointed when she woke up to see him creeping across the room. She wanted to make love with him again. She wanted to know that what she'd felt last night hadn't been a figment of her imagination.

She wanted to know that she could feel that way again, every time she made love with Cord McVane. She wanted to find out if there was more that she could do to give him the kind of wild, unrestrained excitement he had given to her. The more she lay there thinking about it, the more intense her desire to please him grew.

It took her several minutes to realize that he wasn't coming back. She heard him clattering around in the living room, filling the woodstove with logs and running water in the sink. Her ache of anxiety spread, until she felt enveloped in a fog of disappointment. The hollow feeling in her belly intensified, and she scrambled out of bed, determined to confront him.

She swiped her T-shirt up from the floor and slipped it over her head, then padded barefoot into the living room. Cord stood by the oven, staring at the pot of water he'd put on the ring. "Good morning," she said evenly.

He looked up at her, and his wary expression compounded her fears. "I figured you'd want coffee."

Something was definitely wrong. She could see it in his face, hear it in his voice. She tried to remember if she'd said something last night to upset him but could think of nothing that would have brought about this drastic change in his attitude. "Not until I know what's bugging you," she said quietly.

"Coffee first," he said, reaching up to the cupboard. "Then we'll talk."

"I'd rather we talked now."

He lowered his hand slowly, his set expression wiping out her anticipation. "All right. I'm sorry about last night. I reckon I took advantage of you. It was wrong and it was stupid, and I apologize."

She stared at him, willing herself not to cry. "I didn't think you took advantage of anything. I was a willing partner. I told you that. I wanted what happened."

"Yeah, well, I should have known better. I've been around a lot more than you have. I should have stopped it before it even got started."

She struggled with the words, while her throat threatened to close up on her. "You didn't seem sorry last night."

His eyes narrowed. "That's because I didn't have my head on straight."

"I thought I had something to do with that."

"Well, I should have been thinking for both of us."

She drew a deep breath. "Are you telling me I should forget what happened?"

"I reckon that's what I'm saying," he said deliberately. "I think the best thing we can do is forget about it. It'll make it easier to keep things casual if we don't mention it anymore."

"I see." She couldn't believe he was rejecting her. She should have known that she couldn't please him. No doubt he had a lot of women far more experienced than she was, who'd know how to excite a man like Cord McVane. He'd treated her like a kid all along, and he was still doing it.

"Lori...I'm sorry."

She shook her head and intentionally made her voice bright. "Hey, it's okay. It's just something that happens. You're right. Let's just forget it." She turned away, before he could see the tears brimming in her eyes.

"Lori, why don't you go home. You've got people there who love you and care about you—"

And it would let him off the hook, she thought bitterly. "I'm not going home." Her voice wobbled and she paused, fighting for control. "You don't have to worry, Cord. I won't get in your way. No one need ever know what happened."

"Well, I sure as hell won't tell anyone. You can bet your boots on that."

Of course not, she told herself. He wouldn't want his friends to find out he'd made love to an inexperienced virgin who didn't know how to please him. They'd probably make his life miserable with their teasing. "Thank you," she said quietly. "I guess I'll get my things together and take a shower." She pushed the bedroom door open and closed it firmly behind her.

She wasn't going to cry, she promised herself. The pain

would go away eventually. She'd never faced rejection before. It was natural that she'd have trouble dealing with it. By tomorrow she'd feel better, and the sooner she found a job and started her new life, the quicker she could forget about her stupid crush on an experienced heartbreaker who thought she wasn't woman enough for him.

As she finished making the bed and headed for the bathroom, the muffled sound of a rapping on the front door made her jump. Cord had told her that Jed would be there midday. It was still early morning.

She paused, her heart thumping, and strained to hear the low voices from the next room. For a moment she worried that Cord might have called her family after all and her brothers had come to take her back. Then common sense kicked in.

In the first place, she could hear only one other voice and it sounded quite calm. If her brothers had been out there they would have been yelling and firing questions over the top of one another. It had to be Jed.

She cautiously opened the door. The stranger had his back to her, but she saw Cord's eyes widen at the sight of her, and he gave her a quick warning shake of his head. Unnerved, she was about to withdraw again, when the stranger turned.

He was a tall man...taller than Cord by about three inches. He had a nice face, with attractive even features and a kind mouth. His eyes were unusual, a light gold in color, and right now they were staring at her with a mixture of curiosity and amusement.

"Well, hi there," he said softly. "So this is the company ol' Cord was hedging about."

His glance skimmed down to her bare thighs beneath her T-shirt, and she suddenly realized how she must look. She hadn't combed her hair, and it was probably sticking up all over her head in tangles after all the activity last night. No wonder Cord hadn't wanted Jed to see her in this state. She should have at least put some clothes on.

At the thought of how this must appear to Cord's friend, she felt her cheeks begin to burn. "You must be Jed," she said, making an effort to sound as if she were greeting members of a ladies' group at a charity meeting instead of a roguish-looking cowboy with a glint in his eye.

"That'll be me, ma'am. And who are you?"

"This is Lori," Cord said quickly, before she could answer. "You woke us…er…her up." He jerked his head at Lori as if ordering a child into the bathroom and out of sight.

Her resentment rose swiftly, taking her by surprise. An intense desire to cut him down a peg or two made her reckless. Ignoring his fierce frown, she smiled at the obviously intrigued cowboy. "I'm pleased to meet you, Jed." She walked toward him with her free hand outstretched. "It's always a very real pleasure to meet one of Cord's friends."

Jed's eyebrows raised, and he grasped her hand in his, while Cord sent her a look designed to cut her in half. "Lori was just going to pack up her things," he said, scowling at her. "And take a shower. You want a cup of coffee, J.C.?"

"Oh, packing can wait. I haven't got much stuff anyway. I'll be happy to get you a cup of coffee, Jed. Then you can tell me all about the rodeo. Cord has told me some things, but he's not very good with all the details."

"I'll say he's not." Jed's gaze moved over her again. "It'll be my pleasure, ma'am. And I sure could use a hot cup of coffee."

Lori sauntered over to the oven, aware of Cord's gaze

burning into her back. She deliberately avoided looking at him while she fixed Jed's coffee and carried it over to him.

"I thought you were gonna be here at noon," Cord said irritably, breaking the tense silence.

Jed took the coffee from Lori and winked at her. "I figured on getting an early start. Of course, if I'd known I'd be...interrupting something, I'd have held off for an hour or two."

"You're not interrupting anything," Cord said through his teeth.

"Oh, yeah? If I were in your shoes I'd sure as hell be interrupting something." Jed took a sip of the steaming coffee, then grinned at Lori. "Tastes real good, ma'am."

"Thank you." She beamed up at him. "Can I offer you some cereal? We only have canned milk—"

"You'd better be taking that shower, Lori," Cord muttered, his voice lethal. "We'll be heading back real soon, and I reckon you'll want to freshen up."

She heard the threat behind his words and decided she'd better not push him too far. "Okay, but I'll have to wear your clothes again." She almost laughed at Jed's fascinated expression as she crossed the room to the bathroom.

Before she closed the door behind her, she heard Cord explaining, in somewhat strained tones, how she'd been robbed and had ended up at his cabin. He didn't mention her family, she was happy to note. At least he'd done her that favor.

She took her shower quickly. The clothes she'd washed and dried the day before were stacked on top of the toilet tank. She sorted through them and chose a pair of Cord's jeans and the cream shirt she'd worn the day after she'd arrived.

Cord must have taken his shower in cold water, she thought, since he was already dressed. Which was just as well. She could just imagine Jed's comments if he'd arrived to see his partner walking around in his boxers.

Her heart ached when she remembered how wonderful Cord had been last night. Everything had seemed so right, so perfect. She knew enough to understand that men didn't attach as much importance to making love as a woman did, but last night she had been convinced that Cord had been as overwhelmed as she was by the fierce passion between them.

She hadn't expected him to propose, exactly. She knew him well enough to realize that Cord McVane was the last person to get that deeply involved with a woman again. But she had imagined that he cared about her and saw her as an inviting, exciting woman. Obviously she'd been wrong.

Which just went to show how little she understood about making love. It was all too easy to mistake a man's need to satisfy his urges for something deeper and more meaningful. What to her had been beautiful and glorious, had been simply a case of answering nature's call in Cord's eyes.

Well, she thought bitterly, as she pulled on the jeans, she wouldn't make that mistake anymore. If and when she made love with a man again, she'd be darn sure he cared for her as much as she cared for him. As for Cord, he needn't worry. She wouldn't sleep with him again if he were the last man left on earth.

It would be hard to leave the cabin and all its tender memories behind, but she had an exciting new life ahead of her, and she wasn't about to waste it mourning over something that couldn't be changed. From now on, she was going to look forward and put the past behind her. And that included any feelings she might have had for Cord Mc-Vane.

Out in the living room, Cord watched Jed settle himself

in one of the armchairs. He was in no mood for his partner's teasing, no matter how harmless Jed meant to be. "How'd the competition go?" he asked, in a determined effort to keep Jed's mind off Lori.

"Fine. I got a couple of wins."

"What about Denver? Did he ride?"

"Nope." Jed stretched his booted feet out in front of him and studied the scuffed toes. "I don't think Denver's gonna be doing any more riding. I wouldn't be surprised to see him leave the circuit and move in with April until the wedding. I think he's getting tired of hanging around the arena."

Cord nodded. "I figured as much. That'll give us more room, though."

Jed shot him a sly look. "I reckon that will leave some space for Lori in the trailer."

Cord mentally counted to three before answering. "Lori won't be living in the trailer, Jed. I told you, it's not like that."

"Well, that's your story, and I guess you're gonna stick to it." Jed took a gulp of his coffee. "I tell you something, though," he said, lowering the mug, "that little lady has stars in her eyes, and I'm willing to bet it ain't from staring up at the night sky."

"Whatever it is, J.C., it's none of your damn business. I don't want you shooting your fool mouth off when we get back, neither. If I hear talk around the circuit bad-mouthing Lori in any way, I'll cut you up in little pieces and feed you to the hogs."

Jed looked at him in surprise. "Simmer down, pardner. I'm not gonna say nothing. Reckon I won't have to, if you go around making such a fuss about defending her honor. Why didn't you tell me you were hooked?"

Cord jutted his jaw. "You don't know what in hell you're talking about, J.C."

"The hell I don't. You have it written all over you. That's the first time I ever heard you defending a woman. Why don't you just admit it, Cord...you're soft on that little gal."

"And you're out of your cotton-picking mind." Cord made a monumental effort to control his temper. "I feel responsible for her, that's all. She's a good kid, but she hasn't been around much. I just don't want some horny stud out there getting the wrong idea, that's all."

He shifted uncomfortably as Jed studied him with knowing eyes. "How do you figure on keeping an eye on her if she's not living in the trailer?"

Cord shrugged. "I was figuring on Kristi taking her in. Just until she gets on her feet."

Jed stared at him, then threw back his head and roared with laughter. "Kristi?" he spluttered, when he could talk. "Can you see Kristi putting up with another woman hanging around her? She'd rather live with a bunch of hogs. You know Kristi's got no time for no females. She's too damn busy trying to prove she's a man. She'll scare the pants off your little woman."

"She's not my 'little woman,'" Cord said through his teeth. "And you'd better quit calling her that, J.C., or I'll ram the words down your freaking throat."

Jed held up his hand. "Okay, no need to get all riled up—I was just joshing. But I'm right about Kristi. I reckon she'd eat that little lady up alive."

"Maybe not," Cord said thoughtfully. "Kristi isn't half as bad as you make her out to be, and I reckon those two could learn something from each other."

"If they don't kill each other first."

"It'll work out, you'll see," Cord assured him, with

more confidence than he felt. "I figure on asking Kristi's pa to give Lori a job in the office. Just to get her started until she finds her feet. She's got nothing right now, except the clothes on her back, thanks to that no-good son-of-a-bitch who robbed her."

Jed eyed him curiously. "How'd she get robbed?"

"Ran out of gas on the highway and some jerk picked her up."

"What about her family? Can't they help her out?"

"She doesn't have family," Cord said slowly, remembering his promise. "I reckon Lori doesn't have anyone in the world except me. That's why I have to watch out for her—just until she's on her feet. I feel kind of responsible for her. What I don't need is you or anyone else giving me a hassle about it."

Jed shook his head. "Like you said, pardner, it's none of my business. Just watch your back, okay? Men have stood taller than you and been cut down by a helpless female. I wouldn't want to see it happen to you."

"Don't worry yourself on that score," Cord said dryly. "I know what I'm doing. I'm not about to get caught in that trap again. There isn't a woman alive who can change my mind on that score."

The bathroom door opened on his last words, and he looked up to see Lori standing in the doorway. She'd tied her damp hair back with his bandanna, and wore a pair of his jeans cinched in at the waist, with the tails of his cream shirt tied above them. She looked young and vulnerable, and mad as hell.

His heart turned over at the sight of her. He knew she was hurt, and he hated having been the one to put that look in her eyes. But one day she'd thank him. He was doing her a big favor. If he'd allowed things to go on the way they were, she would have ended up hurting a lot more than she was now. It was better for both of them this way, and one day—soon, he hoped—they could forget what had happened and be friends again.

He'd rather enjoyed having her around, he thought wistfully. It would be good to have her friendship for a while. At least he would know she was doing all right if she worked and lived on the circuit.

"Did you want to eat breakfast before we leave?" she asked, and he winced at the chill in her voice.

"I reckon we can pick something up on the road." He got to his feet, and Jed rose at the same time.

"Need some help packing?" Jed asked, nodding at the cupboards.

"Thanks," Lori said quietly, "but I can manage. You finish your conversation."

Again Cord felt a stab of remorse. He hadn't meant to hurt her. He just hadn't been able to resist the temptation that had tortured him for days. Any red-blooded cowboy would have done the same thing. Hell, he'd done more or less the same thing plenty of times before.

Only, this time was different. This wasn't some bar-hopping, man-hungry groupie looking for cheap thrills. This was an innocent, classy young woman who hadn't realized what she was getting herself into, until it was too late.

Now it was up to him to see that her reputation remained untarnished, even if he had to bind and gag his travel partner. Although he was satisfied that Jed wouldn't say anything. He was a tormenting joker at times, but he would never deliberately hurt someone, and his teasing never hit below the belt.

He had nothing to worry about on that score, Cord assured himself. As for Kristi, well, there might be a grain of truth in what Jed said about her, but Cord was willing to bet his life on Lori making it work. Anyone who couldn't get along with Lori Ashford just didn't deserve to know her.

Lori barely spoke to him on the way back to town. She seemed to have plenty to say to his partner, though. She sat between the two of them, ignoring the lush green forest and farmlands they passed and chattered on to Jed about the rodeo and the people who worked there, until Cord was ready to explode.

When Jed parked the truck in front of a fast-food restaurant and disappeared into the men's room, Cord finally had Lori to himself. He sat with her at a table in the corner, after ordering hamburgers and fries for all three of them. "You're gonna need some money," he said, reaching for his wallet. "I don't carry much cash around with me, but this will do for now. We'll open up a checking account for you once we get back to town. Then you can buy clothes and whatever else you need."

Lori took the bills he offered her and gave him the kind of look that always melted his insides. "You know I'll pay you back, Cord."

"Sure," he said gruffly. "I trust you."

She seemed sad for a moment, then her face brightened, as if she'd determined to forget her troubles. "It will be fun shopping for new clothes. Especially now that I can choose my own. My mother always came shopping with me and told me what to buy."

He raised his eyebrows. "You never picked out your own clothes? Didn't that bother you?"

She shrugged. "It used to, but I soon learned there was no point in arguing with my mother. Actually, she has pretty good taste, and I usually liked the clothes she bought."

Cord studied her for a moment. She'd never had to make

Here's a **HOT** offer for you!

Get set for a sizzling summer read...

with **2 FREE ROMANCE BOOKS**

and a **FREE MYSTERY GIFT!**

NO CATCH!   NO OBLIGATION TO BUY!

Simply complete and return this card and you'll get **FREE BOOKS, A FREE GIFT** and much more!

- The first shipment is yours to keep, **absolutely free!**
- Enjoy the convenience of romance books, delivered right to your door, before they're available in the stores!
- Take advantage of special low pricing for **Reader Service Members only!**
- After receiving your free books we hope you'll want to remain a subscriber. But the choice is always yours—to continue or cancel anytime at all! So why not take us up on this fabulous invitation with no risk of any kind. You'll be glad you did!

345 SDL CPST

245 SDL CPSL
S-IM-05/99

▼ DETACH HERE AND MAIL CARD TODAY! ▼

Name:
(Please Print)

Address: Apt.#:

City:

State/Prov.: Zip/ Postal Code:

her own decisions about anything. Not even the clothes she wore. How was she going to deal with all the hassles of going it alone? He had a bad feeling in his gut about all this. He just wished he could have talked her into going back and standing up to her bossy family instead of running away from the problem.

"She'd have a coronary if she saw me now," Lori was saying, glancing at her belted waist. "She'd be screaming at me for looking like this in public, letting down the family image."

Cord shook his head. It was hard to think of this determined young woman being so securely under her mother's thumb. Her mother had to be some formidable woman. He hoped he never had to meet her. "What does your father do?"

"He's a lawyer. Mike and Dennis work for him."

"What about the other brother?"

"Gary?" She shrugged. "He's not interested in law. He's a computer technician." She glanced out the window. "What kind of clothes do you think I should buy?"

She'd deliberately changed the subject. Obviously she didn't want to talk about her family, and he couldn't blame her. They sounded like a bunch of dictators who still treated her like the kid of the family, when all she wanted was to be treated like a grown-up woman. The problem was, she'd had no practice being a woman. She'd never been allowed to trust her own judgment, which was why she'd gotten herself into this mess in the beginning.

Now he felt bound to help her out of it. But how the hell was he going to teach her how to survive in his world? It was tough enough for women like Kristi, who'd grown up in the demanding, frenzied, sometimes brutal life-style of the rodeo. How would someone with Lori's background stand up to the hardships and loneliness, the heartbreak of life on the road as a perpetual vagabond?

He was the last person she should be depending on to help her find her independence. He'd just have to leave it up to Kristi, he thought uneasily. Although she had a lot to learn herself.

He sighed and leaned back in his chair. He was just beginning to realize what a monumental task he'd set for himself. He could only hope that everything would work out right for Lori, and that he wasn't just leading her down the road to total disaster.

Chapter 7

An hour later Jed pulled off the road and drove the pickup into a large field. Lori stared at the numerous vehicles scattered about. People wandered back and forth, sometimes pausing to chat, while others sat on the steps of their campers, apparently enjoying a break from all the commotion.

Some of the men carried equipment and boxes across the road to a the large white building, where flags and streamers flew from every conceivable corner. An enormous banner advertising the rodeo fluttered in the afternoon breeze. Lori watched a brawny cowboy stroll easily past the truck with a saddle, ropes and tackle slung across his back.

Clothing fluttered from a clothesline slung between two trees, and children darted about, chasing a small, yapping dog. The throbbing beat of country music blared from the windows of a camper nearby, and the smell of barbecued beef made Lori forget the light lunch she'd eaten.

This was an alien world to her, as far removed from everything familiar as another planet. It was exciting, and more than a little intimidating. She just hoped she could fit in and find a place for herself in this new life awaiting her.

Jed had parked the pickup alongside a trailer with flower print curtains at the windows. "I need to take the truck for a while," Cord said, watching him clamber down from the driver's seat. "We've got some running around to do."

"Yeah," Jed said dryly. "I reckon you do. I wish you luck. I gotta feeling you're going to need it." He jumped to the ground and Cord headed around the truck to take his place at the wheel.

"What did he mean by that?" Lori asked uneasily, as they drove back onto the highway.

Cord shrugged. "Jed's real fond of looking for trouble where there isn't any." He nodded at a gleaming white motor home sitting by itself at the edge of the parking lot beneath the shade of a huge maple. "That's Kristi's rig. It's the last day of competition so she's probably out back of the arena with the horses."

Lori gazed at the expensive-looking vehicle. This could be her future home, if Kristi agreed. A cold knot of uncertainty settled in her stomach. There were so many hurdles to cross before she could settle into her new life. Trying to banish her misgivings, she turned back to Cord. "Are you going to ride today?"

He shook his head. "I was supposed to, but I didn't get to register in time. This is one ride I'm gonna miss, I guess. I'll have to wait for the next stop in Idaho."

She stared at him in dismay. "You're going to Idaho?"

He gave her a sideways glance. "I reckon we all are. We travel where the rodeos are—I told you that."

Her pulse skipped a beat. "Does that mean I'll be traveling, too?"

"If you're going to work for the rodeo, you'd better get

used to being on the road. You'll spend half your time traveling.''

She leaned back, intrigued at the prospect. "I think I'm going to enjoy working for the rodeo.''

"We've got to get you the job first.''

"I'm going to need clothes.''

"Yeah, I know. First the bank, then I'll drop you off while I go talk to Kristi. If she's okay with having you move in, I'll ask her to put in a word for you with her pa.''

Lori nodded, her mind already working on where to buy her clothes. Obviously she wouldn't shop at the kind of stores she was used to...she'd have to find somewhere a little less expensive. "How about a mall?" she suggested. "I'll be able to get everything I need there.''

"Good idea. I think there's one on the edge of town.'' He drove fast down a busy highway, then turned off and headed toward a group of rustic, redbrick buildings. The bank was on the main street, which wasn't much longer than a dozen blocks, from what Lori could see. She followed Cord into the gloomy interior of the bank, feeling self-conscious in her roomy jeans and oversized shirt. She was really eager to buy clothes that fit. It would be great to look respectable once more.

She sat on the edge of her chair in front of a large desk and listened to Cord explain to the bespectacled young man on the other side the reason he wanted to open a new account. He talked about transfers and discussed the various kinds of accounts, while Lori sat there feeling strangely detached, as if she were watching herself from a long distance. She was going through all the motions, yet none of it seemed real.

Part of her feared the thought of all the complications ahead of her, while another part of her marveled at her own courage. It was like jumping into the deep end of a swimming pool without really knowing how to swim. She'd learn, she promised herself. She'd learn fast, and all she had to do was keep herself afloat until then.

"Here," Cord said, breaking into her thoughts. "This should be enough to keep you going for a while."

She took the checkbook he handed her and flipped it open. The sum she saw written there made her gasp. "This is too much," she protested. "I won't need half this."

"Then you can give it back to me once you start earning enough yourself. In the meantime, it will be there for emergencies." He handed her a pen and pushed a sheet of paper over to her. "You have to sign here and here, so it's legal for you to write checks."

She signed her name, watched by the curious young man opposite, and handed the pen back to Cord. "Thank you," she said simply.

His mouth twitched in a reluctant smile. "You're entirely welcome, ma'am. Now I guess you can shop till you drop." He rose to his feet, thanked the young man, then led her out of the bank into the street.

"Shouldn't I be going with you to see about the job?" she asked him anxiously, as he pulled away from the curb.

"They might want to interview you later." Cord swung the wheel and drove up onto the highway. "Just for appearances. Paul Ramsett owes me a favor. Besides, I reckon he'll be happy to take you on. He usually has to hire temps when he's in town."

"Paul Ramsett? He's the producer?"

"And the stock contractor, among other things. He's Kristi's pa. He's a good man. Has his hands full with that daughter of his, I reckon. The story goes that he was real disappointed he didn't get a boy when she was born. I guess he let Kristi know that, and she's been trying to prove she's as good as any boy ever since."

Lori immediately felt sorry for the young woman. "That's a shame. Is she an only child, then?"

"Yep. Mother died when she was real young. Paul Ramsett brought her up himself. Never married again. Must have been a heck of a lonely life for her."

"There's a lot to be said for being an only child," Lori said grimly.

Cord glanced at her. "Well, I reckon you can stop worrying about those brothers of yours. It will take them a while to catch up with you once you're on the road."

"I hope they never do." She wasn't about to admit it to him, but there were times when she really missed her rambunctious family. Whenever she felt insecure or apprehensive, she found herself wishing that she were still at home, letting everyone think for her and take care of her.

Those were the times she needed her courage the most—to strengthen her resolve and bolster her pride. She couldn't go back now after all she'd been through. She wasn't the same person she'd been then, either emotionally or physically. She was on her own now, and she would have to sink or swim on her own merits.

She said goodbye to Cord in the parking lot of the mall, and spent a wonderful two hours or so wandering around the stores, trying on clothes, some of them far too outlandish to wear but definitely fun to experiment with.

She finally settled on three pairs of jeans, two pairs of shorts, a half-dozen tops to go with them, a pair of black slacks, three skirts and silk shirts and a couple of dresses with a coordinating jacket. She also bought cosmetics and perfume, shampoo and conditioner, an assortment of combs and brushes, one pair of shoes with heels and a pair of sandals.

By the time she had stocked up on underwear and hosiery, she was weighed down with packages. Cord's expression, when he met her at the appointed place under the main clock tower, was a mixture of amusement and disbelief.

"Looks like you had fun," he commented, as he took some of the packages from her. "I hope Kristi has room in her trailer for all this stuff."

Lori looked up at him eagerly. "You talked to her?"

"Yep. She's happy to have you stay with her for as long as you like. I think she's looking forward to the company."

Lori's pulse skipped in anticipation. "And the job?"

"It's yours. You don't even have to interview. You can start tomorrow, helping them pack up for Idaho. We leave on Friday."

She stared at him in shocked delight. "How did you do that? What about my social security card?"

He shrugged. "I worked it out with Paul. Don't worry about it for now."

She was in awe. "It must have been some favor."

"It was." He looked down at her, his eyes narrowed against the sun as they crossed the parking lot to the truck. "Don't let me down."

"I won't." She grinned happily at him. "Thank you, Cord. I owe you a lot."

His expression changed, and he looked quickly away. "We'd better get back to the arena. Kristi gave me the key to her rig, so we can drop all this stuff off there before you go meet her."

"Will I have time for a shower? I'd really like to change into my own clothes before I meet anyone else."

He gave a curt nod without turning to her. "Sure. But you'll have to make it a quick one. We need to grab something to eat before the show starts."

Her heart jumped. "I'm going to see the rodeo tonight?"

"From the best seat in the house." He opened the door

of the truck and threw the packages in behind the seat. Lori gave him the rest of the packages, which he piled on top of the others.

She sat beside him on the way back to the arena, aware that his mood had changed since he'd met her in the mall. She knew him well enough by now to tell when he was worrying about something.

All her excitement vanished as she contemplated the reason for his concern. He was probably dealing with the prospect of explaining her presence to his friends and colleagues. And he obviously wasn't looking forward to it.

Kristi's motor home was quite luxurious, and to Lori it seemed like paradise after the primitive conditions in Cord's cabin. Although the shower was actually smaller than the one in the cabin's bathroom, it more than made up for the size, with its massager showerhead and modern sculpted plastic walls.

While Cord waited for her in the living area, Lori luxuriated in the cascade of hot water, the perfumed soap that smelled of flowers rather than male deodorant and the fragrant body cream she smoothed on her skin after she'd toweled it dry. Kristi's hair dryer was another luxury, finally allowing Lori to fluff her hair instead of tying it back from her face.

Eager to try out her new makeup, she dabbed a touch of rose on her lips, added a faint smear of green eye shadow and darkened her eyelashes with mascara. She'd chosen a pair of the new jeans and a simple white cotton top to wear. Now she was ready to face the world. Feeling more like herself than she had in days, she emerged from the bathroom.

Cord sat reading a newspaper on a long bench seat in the living section of the camper. He looked up when she closed the door behind her. The newspaper shook in his hands, and for a moment or two he stared at her, his face studiously devoid of expression.

She felt self-conscious under his scrutiny and said lightly, "What's the matter? Do I have lipstick on my teeth?"

He gave his head a slight shake, as if to dislodge a disturbing thought, then said gruffly, "You look different in that getup."

She eyed him warily, wondering if that was supposed to be a compliment. She decided to ask him. "Is that good or bad?"

"Depends on who's looking, I reckon."

"Right now I'd like to know what you're thinking."

She wished she hadn't asked when his gaze traveled over her with a thoroughness that made her skin tingle. "I reckon you look good enough to pass inspection."

"Well, thanks. I think."

He seemed uncomfortable. "I'm not real used to handing out compliments to women."

"I assumed that much," she said dryly.

"I guess I'm not used to seeing you all prettied up, neither. Kind of took me by surprise, that's all."

She smiled. "You should see me when I'm dressed for a dinner date. You probably wouldn't recognize me at all."

A gleam appeared in his dark eyes. "Reckon I wouldn't at that." He shook out the newspaper and folded it, his movements slow and deliberate. "We'd better get on over to the arena if we're gonna talk to Kristi before the show starts."

She followed him out of the trailer, still uncertain whether he approved of her appearance. Not that it really mattered what he thought, she reminded herself sternly. It was her choice what to wear, and she was happy with it. That's all that mattered.

They found Kristi in the pens that housed the horses and cattle for the rodeo. Kristi turned out to be a little older than Lori had imagined. Probably closer to thirty or so. She was a small, vigorous young woman, with pert features and blond hair pulled back into a short ponytail. Her slightly aggressive manner suggested an underlying insecurity, Lori guessed, judging from what Cord had told her about the producer's daughter.

In spite of that, Kristi's smile was friendly and welcoming, easing some of Lori's apprehension about sharing the stranger's home.

"I hear you're all set to join up with these here ruffians," she said, gesturing at a boisterous group of cowboys joking with one another over by the railings.

"I guess so." Lori cast an apprehensive glance around. "I hope I can cope with it all. I've never even seen a rodeo before. I don't really know that much about it."

"Then you'll have to get Cord to show you it." Kristi came through the gate and closed it behind her. A horse followed her, apparently wanting out of the pen. Kristi gave it a pat on the neck and it obediently trotted away.

Lori watched it in surprise. "I thought that all rodeo horses were wild."

Kristi grinned. "Some of them are pretty feisty. These are trained working horses, used for roping. The bucking broncs are over there." She nodded at a group of horses quietly standing in another pen.

"They seem harmless enough." Lori looked up at Cord, who was reading a large notice pinned to the wall. "Are these the horses that you ride?"

"Don't let them fool you," he muttered, his gaze still on the notice. "They're harmless enough until you try to ride them. Then they turn into raw, stomping, hotheaded savages who'd stop at nothing to get you off their backs."

"Sounds a lot like some of the cowboys around here," Kristi said darkly.

Lori grinned. She was going to like Kristi, she decided.

"Well, I've got to go round up my partners." Cord gave Kristi one of his narrowed glances, then faced Lori. "You want to stay and get acquainted with your new roommate for a spell?"

"I'll take her to see the office." Kristi thrust a hand under a faucet set in the wall and turned on the spigot. "Just let me get washed up here."

Cord raised an eyebrow at Lori. "I guess I'll catch you later, then. Meet me back here in about a half hour and we'll get something to eat before the show."

Lori watched him go, trying not to feel a ridiculous sense of being abandoned. She was on her own now, she reminded herself. She could no longer rely on him to lead her around. The sooner she got used to it, the better. After all, this is what she wanted...to be independent and free. Wasn't it?

"Let's go, then," Kristi said, with a note of impatience.

Shaking off her momentary depression, Lori followed her into a narrow covered passageway.

"Cord said this is your first job," Kristi remarked, as the hollow sound of their footsteps echoed down the tunnel-like corridor. "You picked a good one. Rodeo work is interesting and always a challenge. You'll enjoy it once you get used to the smell and the noise."

Lori had to admit the barnyard odors would take some getting used to, but she wasn't about to voice her misgivings. "I'm looking forward to it," she assured Kristi.

She followed the petite woman through a door and into a small office, where a heavyset middle-aged woman in jeans and a plaid shirt sat at a desk littered with papers and files. Her dark hair was thick and straight, blunt-cut at her jaw and slashed with gray. The deep creases in her tanned face spoke of long hours in the sun.

"This is Grace," Kristi explained. "She's the secretary, among other things. She also helps out with the promotion work. You'll be her assistant."

Grace held out her hand and smiled. "Howdy. We're mighty pleased to have you along. There's plenty of work here to keep you busy." Her voice was deep and harsh, but she sounded as friendly and warm as her welcome. She spent the next few minutes briefly explaining what the job entailed.

"I hope I can handle it," Lori said nervously.

"Oh, it ain't that hard." Grace waved a hand across the cluttered desk. "Mostly filing, answering the phone, typing up notices on the computer...easy stuff."

"You'll do fine," Kristi informed her. "Just relax and enjoy it."

Lori nodded. "I'm certainly going to try."

"We'd better get back," Kristi said, checking her watch. "I have some stuff to take care of before the show. I reckon Cord will be looking for you, Lori. Never keep a hungry man waiting."

Grace looked at Lori in obvious surprise. "You with Cord?"

Lori glanced at Kristi, not sure what "with Cord" meant.

"Oh, he's just helping her learn the ropes for a while," Kristi said airily.

"Son of a gun," Grace murmured. "I didn't think that black heart of his had any chinks in it. Reckon I was wrong."

"He's just a friend," Lori said quickly, anxious that this woman not start any rumors.

Grace shook her head. "Honey, Cord McVane ain't got no women friends. He ain't got that many friends, period, 'cept for those two travel partners of his, and even they can't crack that thick skull of his. I don't know what you did to get his attention, but there are more than a few women out there who'd sure like to know that secret.'' She uttered a dry chuckle at the thought.

"We'd better get going," Kristi urged, nudging Lori toward the door.

"I'll see you in the morning," Lori called out, just before Kristi swept her down the steps.

"Don't let Grace rile you," Kristi muttered. "Some people around here have nothing better to do than gossip all day. Always reading something into things that are not there. Everyone knows Cord's got no time for women." She sent Lori a sideways glance. "Not women like you, anyhow."

Lori nodded miserably. "I know."

Kristi halted in her tracks, oblivious to the group of cowboys hustling past them. "Have you got feelings for Cord McVane?" she demanded.

Lori shook her head hastily. "No, of course not. It's just, well...he's been good to me...and..." Her voice trailed off as Kristi continued to study her with narrowed eyes.

"Oh, shoot, don't go thinking about him that way. That's a good way to get your heart broken." She tilted up her chin and cursed. "Men. Can't get along with 'em or without 'em. Aren't they the pits?"

Her snort of disgust made Lori smile, in spite of her heartache. "Don't worry," she said, forcing a casual tone. "I'll survive very well without Cord McVane."

"Yeah, won't we all." Kristi linked her arm through Lori's and headed over to the pens, where Cord stood talking to Jed and another tall, good-looking cowboy. "There's Denver," she said, nodding in their direction. "He's getting married at the end of the year. At least one of them had the good sense to get over his feud with women. I give up on the other two.''

Remembering what Cord had told her about Kristi's hopeless hankering after Jed, Lori sent her a look of sympathy.

Cord turned to greet them as they reached the small group. ''There you are,'' he said, his gaze flicking over Lori. ''The show should be starting soon.'' He nodded at the tall man who was studying her with undisguised curiosity. ''This here's Denver Briggs, the third member of our team and the best darn bull rider this side of the Mississippi.''

Denver smiled as he shook Lori's hand. ''Not anymore,'' he murmured, in a deep, pleasant drawl. ''I'm about to retire from the rodeo. Let the young 'uns have a chance at the title.''

Deciding she liked the good-looking cowboy, Lori smiled back. ''Your future wife must be happy to hear that.''

''She sure is,'' Denver assured her. ''She'll be around later. I'd like you to meet her and Josh. He's just ten years old, but he has all the makings of a champion cowboy when he grows up.''

''Poor kid,'' Kristi muttered.

Jed, who'd been listening to the conversation with a preoccupied expression, suddenly joined in. ''That a case of sour grapes, Kristi?''

She tossed her head at him. ''Watch your tongue. You wag it too much and one of them bulls is gonna charge right in and tear that sucker off.''

''Is that a fact.'' Jed smiled lazily at her. ''Well, I reckon I can count on you to haul him right out of here without any hassle at all, then.''

Kristi scowled back at him. "Don't flatter yourself, J.C. I've got better things to do than play nursemaid to you."

"Really?" Jed shook his head in mock dismay. "And here I was thinking of hiring you to be my special pickup man."

"I could do it, too. And you well know it. One of these days, Jed Cullen, I'm gonna show you—" She broke off with a snort of disgust.

"You're gonna show me what, Kristi? I'd be real interested in seeing anything you got to offer."

She jammed her fists into her hips. "If there wasn't a lady present I'd sure as hell tell you, J.C." She glanced at Lori. "I have to get to my horses. I'll see you back at the camper."

Lori nodded, a little unnerved by the intense exchange between the two of them.

"Come on, J.C.," Denver said, clapping the younger cowboy on the shoulder. "If you want me to help you in the chutes tonight we'd better get over there."

Jed looked at Cord. "You coming, too?"

"No, I'm gonna get something to eat. Since I don't have a ride tonight I reckon I'll stay with Lori at the fence to watch. She's never seen a rodeo before. She'll get a better view from there."

Jed nodded, then winked at Lori. "Have fun."

Denver touched the brim of his hat with his fingers. "Reckon we'll see you later, Lori."

She waved at them, then turned to Cord with a smile. "I like your friends."

He nodded, his expression thoughtful. "How about Kristi? You like her, too?"

"Yes, I do. I think we're going to get along just fine."

Apparently satisfied with that, he took her arm with a proprietary gesture that normally she would have resented.

Tonight, however, she was content just to be with him, and she went willingly as he led her across the road to where the pickup was parked in the field.

He took her to a small, cheerful restaurant that served wonderful barbecued ribs and chicken. He kept the conversation firmly on the competition that evening, telling her more than she wanted to know about the various aspects of the different categories. She guessed that he was making a deliberate effort not to touch on anything in the least personal, and she didn't know whether to be glad or sorry about that.

It was something of a relief to her when the meal was over and they were once more in the noisy, colorful, distracting atmosphere of the rodeo arena.

Cord offered her a hand when she climbed up to the top rail of the fence. She ignored him, anxious to display the fact that she could do quite well without his help. From her rather precarious perch, she had a full view of the arena as well as the chutes.

The lower rows of seats were filled with eager spectators, while the ones farther up had several spaces in between. The evening breeze felt cool on her back, and she glanced up at the sky, concerned that it might rain. She'd noticed that Cord had brought his leather jacket with him. The clouds scudded harmlessly by, however, as the sun gradually slipped below the thick rows of pines.

Lori enjoyed the colorful opening parade and watched with interest as women in colorful shirts and wide-brimmed hats rode into the ring. The lead rider wore a white hat with a large silver badge on the front and carried the national flag. Cowboys on horseback followed them, while three clowns tumbled and leaped alongside.

The horses halted, and the announcer asked everyone to stand for Old Glory.

Lori straightened her knees and clung to the fence while the familiar chords of the national anthem rung out across the arena, until cheers from the crowd drowned the last dying note.

Lori's attention was drawn to the chutes, where a flurry of noise signaled the arrival of the first horses. Men scrambled above the chutes to ready a horse, then the rider clambered up and positioned himself. Lori held her breath as he lowered himself onto the animal, who immediately started thrashing around in the chute. The cowboy handed a rope to the man on his left, who passed it under the horse to another cowboy the other side. The rider then took the end and wound it tight around his hand.

He slid forward on the stomping horse, jammed his hat down on his head with his left hand, then raised his arm and nodded. The gate opened, and the bucking, writhing, leaping animal exploded into the ring.

Lori gasped and grabbed hold of Cord's arm. "He's going to fall off."

"That's the general idea," Cord said dryly. "The tough part is hanging on long enough to beat the buzzer."

Lori glanced up to where a large screen marked off the seconds. "How long does he have to stay on there?"

"Eight seconds."

She relaxed her grip on his arm. "Oh, that's not very long."

He gave her a wry look. "Try it sitting on a horse that's doing its damnedest to kick you off his back. Eight seconds can seem like a mighty long time."

The buzzer sounded as he spoke, and the crowd cheered. Lori watched another rider come alongside the cowboy and grab his arm to help him off the horse, while a clown dashed into the ring and herded the horse through the gate alongside where she sat.

The thunder of hooves sent up a cloud of dust as the horse thudded by, and the clown looked up and gave her a comical grin before chasing after the animal.

"That's Sam," Cord told her, as another rider prepared to clamber up on the chutes for his ride. "He hasn't been back too long. Got gored by a bull a while back."

Lori looked at him in dismay. "How did that happen?"

"He was trying to get the bull's attention away from Denver, and wasn't quite fast enough to get out of the way of the horns."

Lori shuddered. "How awful. That was brave of him, though, to come to Denver's rescue."

"That's his job," Cord said, sounding matter-of-fact.

Lori stared at him. "He baits bulls for a living?"

Cord's mouth twisted in wry humor. "Well, I've never heard it put that way before, but I reckon that's about the size of it."

"Why would anyone want to do that?"

"Same reason anyone rides rodeo. The challenge of it, I reckon."

She thought about that for the next hour or two as she watched tough, rugged men tossed from the backs of horses, thudding to the ground, then limping out of the ring to prepare for the next round of punishment. She saw cowboys rolling in the dust with struggling calves while they tried to tie their feet. She watched women lean perilously close to the ground as they rounded barrels in a thick haze of dust, and she stared in horror as men fought to cling to the backs of snorting, rampaging bulls.

The noise at times was deafening as the announcer strove to be heard above the roar from the spectators. Animal hooves pounded the ground, while others kicked at the gates penning them in the chutes. Dust stung her eyes and throat, while the breeze wafted smells of horse manure, popcorn and hotdogs.

By the time it was over she felt as if she herself had been out there competing. She felt a whole new respect for the riders, and more than a little apprehension when she thought about Cord riding in the next competition. Somehow, when he'd talked to her about the rodeo before, none of it had seemed tangible. Now it was all too real, and for the first time she truly understood the risks involved.

It was a very different world from the one she was accustomed to, and she wondered if she'd be able to fit into this rough, gritty environment of professional rodeo.

"So what did you think of it?" Cord asked her, as he picked up his jacket from the fence and slung it over his shoulder.

"I'm still trying to make up my mind," she told him honestly. "How do you stand being jarred around like that? Doesn't it hurt? Don't you ache afterward?"

"Yeah, it hurts. 'Specially when you hit the ground."

"It seems a strange way to make a living."

"For most of us it's the only way. It's all we know."

Or all they wanted, she thought, remembering the reason Cord had joined the rodeo. "I can't help feeling sorry for the animals out there," she said. "Don't they get hurt by all this rough handling?"

Cord shook his head. "The PRCA has some pretty strict rules when it comes to handling the critters.

"PRCA?"

"Professional Rodeo Cowboys Association. The judges inspect all the animals before and after the competition. There's no ill-treatment allowed, and you'll find Kristi feeding and watering the horses before she chows down herself."

"Well, I don't know how anyone rides those bulls," Lori

said, as they made their way to the back of the arena where Kristi was attending to the horses. ''No wonder Denver hurt his back. It's a wonder he hasn't broken every bone in his body.''

''He probably has at one time or another.''

He'd sounded so casual about it Lori thought he must be joking. He seemed perfectly serious, however, and once again she felt a twinge of anxiety. She didn't know if she could watch Cord ride, realizing he could fall under those lethal hooves at any time.

As they approached the pens, she saw Denver standing by the fence, talking to Jed. A slender, attractive woman stood by his side, laughing up at him, while a young boy hung over the rail, talking to Kristi.

''There's April,'' Cord said, and quickened his stride.

He reached the small group ahead of her, and Lori felt self-conscious as they all watched her approach. She wondered what Jed had told his friends about her and hoped he hadn't told them about seeing her in the cabin dressed only in a T-shirt.

April greeted her with a smile when she was introduced, and Josh, April's son, asked her if she was riding in the barrel races.

''Heavens, no!'' Lori exclaimed. ''I've never been on a horse in my life. I'd fall off the second it moved.''

Josh was highly amused by this statement, but Jed eyed her thoughtfully. ''You gotta know how to ride a horse if you're gonna work around here. I reckon I could give you a couple of lessons, just to get you started.''

Lori opened her mouth to politely decline, but Cord beat her to it.

''Lori's not going to have time to ride horses,'' he said shortly. ''Reckon she'll be too busy with her office work.''

Lori sent him a scowl, while Jed raised his eyebrows. "I don't reckon she'll be working all the time."

"Maybe not," Cord said a little too softly, "but she'll have plenty to keep her amused without getting herself tangled up with horses."

Jed grinned. "You gonna do the amusing, Cord?"

Cord's face looked as if it had been chiseled out of stone. "Watch your step, J.C."

"Cut it out, Jed," Denver said quietly. "You're embarrassing Lori."

Lori sent him a grateful glance, though she wasn't so much embarrassed by Jed as annoyed with Cord's high-handed rejection on her behalf of Jed's offer. If they had been alone she would have said something, but she didn't want to make everyone uncomfortable.

Kristi chose that moment to join the group, much to Lori's relief. "I'm just about through," she announced to no one in particular, though Lori noticed she flicked a glance at Jed. "Anyone want to go down to the Red Horn for a bite to eat?"

Denver shook his head. "I have to get April back to Portland. Josh has to go to school tomorrow. I reckon I'll join up with you folks in Lewiston next week."

Kristi nodded. She waited until all the goodbyes were said and Denver had moved off, then looked at Cord. "How about you and Lori coming with me, then? They've got a good band down there. Just right for dancing."

"You know darn well I don't dance," Cord said, shoving a thumb into the pocket of his jeans. "And Lori needs to get some shut-eye. She has to start a new job in the morning."

Lori gritted her teeth, making a mental note to talk to him just as soon as the opportunity arose. Obviously he had forgotten everything she'd said to him. Either that, or he was choosing to ignore it. She would have to remind him again, and next time she'd have to make sure it was in a way he wouldn't soon forget. Lori Ashford was not going to let anyone run her life anymore. Especially someone like Cord McVane.

Chapter 8

"Well, if you're not going to come with me," Kristi said, with a resigned shrug, "I guess I'll go on my own. Let yourself into the camper, Lori. I'll try not to wake you when I get in."

Before Lori could answer her, Jed said plaintively, "So what about me? Am I invisible or something?"

Kristi's smile had no humor in it. "I'm not going to ask you, J.C., just so's you can have the pleasure of turning me down. I'd rather go on my own, anyhow. I have more fun that way."

She stalked off, leaving Lori to wonder uncomfortably if Kristi was upset with her for not insisting on going with her.

Jed must have seen her worried expression. He touched her on the shoulder, murmuring, "Don't fret over Kristi. She's used to doing things on her own."

Lori gave him a reluctant smile. She was still seething inside at Cord's domineering attitude. It was true; she was tired and ready to get some sleep. It had been a long and eventful day and she needed to be fresh for tomorrow. It was, however, her decision to make. Not Cord's.

"Well, I reckon I'll drop by the Pit Stop for a nightcap before turning in," Jed said, giving Cord a meaningful look. "I'll be there for a while if you want to join me later."

"I might just do that," Cord murmured, intensifying Lori's resentment. Apparently she wasn't to be invited there, either. It would just serve Cord McVane right if she walked in on her own.

She was quiet on the way back to the camper, pretending to be absorbed in watching the dark branches of the pines swaying in the wind against the starlit sky. Now that she was away from the shelter of the arena, the chill night air penetrated the thin cotton of her shirt and she shivered.

Cord must have seen the movement. He swung his jacket off his shoulder and placed its heavy folds around her shoulders. "Next time," he said quietly, "bring a jacket. The nights get cold now."

"I don't have a jacket." He'd sounded so much like her mother she'd had to bite back the retort. This wasn't the time for a discussion, she warned herself. She was tired, and it would be too easy to lose her temper. Somehow she had to get through to Cord, in as mature a manner as possible, that she was an adult, and perfectly capable of taking care of herself. She just couldn't let him go around giving everyone the impression that he was her guardian or something. The fact that she'd already stressed that point—several times—did not bode well for success.

Somehow she would have to find a way to prove it to him, since mere words seemed to have no effect whatsoever. Although how she was going to do that when he kept such a close eye on her was going to prove quite a challenge.

"Hope you sleep well," Cord said, as they reached the door of Kristi's motor home. His gaze met hers, then slid away. "Good luck with the job tomorrow. You'll probably spend the morning packing up. Most of us will be moving out tomorrow afternoon."

She felt a sharp stab of dismay. She hadn't thought about the travel arrangements until now. Of course she'd be traveling with Kristi. She wouldn't see Cord again until they reached Idaho.

"Hope you have a good trip," she said, doing her best to sound indifferent. Inside, her heart felt as heavy as lead. They were like strangers again. Where was the man who had made such passionate love to her—the first and only man to bare the secrets of her body and teach her how to love like a woman?

Was this how it happened in real life? One night and then forget it? Had all her wonderful dreams been nothing but fantasy? Had she been fooling herself about what making love was all about? Maybe there was no such thing as real love and she'd been chasing after rainbows the night she'd run away from Richard.

In the next instant she rejected that thought. She refused to give up her dream. Cord had dismissed their wonderful night together because she hadn't been exciting enough for him—because she lacked the experience to make a man like Cord McVane happy. Because, as Kristi had so aptly put it, he just didn't have time for women like her. The sooner she accepted that, the less heartache she'd cause herself.

She slid his warm jacket from her shoulders and handed it to him. "Thank you," she said quietly. "I enjoyed the evening. I guess I'll see you in Idaho."

He looked down at the jacket in his hands for a long moment, then looked back at her. "Good night, Lori."

The sound of her name on his lips would always give her a jolt. She pressed her own lips together and nodded, not trusting herself to speak. Instead, she fitted the key into the lock and, without looking at him again, let herself into the camper.

In spite of her weariness, she found it difficult to fall asleep. After the quiet peacefulness of the forest, the street noises intruded on her, disturbing her efforts to shut them out. The sound of a car engine revving, the blast of a horn, the wail of a police siren somewhere on the highway, a dog howling in indignation at being left outside—it all sounded as loud as if she'd left the volume up on the TV.

The narrow guest bed that Cord had indicated as hers felt restricting, and she kept throwing the covers off, only to retrieve them when the cold chilled her shoulders. It was relief to hear a car door slam outside the camper, then the sound of Kristi's spare key in the lock.

Lori feigned sleep while Kristi crept to her bedroom. She didn't feel like talking, and she didn't want to hear about Kristi's adventures down at the Red Horn. The very next time Kristi invited her, she promised herself, she'd go. No matter where it was. She wasn't going to miss out on life just because Cord McVane thought he had to protect her from herself.

She fell asleep soon after that and woke up in the middle of the night with a strange ache that wouldn't go away. Although subconsciously she knew it had to do with Cord, she refused to think about him. She missed him, but she'd get used to that.

Instead, she thought about her parents and what they would think if they knew she was sleeping in a camper belonging to a stock contractor's daughter and tomorrow

would be starting work as a producer's assistant with the
rodeo. Her mother would have a convulsion. The thought
brought her a small measure of satisfaction.

She wouldn't allow herself to wonder what her parents
would think if they knew their only daughter had given up
her virginity to a rodeo cowboy. The experience was too
new, too precious, to tarnish with thoughts of her family's
displeasure. No matter what her family would think of her,
no matter how little that night had meant to Cord, she
would never regret those stolen hours. No matter whom she
might meet in the future, there would never be anyone quite
as special as the man who had shown her for the first time
the secrets of making love. She fell asleep again, clutching
her pillow to her tearstained cheeks.

Lori awoke refreshed the next morning, despite her restless night. Kristi advised her to wear jeans to work, since
they would be packing up. "Most of us wear jeans all the
time, anyway," she told Lori. "You'd look out of place at
a rodeo dressed in a skirt and heels."

She'd have to spend some more of Cord's money, Lori
thought ruefully, if she was going to live in jeans. According to Grace, she wouldn't get her first paycheck for two
weeks. She still had to eat, and there was the little matter
of paying rent for her space in Kristi's camper.

When she broached the subject over a breakfast of melon
and scrambled eggs, fixed by Kristi on the miniature stove,
the other woman dismissed the subject with a wave of her
hand. "Cord has been a good friend to me," she said,
reaching for a slice of toast. "I'm happy to return the favor."

Lori looked at her in surprise. "I got the impression that
Cord was a loner. Didn't Grace say he didn't have any

friends? Yet both you and your father seem to be in his debt.''

Kristi smiled. ''Cord doesn't wave his friendship around like a flag. He's the deep and silent type, like a river that you don't even know is there until you need water. He's had his problems with women, and he doesn't trust anyone, except Jed and Denver. But he's the kind of man who could never turn his back on someone in trouble.''

Lori thought about the night Cord had found her in his cabin. He thought she'd broken in, yet he didn't call the police and he hadn't turned her out. She sipped the hot coffee and put down the mug. ''You're right,'' she said quietly. ''He's a good man.''

''Oh, he's got his problems,'' Kristi said airily. ''Don't all men? Look at J.C., for instance. That man is a walking disaster. It's impossible to get through to him. He never takes anything seriously.''

Including Kristi, Lori thought privately. She knew, only too well, how that felt.

She helped her new friend to wash the dishes and put them away before leaving for the office. When she got there, she saw that Grace's desk was piled high with boxes, rolled-up posters and bulging files. She had a file box in front of her and was sorting through a wad of forms.

''We have to get this stuff packed in the trailer,'' she told Lori, waving her chunky hand at the mess. ''Paul wants us out of here and on the road by noon.''

''Is he here?'' Lori asked, eager to meet Kristi's father.

Grace shook her head. ''He's at the ranch in eastern Oregon. He catches up with us now and again, to check up on Kristi and the boys. But he knows what's going on all the time. Doesn't miss a thing, that Paul Ramsett, except maybe the way his daughter spends her life trying to get his attention.''

"He must trust her if he lets her handle the animals without him."

Grace shrugged. "He's got some good men on the payroll, and the rodeo guys look out for one another and help out. Paul knows that."

Lori piled the files into one of the empty boxes. "What's he like?"

"Paul?" Grace wrinkled her brow. "Good-looking man. Looks younger than his age. Been single too long. He was only twenty-six when Kristi's mom died. That was twenty-five years ago. He's still a young man...he should get married again. It's not right for a man like that to live such a lonely life on that ranch of his."

Lori glanced at Grace, intrigued to hear a wistful note in the other woman's voice. Maybe she wasn't the only one with unfulfilled dreams, she thought wryly. "What's he like to work with?"

"Huh?" Grace stared at her for a moment, then went on sorting through the forms. "Oh, he's a tough man to please, but he lets you know when you've done it. He doesn't give praise very often, but when he does you can tell it's genuine. I like that."

Lori had to agree that the best praise was the honest kind.

She spent an enjoyable morning packing up the office files and helping Grace load them in the trailer. All morning long cowboys stopped by to pick up their winnings, and the phone rang constantly. Grace insisted on answering it, telling Lori she would have her turn soon enough once she learned a little more about what was going on.

From those phone conversations, Lori concluded that the booking of one of the opening acts for the next rodeo was not going as planned. The trick rider who was supposed to perform had fallen from her horse and broken her foot.

Grace spent a good part of the morning calling talent agents in the area.

"It's tough to find an act at this short notice," she grumbled, as she slapped the phone down for the fifth or sixth time. "That gal has been booked for two months. You'd think she could have stayed on her horse for another week or two."

Lori hid a grin. "What happens if you don't find anyone?"

Grace shuddered. "I catch hell from Paul, that's what happens. He don't like hitches in his productions."

"But if it's not your fault—"

"Someone has to take the heat." Grace wagged a finger at her. "Remember that when you start taking on some responsibility. Sometimes you have to swallow your pride and figure it's all part of the job."

Lori looked at her in dismay. "But that doesn't seem fair."

"Honey, life ain't fair. You'll learn to accept it just like the rest of us."

Lori frowned at the posters she was stacking into a box. Life in the real world was turning out to be very different from the way she'd imagined. That didn't mean she regretted her decision to leave home, she thought hastily. It was just that it would take some getting used to, that was all.

After all, she'd dealt with everything pretty well so far. The memory of Cord's strong body covering hers momentarily distracted her. While she was still struggling to erase the memory from her mind, the phone rang once more.

"It's for you," Grace said, handing her the receiver.

Aware of the woman's curious glances, Lori spoke cautiously into the mouthpiece. "Hello?"

"So, how's it going in the working world?"

Cord's deep voice seemed to spread like wildfire through her veins. She felt the heat creeping over her cheeks as she answered a little breathlessly, "Fine. We're almost done packing, and Grace should be ready to leave by noon."

"Good. That's what I wanted to talk to you about."

He paused, and she waited, her heart thumping anxiously, for him to continue. "I talked to Kristi," he said at last, "and she's planning on moving out around two. I thought you might like to grab a bite to eat before you go."

Thrilled at the thought of seeing him again, she answered eagerly. "I'd love to. When?"

"I'll pick you up at the office in about half an hour."

She replaced the receiver and smiled happily at Grace. "That was Cord. He's taking me to lunch."

Grace nodded. "So I gathered." She went on packing in silence for a moment, then added quietly, "Honey, I know it's none of my business, and you can tell me to shut up if I'm out of line but…"

She hesitated, and Lori regarded her anxiously. "What is it?"

Grace laid one of her large hands over Lori's. "Just watch your step with Cord, okay? Don't let him break your heart. Believe me, it ain't worth it."

Flustered, Lori pulled her hand away. "I don't know what you mean."

Grace sighed. "Look, I've got no idea what's happened in your life, and like I said, it's none of my business. I just figure you don't belong in a place like this. You're not like the rest of us, you know? You have to be tough and just a little mean to survive in rodeo, and I don't think you've got a mean bone in your body. I don't want to see you get hurt, that's all."

She was just a little too late, Lori thought dryly. "Thanks, Grace," she said, tempering her words with a smile, "but you don't have to worry about me. I'm tougher than I look."

Grace gave her a doubtful nod. "I sure hope so, honey," she murmured, "because you're sure as hell gonna need to be before you're through here." She picked up the box and headed for the door. "This is the last one, I reckon. We'll just finish cleaning up here and then I guess I'll see you in Lewiston tomorrow?"

Lori nodded, only half registering what she'd said. She was too busy wondering exactly what Grace had meant by her ominous-sounding warning.

Cord arrived at the office just as Grace was dusting off the last shelf. "I don't know why we can't just run the office from the trailer instead of moving the office every time," she grumbled as he came through the door.

"You'd still have to drag records out there," Cord reminded her. "Besides, it gets you out of your trailer for a spell."

Grace grinned at him. "It does that. Always got a ready answer, you handsome devil." She winked at Lori. "See you in Lewiston."

Lori watched her leave, feeling ridiculously self-conscious now that she was alone with Cord again.

"Thought we might stop by the steak house," he said, as he opened the door of the truck. "I can't go far. I want to get hooked up again by the time Jed gets back from town."

"A steak house sounds good." Lori sent him a sideways glance. His jaw was freshly shaven and he wore a black shirt with his jeans. He'd pulled the black hat low over his eyes. He looked even more imposing than she remembered.

"So how'd you like the job?" he asked, as the truck bowled along the main highway.

"It's hard to tell yet," she said cautiously, "but I think

I'm really going to enjoy working for the rodeo. It's interesting, varied and you can't beat the change of scenery."

He glanced at her. "Hell-bent on making a go of it, huh?"

"Something like that."

He nodded. "Well, you could do worse, I guess. How's it working out with Kristi?"

"Great so far." She hesitated, then decided now was as good a time as any. "I felt bad about not going with her last night, though. I think she was disappointed in me."

"Yeah, well, she'll have to swallow her disappointment. The kind of places Kristi goes to are not the kind of places I want to see you in."

"And what about what I want?" she asked evenly.

He sent her a quick frown, then turned back to the road. "Look, I know you had problems with your family running your life, but let's not get that mixed up with what I'm trying to do here."

She shifted her body so that she could face him. "Exactly what are you trying to do?"

He didn't answer her at first. He appeared to be giving her question some deep thought. Finally, he said carefully, "I'm just trying to protect you from a world you're not ready for. The rodeo is a great place to be, but there are some, including me, who'll tell you it's no place for a woman like you."

She was beginning to get irritated with that phrase. "What does that mean, precisely—a woman like me?"

"A woman who hasn't been around, and doesn't know the score. There are some men who would be only too happy to take advantage of that."

"Like you, for instance?" The words were out before she could stop them. "I'm sorry," she added quickly, "I didn't mean that."

She could tell by his grim profile that she'd hit a button. "No," he said gruffly. "You don't have to apologize. You're right, and believe me, I'll never stop regretting it. I should be apologizing to you."

"You already did." This wasn't the way she'd wanted this discussion to go, she thought desperately. Struggling to get back on track, she added, "There are men in all kinds of jobs who would take advantage of…someone like me. If I'm going to have problems, then I'll have to get out there and face them. I have to learn by my own mistakes. I'm not going to learn anything if you insist on wrapping a cocoon around me the way my family did." She took a deep breath. "I don't want to be dependent on you forever, Cord. That isn't fair to either of us."

He seemed to be searching for words as he swung the wheel, turning the truck into a parking lot. Lori looked up and saw a low-lying, wooden building with lit beer signs in the windows. The truck shuddered to a halt, and the silence seemed startling after he cut the engine. Finally, he uttered a long, heavy sigh. "You're right," he muttered. "I reckon I have been pretty heavy-handed at that. From now on you go where you want. I'll try not to stick my nose in again."

She wasn't at all sure this was what she wanted, either. Damn him, she thought furiously. How could he tie her up in knots like that and not even know it? She studied his face, trying to tell if he was mad at her. His expression revealed nothing, and she gave up. "Fine," she said miserably. "From now on you can quit worrying about me."

He managed a brief nod. "Come on, let's go eat. I'm starving."

She followed him into the busy restaurant, wondering how he could be hungry when her own stomach churned so badly she didn't know if she'd ever feel like eating again.

"You're mighty quiet," Jed observed, after he and Cord had sat in silence in the cab of the truck for several minutes.

Cord gripped the wheel, his eyes narrowed against the setting sun, and did his best to clear his mind of his troubles. They had been on the road for two hours, and still he couldn't stop thinking about Lori. "Just tired, I guess," he mumbled. "I need to get back to riding again. Take my mind off other things."

"Other things wouldn't be a classy young lady by the name of Lori, now would it?" Jed asked slyly.

Cord sent him a warning glance. "Don't start on me, J.C. I'm not in the mood."

"Strikes me you haven't been in any kind of mood except a black one ever since you got back from the cabin."

"I'm just worrying about the standings, that's all. If I don't get a win in Idaho I'm gonna lose my place for the title."

"You'll make it up. We've got the Cow Palace coming up next month. That carries a pretty good purse, and you always do well in San Francisco. How's the shoulder, anyway?"

Cord shrugged. "About as good as it's going to get, I reckon."

"Then you've got nothing to worry about, pardner. Except maybe your little protégée. Strikes me she's the one who's getting under your skin. Not the standings."

Cord gritted his teeth. "You're not funny, J.C."

"I'm not trying to be funny." Jed leaned forward to peer into Cord's face. "Truth is, I'm worried about you. You don't usually let a little filly like that throw you."

Cord kept his gaze squarely on the road. "Nobody's throwing me. Not unless I want to get thrown."

"Well, do you?"

"Do I what?" Cord braked as a sleek BMW cut in front of him.

"Wanna get hooked?"

Cord uttered a derisive snort. "Do I look like I'm ready to commit suicide?"

Jed sighed and leaned back in his seat. "I don't know, Cord," he murmured. "You worry me. I was talking to Denver about it—"

"Just what were you talking about, J.C.?"

Jed must have heard the dangerous note in his friend's voice. He sounded wary when he answered. "Aw, come on, Cord. You know me and Denver are like family."

"All I know," Cord said, taking care to keep his voice even, "is that the two of you are discussing something that is none of your damn business. I want the subject closed once and for all. Is that understood?"

"All we're trying to do—"

"I know what you're trying to do, and I appreciate it. What I'm telling you is that you're wasting your time worrying about something that doesn't exist. Now, I don't want to hear another word about it. Period."

"But—"

"Not one word, J.C."

Jed lapsed into silence, and Cord let out his breath. His partners meant well, but he just didn't know how much more he could stand of J.C.'s constant heckling. The problem was, Jed had seen Lori coming out of the bedroom that day at the cabin, and it was pretty obvious she'd just climbed out of bed. It didn't take someone like Jed long to make a federal case out of it.

He'd tried to convince his younger partner that Lori had

slept alone in the bedroom, while he'd taken the chair. More to protect Lori's reputation than for any concern about his own. It was a little late to worry about his image now. He'd blown that a long time ago. But he was bound and determined that no one should realize Lori had compromised herself that way. Especially with an old reprobate like Cord McVane.

He just didn't know what to do about Lori. Most of the men he met on the circuit were decent guys, intent on minding their own business and concentrating on their careers. But there were always one or two bad apples in the barrel. Riding the rodeo circuit was a solitary life, and passing a few hours with a woman could go a long way toward helping a man feel less lonely.

Now and again a cowboy would fill himself full of beer and get persistent. Most women knew how to handle a situation like that, but there were some who were either too hungry themselves or too naive to understand what was happening until it was too late. Knowing firsthand how vulnerable Lori was, Cord felt he had good reason to worry about her.

But now he'd promised not to interfere in her life. That was going to make it a little tough to protect her. He could understand how she felt, having just gotten out from under the heavy hand of her family. But she had a lot to learn about men and taking care of herself. All he could do was hang around and keep an eye on her from a distance. If he saw trouble brewing, maybe he could step in without her noticing.

Either way, he thought gloomily, he saw a rocky road ahead. He couldn't forget that he was her first man, and he couldn't help feeling possessive about her. It kind of went with the territory. He knew full well that just because she gave up her innocence for him, that didn't make her his property.

Which was just as well, he hastily assured himself, seeing as how he didn't want to get tangled up with a woman ever again. Which made it all the more important that she learn to stand on her own two feet. It was just damn hard watching her test the waters, knowing she could get in over her head at any time.

Maybe if he could forget that night in the cabin he'd have an easier time of it. But every time he laid eyes on her his body ached to make love to her again. He couldn't forget how she'd driven him wild with her special brand of innocence and passion and how his body had craved her, needing her as he'd never wanted a woman before. How he still needed her, with a fierce yearning that threatened to drive him out of his mind at times.

It didn't seem to help much when he reminded himself of how dangerous that could be. He'd even gone so far as to open up the memories he'd kept buried for so long…hoping that the pain of remembering would bring him to his senses.

Instead he'd discovered a startling fact. Although the agony of losing the child he'd loved more than life itself still cut him to the core, the feelings he'd had for Ellie seemed to have faded with time. He couldn't forget her betrayal, or forgive, but now he could understand.

Even so, he knew better than to give in to the powerful emotions that drove him whenever he was near Lori. He'd been through too much to lay his heart on the line again, and Lori deserved more. Lori deserved a man whose heart was whole…a man who could love…a man who could trust. For without trust, there could never be the kind of love that Lori was looking for. And that was sad.

"Are you gonna sit there scowling at the road like that

for the next two hours?'' Jed demanded at his side. ''If so, I might as well try to catch some shut-eye.''

Cord dragged his thoughts back to the present. ''As a matter of fact, J.C.,'' he said, pulling off onto the shoulder, ''I'm getting a little sleepy myself. Why don't you take the wheel, and I'll go lie down in the back for a while.''

''Now, you know right well that's illegal.''

Cord snorted. ''Just tell me since when you've been so all-fired concerned about legalities?''

Jed feigned a hurt expression and clamped a hand over his heart. ''That got me right here, pardner. You know I have the deepest respect for the law.''

''As well as I know that pigs fly.'' Cord shut off the engine and opened the cab door. ''Wake me up when we get to Lewiston.'' He climbed down and walked back to the door of the trailer. If he couldn't get Lori Ashford out of his mind, he could at least let sleep shut her out, he told himself as he let himself into the cool living space. Which was ironic, considering memories of her naked body responding to his touch tormented him in his dreams every night.

He slammed the door shut a little harder than necessary. There were some days he just couldn't win.

The days passed quickly for Lori as she learned the various features of her new job. She particularly enjoyed meeting the winners who came to the office to collect their pay, and the many more hopefuls who registered for the rides. She became adept at solving the petty little issues that crept up from time to time, and gradually Grace left her alone to handle her work without supervision.

One morning Lori found an e-mail on her computer from Paul Ramsett, complimenting her on her handling of a difficult sponsor whose demands for publicity had been excessive and impossible to meet. Lori had managed a compromise, earning the praise of her unapproachable boss and congratulations from a delighted Grace.

Although she found the pace exhausting at first, Lori learned fast. The job was challenging—always having to be one step ahead—finalizing arrangements for the next town while still mopping up the last-minute details of the one she was in.

The towns became blurred names on the map as days flew by, until it became hard to distinguish one from the other. The highways were mostly straight, seemingly unending and unbearably boring.

One morning, after a particularly long stretch of dead straight highway, Kristi pulled off the road and raised her arms above her head with a groan. "I've got to get out and stretch my legs. I'm going cross-eyed."

Lori glanced uneasily at the wheel. She'd never driven anything bigger than her car, and the thought of steering the huge motor home terrified her, but she'd been feeling guilty about letting Kristi do all the driving for some time. Now seemed as good a moment as any to mention her idea.

"Do you think I could drive this thing?"

Kristi shrugged. "Don't see why not. It's pretty much the same as driving a car."

"It's a lot bigger than a car."

"You just have to give yourself enough space, that's all."

"I'd like to try it."

"Be my guest." Kristi opened the door and jumped out.

Lori sat behind the wheel and waited for Kristi to climb back in the other side. It seemed to be an awfully long way down to the ground, she thought nervously, staring through the window at the road ahead.

"There's one thing about it," Kristi said cheerfully as

she flung herself into the passenger seat. "You're not likely to hit anything but a stray rabbit on this road. Not unless we catch up with some of the boys, anyway."

"Thanks," Lori said dryly. "That's a comforting thought."

She started off slowly, afraid to press down too hard on the accelerator, until Kristi pointed out that it would take them a week to get to their destination if she didn't put her foot down.

At first she was terrified she'd land them in a ditch, but eventually she began to relax. She drove for two hours, then thankfully handed the wheel back to Kristi when they reached the outskirts of town.

"You just need some practice in parking" Kristi told her, "and you'll be handling this baby like a pro."

Lori felt immensely pleased with herself. Bit by bit she was conquering her reservations about her own abilities. Day by day she was growing more confident, more sure of herself. She would have been utterly content if it hadn't been for the feeling that Cord was doing his best to avoid her.

She saw him at the office when he came to register, and now and again she'd sit on the fence and watch him ride, always with her heart in her mouth until he was safely back behind the chutes. Sometimes he'd win; more often he wouldn't; and she knew that Jed and Denver were worried about him. Cord seemed to have lost his fire, Jed told her, and was losing his place in the standings.

Now and again she'd see him talking to women—women who laughed and flirted with him—women who apparently were not like her. That hurt, especially on the lonely nights when sleep evaded her and she'd lie aching to feel his arms around her and his mouth claiming hers.

She no longer thought about her family, unless something happened to remind her about one of them, and always the thought was fleeting. Several times, while in town, Kristi had asked her to go with her to a roadhouse or the local tavern, but mindful of Cord's disapproval, she'd declined.

The day Denver announced he was officially retiring from the rodeo and going back to open a rodeo school in eastern Oregon, everyone wanted to take him down to the tavern to celebrate.

"This is his last day," Kristi told Lori when she got back to the trailer that evening. "We should all be there to give him a send-off."

"I don't know," Lori murmured automatically. "I'm pretty tired."

"Everyone needs a break now and again." Kristi pulled her hair back and fastened it with a clip. "Come on. It'll do you good. You've been looking a little peaked lately. Take a shower, get into some fresh duds and let your hair down for a change. It'll be fun."

It did sound inviting, but Lori hesitated. She hadn't gone out with the sole intent of having fun since she'd left home. It sounded appealing, in spite of her weariness. In fact, now that she thought about it, she'd felt unusually tired most of the time lately. Maybe a night out on the town was just what she needed.

"Cord will be there," Kristi said casually, as she peered into the mirror on the bathroom door to put on her lipstick. "He offered to take us down in the truck."

Lori's pulse skipped. She should have been disturbed by the thought that he obviously wanted to keep an eye on her, but she couldn't help feeling excited at the prospect of being out on the town with him. "I imagine Jed will be going, too," she said lightly.

"Reckon he will. He owes me a beer. I'll have to make sure to collect it."

"I don't feel much like drinking, but I'll go with you and toast Denver with soda." Lori pulled a pair of jeans off their hanger and studied the silk shirts. "My stomach hasn't felt too good the past few days."

Kristi sent her a concerned look. "Not coming down with something, are you? It's that time of year. Seems like everyone gets a bug around Halloween."

"I don't know." Lori frowned at the shirts, trying to decide between a pale peach or a royal blue.

"You gotta take care of yourself," Kristi said earnestly. "You've been working long hours. Maybe a drink or two will help you feel better."

Lori smiled. "I'll be fine. Probably a bug, as you said." She pulled the peach shirt off its hanger. "I'll take a shower and be right with you."

She dressed hurriedly, her pulse racing at the thought of spending some time with Cord. At least while they were driving down there. He'd probably ignore her again once they were there, she thought wryly, as she carefully applied just a touch of eye shadow.

The thought depressed her, and she brushed it aside. She wasn't going to let anything spoil her first real night out since she became a liberated woman. She certainly didn't need anyone paying attention to her all night to have a good time. She was going to have fun, and to hell with Cord McVane.

Chapter 9

Lori's confidence faltered a little under the intense appraisal Cord gave her when he pulled up in front of the camper and leaned out the window of the truck.

"I managed to talk her into going," Kristi said, as she waited for Lori to climb up next to him.

Lori scooted along the seat and gave him a defiant smile. "I hope that meets with your approval."

His black eyes gleamed at her in the light from the parking lot street lamps. "I reckon." He waited for Kristi to clamber up, then shifted the gear and let out the brake. Squished between Kristi's elbow and Cord's hip, Lori did her best to relax.

"Where's Jed?" Kristi asked, leaning forward to peer at Cord.

"He's gone on ahead with Denver. Sam took them down in his truck."

Apparently satisfied, Kristi leaned back again.

"Will April be there?" Lori asked.

Cord shook his head. "It was too far for her to come and she didn't want to leave Josh overnight."

"Have they decided on the wedding?"

"Yeah, they want a Christmas wedding."

Lori gasped in delight. "Really? That's so neat."

"I hope we all get invites." Kristi reached for the handle and wound the window up tight. "That wind is cold tonight. It'll soon be winter."

Cord didn't answer, and Lori glanced at his harsh profile, trying to gauge his mood. As always, she couldn't tell what he was thinking. Her feeling of expectancy died, and a cold knot settled in her heart. She wished now she hadn't come. It was obvious he didn't want her there. He was probably wishing he'd never got her a job with the rodeo.

She sat the rest of the way in silence, only half listening to Kristi chattering on about her favorite country singer. The current rodeo season ended in December, she thought, beginning to feel depressed again. By then she should have paid back all the money she owed Cord. The new season began right after the new year, but maybe it would be better if she looked for a different job after the finals in Las Vegas. Though what kind of job she hadn't the faintest idea. After working for the rodeo, most jobs would seem terribly dull.

"We're here," Kristi announced, making Lori jump. She'd been so deep in her thoughts she hadn't noticed the truck slowing down.

They were in the parking lot of a tall building that resembled somebody's mansion more than a tavern. Huge windows overlooked the street, and wide steps led up to an impressive heavy oak door banded by enormous old-fashioned wrought-iron hinges.

Lights blazed from the ground-floor windows, spilling out onto the gravel driveway that led up to the steps. The crunching sound of their footsteps seemed to ring out in the cool, crisp air, above the faint echoes of music and laughter coming from inside the building.

A huge sign hung above the portal over the door, hand-painted with the grinning face of a cowboy and a hand holding a foaming mug of beer. The name above the painting said, The Watering Hole.

"Jed's here!" Kristi exclaimed. "There's Sam's truck." She pointed to a red pickup parked a few spaces down.

"He's more'n likely on his fourth beer by now," Cord muttered, sounding grumpy.

Lori glanced at him, remembering Jed's comments the other day about Cord losing his enthusiasm for the rides. Maybe he was coming down with a bug, too, she thought, as she followed him up the steps.

Cord pulled open the door, and Lori was met with a blast of thumping guitars and voices striving to be heard above the racket. The room was huge, like a ballroom, complete with dusty yellow chandeliers hanging from the high ceiling. Wide-beamed rafters crisscrossed above her head from wall to wall, and massive wrought-iron lanterns hung from each end of the crowded bar.

Tables filled the main floor, with the exception of one corner where people danced in long lines, all apparently doing the same step. Smoke hung around the chandeliers in a golden haze, and Lori's stomach churned as the smell of beer and cigar smoke invaded her nose.

"There's Jed," Cord said, his voice raised above the din. He led the way across the floor, threading between the tables until he reached one in the far corner. Jed sat talking to Denver, while a young woman with flaming red hair leaned against his chair, seemingly enthralled by the conversation.

Kristi stopped short at the sight of her and grabbed hold

of Lori's arm. "We don't want to sit with the guys," she said, loud enough for everyone at the table to hear her. "We came down to have some fun. Let's find our own table."

Lori sent Cord a glance, waiting for him to protest. For a moment she thought he was going to say something, but then he pulled out a chair and sat down in it without looking at her.

Pain bit deep into her soul. He couldn't have made things any plainer. True, she had asked him not to order her around, but she hadn't asked to be ignored. He had no reason to act as if she didn't exist. Lifting her chin, she said clearly, "Good idea. Let's go."

Kristi headed for the bar, and Lori followed more slowly, her defiance ebbing faster than it had risen. Cowboys sprawled at the counter, perched on bar stools, while others stood in groups, all talking and laughing above one another. Most of them held mugs of beer, while some tossed back a shot of hard liquor without blinking an eye.

More than one of them watched her and Kristi approach with a gleam in their eyes. Kristi appeared not to notice as she pushed in between them to reach the bar. "Beer," she ordered briefly, when the bartender looked at her. She glanced over her shoulder at Lori. "What're you gonna have?"

"Soda, please," Lori said, giving a husky cowboy a wary smile when he shifted back to let her pass.

"Aw, honey," he said, tilting his head to one side, "you can't have any fun on soda. You need a margarita." He waved his hand at the bartender. "Hey, Bud, give the little lady here a margarita."

Lori's stomach did a nosedive. "No, thank you," she said politely. "I'm not drinking tonight."

"All right, how about a dance, then?"

Lori glanced over to where the lines of dancers performed their synchronized steps. "I don't know how to do that."

"Well, I'll sure be happy to teach you, honey."

She shook her head. "Thanks, but I think I'd rather watch."

He held out his arms. "Come on, sweetheart, give it a shot. You don't know what you're missing."

Kristi turned around and sent the cowboy a hard look. "Back off, buster. You don't hear too good. She doesn't want to dance with you."

Lori held her breath, but the man simply shrugged, then leered at Kristi. "So how about you, doll face? Wanna give it a whirl?"

"I'd rather puke." Kristi handed Lori a glass of soda. "Come on, let's go find us a table."

Amid laughter from the cowboy's companions, Lori escaped from the crowd and followed Kristi to an empty table.

"Jerks," Kristi muttered, as she dropped onto a chair. "You've gotta get tough with them or they walk all over you."

Lori took a sip of her soda. "What are they doing over there?" she asked, nodding in the direction of the dancers.

Kristi glanced over there. "Line dancing. You must have seen them do it on TV."

Lori shook her head. "I've heard of it, but I've never seen anyone do it before. It looks like fun."

"It's real easy. All you have to do is follow everyone else." Kristi swallowed a mouthful of beer and put down the mug. "The nice thing about it is you don't need a partner. Wanna try it?"

Lori looked at the dancers doubtfully. "I don't know if I could do that."

"Sure you can. Wait until they have a simple one and I'll show you the steps. Watch them. See? All they're doing is tapping heel and toe, then the vine, which is just side-cross-side, brush your heel and come back the other way. Simple."

It didn't sound simple to Lori, but after watching the dancers for a few minutes, she began to see a design to their steps. The music ended, and the dancers left the floor, but a couple of minutes later the band started up again, and people drifted back.

"This one will be easy to follow," Kristi said, as the dancers began moving in unison. "Come on, let's join them." She jumped to her feet and headed for the floor.

Lori glanced across the room to where Cord sat talking to his two partners. She saw three women hanging around the table—one, a pretty brunette, with her hand resting possessively on Cord's shoulder.

Lori compressed her lips, then got up and joined Kristi on the dance floor. It took her a while, but by the end of the dance she'd managed a few rounds of the routine. "That was fun," she told Kristi as she followed her off the floor.

The band started playing a tune with a slow, sensuous beat, and the burly cowboy from the bar suddenly appeared in front of her at the edge of the dance area. "Looks like you can boogie real good," he said, catching hold of her arm. "I reckon this one's mine."

Lori pulled her arm free and glared at him. "I'm not interested so quit bugging me. All right?"

She tried to push past him, but he barred her way, his arms outstretched. "Now you don't mean that, little lady. I only want to dance with you, that's all."

"Well, I'm sorry, but I don't want to dance with you,"

she said firmly. "Now, please, get out of my way and let me go back to my table."

"Not until you've danced with me, sweetheart."

She could tell from his slurred speech that he'd had one beer too many. He was a big man—too big to resist if he decided to get persistent. She looked across the floor, hoping to catch Kristi's eye, and instead, saw Cord heading purposefully toward her.

Worried that there might be trouble, she gave him a quick, firm shake of her head. He ignored it and kept on coming.

The cowboy closed his arms around her. "Come on, honey, I'm beginning to lose patience."

Lori acted instinctively. She lifted her foot and stamped down hard with the heel of her boot. The cowboy yelped and let her go.

Cord reached them at that moment and spun the cowboy around by his shoulder. "Beat it," he muttered. "This lady's dancing with me."

Before Lori could utter a word, he grabbed her around the waist, took hold of her hand and pulled her hard against him. Holding her there, he guided her onto the floor. He paused and then began swaying to the beat, his feet barely moving from the spot. She moved with him, her body vibrating with the heavy thump of her heart.

This was the closest she'd been to him since that night in the cabin. The tangy fragrance of his aftershave and the clean smell of the soap he used brought the memories crowding back to torment her. She remembered his hands on her, his mouth exploring her body, arousing sensations that were too incredible to describe. The ache started low in her belly, spreading downward and up, until the gnawing hunger threatened to overwhelm her.

Her left hand lay on his shoulder, and she slid her fingers

closer to his neck, until they curled into the thick, dark hair at his nape. His arm tightened in response, and she pressed herself closer to him, yearning to feel the hard length of his body.

"I thought you couldn't dance," she murmured, looking up at him.

His mouth hovered above hers, mere inches away. All she had to do was raise herself higher on her toes and she could taste the hard warmth of his lips.

"I can't," he muttered, his voice sounding strained. "But someone had to get you away from that big ox."

Her disappointment was so intense she wanted to strike out at him. She dropped her arms and pulled away from his grasp. "Is that the only reason you're dancing with me?"

He stared at her for a moment, his face blank. "Why else would I be up here making a fool of myself?"

Her anger rose, swift and white-hot. "Well, you certainly don't have to make an exhibition of yourself on my account," she snapped. "You can manage that perfectly well all by yourself."

His eyes narrowed. "What the hell does that mean?"

"It means," Lori said quietly, "that once again you've stuck your nose in where it wasn't wanted. Leave me alone, Cord. I don't need you or your damn protection. Just leave me alone."

She spun on her heel and marched back to the table. "I'm going to the camper," she told a surprised Kristi. "I'm not feeling very good."

Kristi jumped to her feet. "Is Cord taking you?"

"No," Lori said evenly, "I'll get a cab."

"I'll come with you—"

"I'd rather go alone." Lori smiled to soften her words. "I'll be fine, Kristi, really. Tell Denver I wish him luck.

I'll see you later." She grabbed up her jacket and purse and hurried off before Kristi could give her any more argument. She had a horrible feeling that she'd break down and cry if she stayed any longer.

Once outside, she paused on the steps to draw a steadying breath. The wind lifted her hair from her shoulders, and she shivered at the chill touch of the breeze on her neck. She slipped her arms into her jacket, then looked around for a phone. The tavern stood on the corner of a small block of shops, and across the street loomed the cold, empty grounds of a warehouse complex. But no public telephone booth.

Cursing herself for not finding a phone inside the tavern, Lori hovered for a moment, bracing herself to return to the noisy, smoky room. The door opened abruptly behind her and a familiar voice said harshly, "I'll take you home."

Without turning around, she muttered, "You don't need to take me home. I can get a cab."

"This is one time I'm not going to take any argument from you." Cord grabbed her arm and marched her down the steps. "I know you don't want me telling you what to do, but I'm damned if I'm going to let you wait out here in the cold for a cab, when I can have you back at the camper in a few minutes."

Too weary and dispirited to argue, she went with him and climbed meekly into the truck.

"Why didn't you tell me you didn't feel well?" he demanded, when they were once more speeding along the highway.

She sighed. She might have known Kristi would tell him. Why couldn't people mind their own business and let her lead her own life? "I'm fine," she said shortly. "I'm just a little tired, that's all."

He didn't answer at first. Just when she thought he was

going to drive the whole way in silence, he said quietly, "Lori, I don't want to fight with you."

"Then stop trying to run my life." She heard the sharpness in her voice, and wondered what on earth was the matter with her. When had she become so irritable and short-tempered?

She heard Cord heave a heavy sigh. "You just won't listen to reason. That guy was trouble. I know him. I know how he gets when he's been drinking."

He was right, of course. If she was honest with herself, she'd admit that she was more upset about his motive for dancing with her than she was about him butting into her life. She struggled to soften her tone when she answered him. "I guess I should thank you for coming to my rescue."

He glanced at her, as if trying to decide if she meant it. "No thanks necessary."

She felt like crying. Things had become so strained between them. It was hard to believe that this was the same man who had opened the doors to a whole new world for her.

She missed the cabin, she thought miserably. She wished they'd never had to leave there. She'd been so happy and content in that broken down old shack with Cord. Now everything was different. She felt lonely and incredibly depressed.

She sat in silence until Cord pulled into the parking lot alongside Kristi's motor home. "You'll be all right?" he asked, as she climbed wearily down from the cab.

"I'll be fine. All I need is some sleep." She made herself give him a wistful smile. "Thanks for the ride."

"You're welcome." He looked at her for a long time, as though he were trying to find something to say, then he nodded and pulled away.

She watched him turn onto the highway again and knew he was going back to the tavern. Her heart felt as if it were coated in lead, and her entire body felt chilled. She let herself into the camper and made herself a cup of tea before climbing into her bed. She didn't remember hearing Kristi come home. She woke up the next morning feeling even worse than she had the night before.

Realizing Kristi must still be asleep, she moved quietly out of bed. The thought of coffee nauseated her, and she opened the door of the miniature fridge to find some orange juice.

With the glass in her hand she sat on the bench seat under the window and tried to think of something to eat that wouldn't upset her stomach. She'd drunk half the juice before she had to make a mad dash for the bathroom.

A few minutes later she emerged, feeling weak and shaken. Something was wrong. Something was dreadfully wrong. She'd been feeling sick for too long. At least two or three weeks.

She stared down at her hands and saw them shaking. She was afraid she knew what the problem was. When she'd missed her period a month ago she'd put it down to all the late nights, irregular meals and exhausting travel. But now she couldn't ignore the facts any longer.

She heard Kristi moving around in her bedroom and felt a moment of panic. Somehow she had to keep her condition a secret. Kristi must never know.

The door opened and Kristi wandered out, yawning and smoothing her hair out of her eyes. "Hi," she said sleepily, then she halted, staring at Lori in concern. "Are you okay? You look terrible."

It was impossible, of course, Lori thought helplessly. She couldn't hope to keep something like this a secret for long. The best thing she could do was take Kristi into her confidence and make her swear not to tell a soul. Especially Cord.

"No, I'm not okay," she said carefully. "Unless I'm badly mistaken, I think I might be pregnant."

"Wow!" Kristi stared at her wide-eyed. "Are you sure?"

Lori tried to stem the wave of panic sweeping over her. Now that the words were actually out in the open, the full enormity of her predicament loomed like a massive mountain of trouble. "Pretty sure," she said shakily. "I know I'm way overdue, and I just threw up."

"Oh, man. We've got to get you to a doctor." She stared thoughtfully at Lori. "I know this is none of my business, but does Cord know?"

Lori shivered. There was no point in denying he was the father. Kristi was aware of how Lori felt about him. "No," she said harshly, "and you mustn't tell him. Swear you won't tell him. I don't want him to know."

Kristi walked over to her and sat down next to her. "Lori, he has to know. Sooner or later he's gonna notice anyway."

"Not if I leave here." Lori rubbed her upper arms, trying to get some warmth in her chilled body. "I'll leave at the end of the month. I should have enough money by then."

"Where will you go? You can't just go off on your own."

"I'll think of something."

"Do you have family you can go to? Cord said you don't have anyone."

"Yes...no...." Lori shuddered, imagining what her parents would say if they knew. Her father would definitely disown her, and her mother would probably never recover from the scandal. Even if they accepted her condition, there was no way she would go crawling back to them just to hear them say they told her so. "Oh, God," she groaned, covering her face with her hands. "What am I going to do?"

"Well, first," Kristi said briskly, "you're going to stop panicking about it. Then we're going to find out if you really are pregnant. It could be a false alarm. I'm going into town today. I'll pick up a pregnancy test."

"Thanks." Lori sighed. "Then what? What if I am pregnant?"

"Then you are going to make an appointment with a doctor. That's the problem with traveling on the road—not having a regular doctor. We'll find one, though. And then you're going to tell Cord."

"No! I can't tell him." To her dismay Lori felt a tear squeeze through her eyelashes. "You've got to promise me, Kristi. Don't tell Cord."

Kristi shook her head. "Cord McVane, of all people. I can't believe he was that stupid. He's been around long enough to know better."

"It was my fault," Lori said tearfully. "All my fault."

Kristi gave her a wry smile. "You didn't get this way all by yourself. He has to accept some of the responsibility."

"That's just it!" Lori wailed. "I don't want to be a responsibility. That's the last thing he needs right now."

"He should have thought about that when he was taking such a stupid risk," Kristi said grimly. "Now he has to pay."

"I don't need his money."

"I'm not just talking about money." Kristi sighed and reached for Lori's hand. "Listen to me, Lori. If you know that Cord's responsible, then it's his baby, too. Apart from anything else, he has a right to know. It isn't fair to him to keep it a secret."

Lori fought to control her tears. She could handle this, she told herself firmly. She'd come a long way since that night she'd packed a bag and left home. She was a different person...stronger, more mature, more responsible. She could handle it.

Just because she had to tell him about the baby didn't mean that she expected anything from him. She'd have to make that quite clear. "You're right," she said, more calmly. "I have to tell him. But not now. Not yet. And I want to tell him in my own way. Please promise you won't say anything to anyone."

Kristi held a hand over her heart. "I swear. As long as you promise to tell Cord."

"All right, I promise." Lori pulled in a shaky breath. "I could be worrying about nothing, I guess. After all, it was only one time. I didn't think it could happen your first time. Guess I was wrong."

Kristi's face was creased in concern. "Oh, you poor kid. What a bum break. Well, if you are pregnant, you must see a doctor. We'll make an appointment and stop off in Portland on our way to San Francisco next week. I know a doctor there who will see you."

Beginning to feel a little better, Lori managed a smile. "Thanks, Kristi. It helps to have someone I can talk to."

"You're gonna need more than talk if that test shows up positive."

"I know." Lori nodded, then got to her feet. "I'd better take a shower. I have to be at work in less than an hour." She grabbed up a pair of jeans and a shirt and headed for the bathroom. There was no point in worrying about anything until she knew for sure, she told herself. Until then, she'd simply try to put her situation out of her mind.

That was easier said than done, as she discovered throughout the next few hours. She felt irritable and out of sorts. Even Grace, who was usually too absorbed in her own work to pay much attention to anyone else, commented on Lori's lack of color and short temper.

By the end of the day Lori felt wound up so tight she wanted to scream. Kristi was waiting for her when she got back to the camper, and showed her how to use the test kit. An hour later the verdict was in.

"I'll make the appointment for you," Kristi said, scowling at the plastic tube in Lori's shaky hand.

"I guess there's no mistake," Lori said unsteadily. "I really am going to have a baby."

"Cord's baby," Kristi reminded her.

"Cord's baby." A rush of tenderness took her by surprise. Part of Cord was growing inside her. It was a strange, and oddly comforting, thought.

The next few days passed in a turmoil of miserable mornings, difficult working hours and restless nights. It was a great relief to Lori when it was finally time to pack up in preparation for the trip to San Francisco.

She'd managed to stay out of Cord's way for most of the week. Although she relied heavily on makeup to hide her wan complexion, he was shrewd enough to detect something wrong.

It was on the last morning when he arrived at the motor home, just as she was carrying the clean laundry back from the Laundromat. "Haven't seen you around," he said, as she reached him. "Just thought I'd come by and check to see if you're okay."

"I'm fine." She dropped the basket of clothes onto the step and fished in her pocket for her key.

"You don't look fine to me."

"It's been a busy week. I'm a little tired, that's all."

He seemed fidgety, shifting from one foot to the other. "How come you haven't been around to see me ride?"

She averted her face, stooping to pick up the heavy basket. "I've been busy."

He took the basket from her hands. "Here, let me get this."

"Thank you." She opened the door with the key and reached for the basket again, but he moved it out of reach.

"I'll bring it in for you."

It was the last thing she wanted him to do, but she could hardly refuse without making a fuss. She walked in ahead of him and waited for him to put the basket on the table. "Thanks," she said awkwardly.

He peered at her face. "You sure you're okay? You look worn out."

"I told you, I'm fine." She'd tried to keep the irritation out of her voice, but she knew she'd sounded tense. She met his gaze defiantly, determined to bluff it out.

He looked worried, but he appeared to accept her assurance. His dark gaze moved over her face and rested briefly on her mouth. "I've missed you," he said quietly.

Any other time that admission would have had her soaring on wings of joy. Now, however, all she could think about was getting rid of him before he tried to probe her about her state of health. "I'm sorry," she said lightly. "There was a lot to get done before we left for San Francisco."

He nodded, gazed out of the window, cleared his throat, then said gruffly, "I hope you get to see the show at the Cow Palace. It's usually worth watching."

In spite of her anxiety, her pulse skipped. He wanted her to watch him ride. He was asking her to be there. She gave him a genuine smile. "I'll look forward to it."

The strained expression on his face seemed to soften. He nodded and stuck his thumbs in his pockets. "I'd better get back. Jed's gonna need a hand with the truck."

"Okay." She looked up at him, suddenly overwhelmed by the knowledge that this man was the father of the child growing inside her. The tenderness seemed to well up inside her, making her long for the warm strength of his arms around her. For an instant she thought about sharing the news with him, then fought the temptation. This was not the time. She wasn't sure if there would ever be a time.

"I'll see you in San Francisco, then," she added casually.

"Yeah, see you then." He directed one last intent look at her face, then disappeared down the steps.

Tears stung her eyes as the door closed behind him, and she fiercely blinked them away. She had to be strong now, for the baby's sake. She would be a good mother, she silently vowed, as she folded the clean clothes and packed them away.

She'd keep a firm hand on her child, but she'd let him have his freedom, too. Freedom to make choices, to learn by his mistakes, to stand on his own two feet and choose his own destiny. She would guide him and advise him but never dictate. And above all, she would love him with all her heart.

Her throat felt tight as she imagined a sturdy little boy— a carbon copy of his father. "We'll make out," she whispered, laying a hand on her belly. "No matter what happens, I'll take care of you. I swear I will."

Chapter 10

Seated in the office of the kind but efficient obstetrician in Portland, the next day, Lori received confirmation of the pregnancy. The young doctor assured her that as long as she took her vitamins, exercised and ate right, there was no reason in the world she shouldn't work up to the last month.

Lori thanked her, and took the prescriptions she gave her to the pharmacy, determined to do everything right from the start. The doctor had also told her that the morning sickness would pass, and although it still plagued her, she was learning to deal with it. She threw herself into her work, with a firm resolution to make the best of things. By the time she and Kristi drove into San Francisco, she was looking and feeling better than she had in days.

She watched Cord ride, and cheered when, for the first time in days, he won the round. He waved to her as he strode out of the ring, and she raised her clenched hand in a gesture of victory. She was on her way out of the arena when he confronted her, stepping silently out of the dark shadows in the parking lot like a night hunter in the forest.

Startled, she gasped and jerked to a halt.

"Sorry," he murmured. "I didn't mean to frighten you."

"You didn't." She steadied her breath. "My mind was on other things."

The wide brim of his hat hid most of his features from her, and she couldn't see his expression in the darkness. She could tell he was uptight about something by the way he fidgeted, as if he didn't quite know what to do with his hands. Finally, he said casually, "I'll see you back to the camper. This isn't too good a place for a woman to be walking around alone at night."

It was on the tip of her tongue to tell him she could take care of herself, but she stopped the words just in time. She so rarely had a chance to see him alone anymore. She'd tried to convince herself that it was for the best. That way she wouldn't miss him so much when it came time to leave the circuit. But some treacherous lingering yearning for him wouldn't let her pass up this chance to be with him, just for a little while. She began walking across the parking lot, and he fell into step beside her.

"I hope you're feeling better now."

She nodded. "Much, thanks."

"Must have been some kind of bug."

Her pulse skipped, and she strove to keep her tone casual when she answered. "I guess so." It was time to change the subject, she thought, searching her mind for a subject. "How are you doing in the standings?"

"Okay. I reckon I'll make it back in the running with this win tonight."

"That's great!" She smiled at him, genuinely pleased.

"Yeah, I thought so, too. I figured I might celebrate." He pulled a small bottle of scotch from the pocket of his jacket. "Single malt. How about joining me in a glass when we get back to the camper?"

"Oh, I'd like to," Lori said hurriedly, "but I never drink anything stronger than wine. You go ahead, though."

"Well, join me with a glass of wine, then. If I know Kristi she's got a bottle or two tucked away in the fridge."

There were two bottles in there, Lori knew. But in view of her condition there was no way she could drink any of it. If she refused him now, though, he'd probably take offense, and she was really reluctant to spoil what could be her last chance to share some time with him.

"I had a couple of glasses earlier," she lied. "That's my quota for the day, but I'll be happy to celebrate with a glass of soda."

He sighed and tucked the bottle back in his pocket. "Why don't we both celebrate with soda. I hate drinking alone."

"Done," she said in relief.

She opened the door of the camper with her key and he followed her inside. The place was in darkness, and she flicked on the lamps, sending a soft glow over the comfortable living area. Slipping out of her jacket, she murmured, "I'll get the soda."

He took the jacket from her, his gaze intent on her face. "I reckon you do look better," he said softly. "I was kind of worried about you."

She shifted her gaze away from those relentless eyes. "I bounce back fast." Anxious to escape from his scrutiny, she moved over to the tiny fridge and opened it. "Cola all right?"

"Sounds good." He wandered restlessly over to the table under the window. "Kristi not here?"

"She's gone into town. Dancing at some nightclub."

"How come you didn't go with her?"

There was a careful note to his voice that she couldn't quite analyze. "I wanted to see the show, and I was too tired to go out afterward." She found the two cans she was searching for and straightened. She was in the act of closing the fridge door when he asked in a strange, tight voice, "What's this?"

She twisted her head to look at him. When she saw what he held in his hand, her heart stopped for an instant, then began pumping furiously. She and Kristi had been discussing the pregnancy, going through all the leaflets the obstetrician had given her. She'd left them on the table, in full view of Cord, who now held the top one, clearly labeled, A Guide to a Safe and Enjoyable Pregnancy.

She'd never been a very good liar. She did her best, waving her hand and saying airily, "Oh, just some stuff Kristi picked up the other day. She likes to be prepared for any emergency."

Cord's eyes narrowed. He pointed to the address stamped on the bottom of the leaflet. "From a doctor's office in Portland?" He picked up another leaflet. "And this one? Protecting Your Unborn Child? And this one?" He waved yet another one at her. "These are pretty serious preparations."

Lori's laugh sounded forced, even to her. "I guess Kristi believes in the theory that being forewarned is being forearmed."

"That's crap and you know it. Is Kristi pregnant?"

Lori felt the heat warming her cheeks. "I think that's Kristi's business."

He stared at her, while the dread crept over her body, drowning her in misery. "It's not Kristi, is it?" he said at last in a strangled voice.

She couldn't go on lying to him forever, she thought

desperately. Sooner or later he had to know. It might as well be now.

While she was still searching for the right words, he said harshly, "So just when were you planning on telling me?"

She heard the anger in his voice and flinched. "I found out myself only a little while ago."

"A little while ago? Long enough ago to visit a doctor in Portland. Dammit, Lori, we've been in San Francisco almost a week."

She looked at him helplessly, still hunting for the right thing to say.

"You weren't going to tell me, is that it?"

"No...I was just waiting for the right time."

"The right time." He swore, turning away from her to tilt his face at the ceiling.

She flinched. "I didn't want to upset you before the finals," she said quietly.

"To hell with the finals." With another muttered oath he flung himself into an armchair and pulled the bottle from his pocket. "And to hell with the soda."

Lori watched him take a mouthful of the scotch, wincing when he almost choked on it.

"We'll get married right away," he said, his voice rough with emotion. "We can be in Reno by tomorrow night. We'll get married the next day."

She felt a lump forming in her throat and swallowed. The words she wanted so badly to hear. Yet for all the wrong reasons. "I'm not going to marry you," she said evenly.

"The hell you're not." He stuffed the bottle back in his pocket, then pulled off his hat and laid it on the small table beside him. "I'm not going to argue with you, Lori. We're getting married, and that's it."

Her legs felt shaky and she sat down on the companion

armchair. "No, that's not it. I will not have you marry me out of some misguided sense of duty."

"Duty?" He shook his head in disbelief. "What the hell does duty have to do with it?" His gaze sharpened, as if an idea had just occurred to him. "Wait a minute. It *is* my baby, isn't it?"

The heat surged into her cheeks again, fueled by resentment. "I won't even dignify that with an answer."

"It happened to me once before," he reminded her dryly.

"Well, not this time. You can believe what you want. It's up to you, but I'm telling you that night was the only night. Ever."

He passed his hand across his eyes in a gesture of weariness. "Of course it was. I know that. I'm sorry. It's just that this is such a damn shock."

"I know," she said miserably.

"All right, then. We get married."

"I'm not going to marry you, Cord."

He must have heard the conviction in her voice this time. His expression grew hard. Although he didn't raise his voice, there was no mistaking his determination.

"You don't have any choice, sweetheart. I've already lost one child. I'm not about to lose this one. This baby is mine. I intend to raise him and you've got no say in it. We'll get married next week in Reno. You can leave your job and live in the cabin until the season's over in two months. After that I'll quit rodeo, buy some acreage and a build a big ol' ranch house somewhere to raise my kid. Maybe I'll breed some horses or something."

She stared at him in astonishment. She had no idea he had that kind of money. Before she could answer, he pushed himself to his feet.

"So that's settled." He reached for his hat and jammed

it on his head. "You give your notice in tomorrow. Grace will have to manage without you for a while."

Her resentment, barely held at bay, exploded in a blaze of temper. "I'll do no such thing. I'm not quitting my job and I'm not going to Reno. This is my life, Cord, and no one is going to tell me how to run it. Not ever again. You can help support the baby if you like, and you can visit him whenever you want to, but I will not marry you. This isn't the Middle Ages. You can't force me to marry you."

His eyes glinted at her. Laying his palms on the table he leaned down until his face was inches from her. "Watch me," he said quietly. "I'll get you in front of a priest if I have to bind and gag you to do it."

"Try it," Lori snapped, "and I'll have you slapped behind bars."

"We'll see about that." He straightened, glared at her for a moment longer, then turned on his heel and slammed out of the camper.

Lori waited just long enough to make sure he wasn't coming back, then she laid her head down on her arms and wept.

When she had no more tears left, she got up and went into the bathroom, where she washed her face in cold water and dabbed it dry with a soft towel. She peered at herself in the mirror, faintly surprised to see the familiar, though somewhat blotchy, face staring back at her. She didn't feel at all like the Lori Ashford who, a few short weeks ago, had had little more to worry about than what to wear for an evening on the town.

She felt a hundred years older and a lifetime wiser. But she also felt stronger than at any time in her life. She was in control, and no one was going to take that away from her.

Much as she longed to marry Cord and settle down with

him and the baby in a big house, she simply couldn't do it on his terms. She couldn't marry a man who insisted on making her decisions for her. She didn't want to quit her job. For the first time in her life she felt she was accomplishing something, and she was proud of what she had achieved. She didn't want to hide away in the cabin by herself while Cord finished out the season.

But more important than anything else, Cord had not once mentioned the word *love.* No matter what other considerations there were, she knew without a shadow of a doubt that she could never marry a man who wasn't as crazy in love with her as she was with him.

She stared at her image in the mirror and the tears pooled up again. She might as well face it. She was crazy in love with Cord McVane, and there wasn't a damn thing she could do about it.

She was in bed and feigning sleep when Kristi came home. She slept fitfully that night, and awoke with the churning feeling in her stomach that she had come to expect these days.

Kristi was still sleeping when Lori let herself out of the camper and crossed the parking lot to the office. Grace greeted her with her usual absentminded wave, one ear clamped to the phone.

Lori managed to lose herself in her work throughout the long day, stopping just long enough to eat the chicken salad that Grace brought in for her from the fast-food restaurant across the street.

It was raining hard when she left the office that afternoon, and she pulled her jacket collar up to shield her neck while she ran across the parking lot to the camper. It would be late before Kristi finished in the covered arena, and Lori had no desire to watch the show. It was the final round that night, and Cord would be out there, trying to boost his earnings high enough to give him a good position in the standings. Much as she wanted to see him win, it would be too heartbreaking to watch him surrounded by all those women fighting to congratulate him.

Instead she settled down in front of the TV, though she couldn't resist tuning in to the local sports station to get the final results of the competition before she went to bed. She was shocked and dismayed when Cord's name wasn't mentioned. At first she hung on to the announcer's every word, terrified that he'd fallen and been hurt.

When she heard no mention of anyone being injured, she convinced herself that he'd just had a bad night. He'd lost the final round. That would make it tougher for him to catch up at the next rodeo.

She was preparing for bed when Kristi tumbled into the camper, shaking raindrops from her blond hair. "Boy," she muttered, "it's really coming down hard out there. I'm just glad the arena was covered. It would have been a real mess if it had been open air."

"I saw the results," Lori told her. "I noticed Jed won the saddle bronc round again."

"Yeah." Kristi grinned. "Looks like he's going to the finals in Las Vegas." Her expression changed. "Too bad Cord didn't turn up. He missed his ride. He was all set to win, too."

Lori's stomach seemed to drop. "Cord wasn't there?"

"He didn't show tonight. I asked Jed and he said Cord took a flight out of here this afternoon. Didn't say where he was going or how long he'd be gone. Jed's really worried about him. He said Cord has never missed a ride except for injury since he's known him."

Lori stared at her in dismay. "Oh, no," she whispered.

Kristi gave her a sharp look. "You know where he might be?"

She shook her head. "He was here last night. He found out about the baby. He was...a little upset when he left."

"I bet he was," Kristi said grimly. "So when's the wedding?"

"There isn't going to be any wedding." Lori moved over to the sink and began rinsing out the glasses that sat there.

"Are you telling me that he walked out on you?" Kristi sounded incredulous. "I don't believe it. Cord's a lot of things, but I never figured him for a lousy, no-good quitter."

"Oh, he asked me to marry him." Lori stood the glass gently on the counter. "I turned him down."

"What! Are you crazy?" Kristi tugged on her arm. "Look at me. Is there something wrong with your mind? Why would you turn down a proposal from Cord Mc-Vane?"

"Because he doesn't love me," Lori said patiently. "He only wants to marry me to give the baby a name."

Kristi made a sound of exasperation. "So? You love him, don't you? Isn't that enough? Isn't that better than going it alone?"

"No, it isn't." Lori gave her friend a rueful smile. "I can't marry a man who doesn't love me. Not even to give my baby a name."

Kristi shook her head. "Well, it's your life. I can't tell you what to do."

"Exactly." And neither could Cord, she added inwardly. The thought gave her no satisfaction at all. He was gone, and the world suddenly seemed unbearably cold and lonely.

Cord squatted in front of the gaping mouth of the wood-stove and fed another log into the hungry flames. Coming to the cabin had been a mistake. He knew that now. If he'd had his head on straight he would have figured that out before he'd grabbed a ride on the plane out of San Francisco.

In the first place, the last leg of the trip from the airport had been an adventure. The snow had come early to the mountains, and the narrow trail through the forest had been almost impassable. Twice he'd had to climb out of the rented Jeep to dig out a path, in spite of the chains he'd put on the wheels when he'd left the highway.

He groaned softly as he straightened, feeling the low ache in his back that had plagued him this past year. He was getting too old for rodeo, he told himself gloomily. It was time to think about retiring.

He wandered over to the window and rubbed a hole in the dust that covered the small square windowpanes. The snow still fell steadily outside, weighing down the thick branches of the firs and settling a fine white layer on the woodpile he'd just cleared.

The forest was quiet and still in its lonely white world, and only the crackling logs in the potbellied stove disturbed the eerie silence. He missed her. He missed her like hell. He never dreamed he could feel this alone in the one place that had always before brought him comfort and peace. Her presence was everywhere.

He saw her scowling at him from the kitchen sink. When he sat in the armchair he saw her across from him, her chin propped on her hand as she listened to his stories about life on the road.

Most of all, he saw her in his bed, smelled his soap on her, felt the cautious touch of her gentle hands and heard the soft, urgent sounds of her passion. For two long, lonely nights he'd tried to sleep in that cold, empty bed, but his mind and his memories would not let him be.

He cursed himself a thousand times for the way he'd handled things. He'd been shocked out of his boots when he'd realized she was having his baby. Stunned with disbelief, he'd acted like a jerk. He could imagine how she felt. It must have been bad enough finding out she was pregnant. Knowing it was his baby must have really piled on the agony.

He wasn't expecting her to marry him out of love. He wasn't fooling himself on that score.

But right out of the blue he'd been presented with a chance to make up the terrible loss he'd suffered all those years ago. The knowledge that she carried his child inside her had opened up a whole new world of opportunities...a lifetime of adventures he'd thought would always be denied him. This time he could be a real father. And a baby needed a father, didn't he? Was it so wrong to want so badly the one thing that could make his heart whole again?

As for Lori, she needed him right now. If she could just get past her pride, she'd see that it was the right thing to do, for the sake of the baby. He didn't even expect her to stay with him for a lifetime. He just wanted to marry her to give her the respectability she deserved and make sure the baby would have his name. This was likely to be the only child he'd ever have. He was determined that his kid would grow up as a McVane.

In his haste to put things right, he'd forgotten that she didn't like to be told what to do. He should have asked her, instead of telling her. Women preferred that. He should have remembered.

Somehow he had to get her to marry him. This was his baby she carried in her belly, and he was not about to let a child of his be born without his name. This was one time when Lori Ashford was not going to get her way. Somehow he had to make her see sense.

He paced around the room, cursing the oppressive walls that imprisoned his memories. He couldn't think straight when everywhere he looked he saw her image. He had to go back. He had to try again, and this time he'd ask her to marry him, the way a woman wants to be asked. He'd let her work as long as she wanted to, just as long as she married him.

Now that the decision was made, he couldn't wait to get out of there. He shut down the stove, packed his bag and slammed the door behind him. The Jeep took a while to start, but the engine finally fired, and he was off, lurching down the snow-packed trail, his mind intent on one thing. He was going to make Lori agree to marry him if it was the last damn thing he did.

It was Lori's turn to drive the motor home on the next leg of the circuit. There were two more rodeos in California and one in Arizona before everyone headed up to Nevada for the national finals rodeo in Las Vegas. Heading south on the freeway, Lori kept an eye out for the signs that would lead her to the town.

Depression had settled over her like a suffocating cloak. All the fun had gone out of the job, now that she had no prospects of bumping into Cord. She kept telling herself that it was for the best, that she'd planned on leaving the circuit anyway after the national finals.

The thought of being around all those people, the horses, the cattle, the noise and the smell that was so uniquely rodeo, was pure torture. The memories would be everywhere. She wouldn't be able to look at a tall cowboy in a black hat, striding across the parking lot, without thinking of Cord. She couldn't bear to watch the riders anymore, knowing that the sight of someone clinging to the bare back of a leaping, bucking horse would remind her of a very special man.

How could she sit in an office, watching the winners file

in, knowing that Cord would not be among them? How could she check on opening acts, arrange transportation, inform the media or confirm appointments for the next rodeo knowing Cord would not be there to compete?

Her depression deepened and she was thankful when she saw the sign she was looking for. She pressed her foot on the brake and took the turn onto the two-lane highway. Kristi's father would not be producing the finals in Las Vegas. Lori's job officially ended for the season with the next rodeo after this one. She'd planned to go to the finals anyway, with Kristi and Grace. But now it seemed pointless. Even if Cord did decide to go, she didn't want to see him. It would only make her feel worse.

She would quit after the last rodeo, she decided. She'd stay in California, get a job somewhere, find a cheap apartment and begin her new life. Somehow she'd make out. Plenty of women had done it before her. She and her baby would do just fine.

Kristi, who had been dozing in the back of the camper, came forward to join her as she drove into the town. "It's down there," she said, pointing to a narrow street that led off to the right. "You have to park behind the arena. There's not much space, so I hope they left room for us." She looked at her watch. "The animals won't be arriving for a couple of hours yet, so that will give us time to get something to eat. It's only a two-day rodeo, so it won't be worth unpacking anything."

Lori parked without much enthusiasm. Maybe it would be better to make the break now, she thought dismally. Thanks to Kristi's generosity, she'd paid back the money she'd owed to Cord, even though he'd tried to insist she keep it for emergencies. She was finally out of debt. She'd managed to save enough to pay for two month's rent on an apartment, and have a modest amount for a down payment on a used car.

Now that she had some experience it would be easier to find a job, and she was sure Grace would give her a good reference. All she had to do was hand in her notice and walk away from the only place where she'd found any real happiness. That was going to be the tough part.

"Are you okay?"

Kristi's concerned voice made her jump, and she turned quickly to her friend to give her a reassuring smile. "I was just working some things out in my mind."

"Well, they must have been big problems." Kristi got up from her seat and moved back into the living area. "I spoke to you twice before you answered."

"Sorry." Lori rose, stretching her aching back. "I won't be sorry to get to bed tonight. I'm really wiped out."

"Me, too." Kristi peered out the window. "At least it's not raining. I guess I'll be able to settle the stock down without too much problem." She looked at her watch. "There's a steak house right across the street. Let's get something to eat. I'm starving."

Lori hadn't had much appetite for days, but it would be good to get out of the cramped environment of the motor home for a while. The drive had been exhausting, and she was longing for a different atmosphere.

The steak house was warm and inviting, with red checkered cloths and oil lamps on each table. It was too early for the dinnertime rush, and there were less than half a dozen people in the large dining room.

The waitress was young, friendly and excited at the thought of all the cowboys coming into town for the rodeo. "This is our busiest time of the year," she told Kristi, who nodded politely with a glazed look in her eyes. "I just love it when the rodeo's in town...oh, my."

Lori looked up as the waitress uttered the soft exclamation. The woman's gaze was on the door at Lori's back, and she was apparently staring at someone who had just come in.

Kristi was staring, too, her eyes wide and her face full of anticipation. "Don't look now," she murmured, as Lori gave her a questioning glance, "but Cord McVane just walked in. He's got a real determined look on his face and he's heading right for this table."

She hadn't expected to see him again. She wasn't even sure she wanted to see him again. Heart pounding, she waited for Cord to reach her. The waitress backed away, still wearing a bemused expression on her face. Kristi seemed to want to be anywhere but where she was right then.

"I want to talk to you."

Cord's deep voice, speaking almost in her ear, made Lori jump. Afraid she'd lose her resolve if she looked up at him, she kept her gaze on the menu in front of her. "We've just ordered dinner," she said evenly. "You're welcome to join us if you want."

Kristi pushed her chair back and stood. "Hey, if you two want to be alone…"

"Sit down, Kristi."

The firm order, coming from Lori, obviously surprised Kristi. She sat down abruptly, with a helpless smile at Cord.

For a moment or two the tense silence appeared to spread out over the entire restaurant, then Cord said easily, "Don't mind if I do." He pulled out the chair next to Lori and sat.

His elbow bumped hers. Deliberately or not, she couldn't tell, but she glanced up at him.

His black gaze met hers, and as always, she couldn't tell what he was thinking. She noticed shadows under his eyes, however, and his mouth looked drawn, as if he were fighting some inner battle. She waited, her apprehension mounting, for him to speak.

He gazed at her for a long moment, then said quietly, "I'll have the T-bone, medium rare."

She compressed her lips. He was a master at creating an anticlimax. "As long as you're paying for it."

"What are you having?"

"Soup and salad."

"That's not a meal—that's a snack."

"It's enough for me."

"Not anymore it's not. I'll buy you a steak."

He was doing it again. Making decisions for her. She scowled at him. "I don't want a steak."

"Are you on some special kind of diet?"

"No, but—"

"Then I'll buy you a steak. You need it now that you've got to eat right."

"I've always eaten right, and a salad is a lot more healthy for the baby than a steak."

He looked startled and shot a glance at Kristi.

"It's all right," Lori said wearily. "She knows."

"Congratulations," Kristi mumbled, obviously embarrassed.

"I suppose Grace knows, too," Cord said grimly. "Which means the whole damn circuit knows by now."

Lori calmly reached for her glass of water and drank from it. "No," she said, putting down the glass again, "Kristi is the only one who knows. She's promised not to tell anyone else and I trust her."

"Then maybe she can put some sense into that hard head of yours."

"The subject is closed," Lori said, glaring at him. "This is not something I want to discuss in public."

"Suits me fine," Cord said, just as lethally. "We'll discuss it in private after we've had dinner."

"Where did you disappear to?" Kristi demanded, in an obvious attempt to change the subject. "Jed's been worried sick about you."

"He had no need to be. He might have known I'd head for the cabin."

"Well, I hope you've told him that you're back and put his mind at ease."

"I saw him." Cord glanced up as the waitress hovered breathlessly over him. "I guess I'll have the T-bone," he told her. "Medium rare."

Lori breathed a sigh of relief as the flustered waitress left to put in his order. At least he hadn't insisted on buying her the steak. She hadn't had much of an appetite when she'd arrived at the restaurant. The thought of having another heated discussion with Cord was enough to destroy what little enthusiasm she had left for dinner.

Kristi managed to keep the conversation going throughout the tense meal, apparently oblivious to the fact that neither Lori nor Cord contributed much to the discussion.

Lori didn't know if she was relieved or nervous when the plates were cleared away. Cord insisted on paying the bill and left a generous tip for the gushing waitress. Kristi led the way out of the restaurant, with Lori following closely after, intensely aware of Cord a step or two behind her.

"I have to go check on the stock now," Kristi said, as they crossed the busy road at the light. "It'll probably take me an hour or two, so don't wait up for me if you're tired."

Lori nodded, wishing that Kristi could have stayed with her so she wouldn't have to face Cord alone. She watched her friend sprint across the parking lot to the arena, then paused at the door of the motor home. "I'd ask you in," she said, as Cord came to a halt in front of her, "but we just arrived a short while ago and I have some unpacking to do."

"This won't take long." He stared up at the sky. "It's getting kind of chilly out here. I think it would be better if we went inside."

"I'd rather talk out here," Lori said firmly.

He gave her a look that told her he wasn't exactly thrilled at the prospect, but he did his best to cover the feeling. "All right, if that's what you want." He glanced around, as if checking to see if anyone was close by. A couple of wranglers were unhitching a pickup from their trailer across the parking lot, but otherwise everyone else was inside or out on the town.

"Well, this wasn't the way I'd planned it," Cord said, taking off his hat, "but since you insist, here goes."

Lori watched him curl the brim between his hands. His tension warned her what was coming, and she could only wait, hoping for the words she longed to hear.

Cord cleared his throat. "I know I upset you the other night by proposing all wrong, so I wanted to do it right this time. I want us to get married, Lori. That baby needs a father and you need a husband. I'm figuring on trying to be both."

Her ache of disappointment almost destroyed her fragile composure. If only he could have said he loved her. Just three words. It was such a simple thing to say. And so damn impossible if the feelings weren't there.

"I'm sorry, Cord, the answer is no. I am not going to marry you."

She almost capitulated when she saw his stricken expression. For a moment hope soared when she read genuine grief in his eyes. Was it possible he really cared for her after all?

"Dammit, Lori, am I that repulsive? Can't you at least give it a shot for the sake of that baby? I won't ask for anything from you, just as long as my child has my name."

She nodded, all hope draining away at his words. The baby. That was all it meant to him. He felt responsible for the baby's welfare and he was willing to put up with her to take care of it. Well, there was one thing she could do for herself to salvage her pride. She must never let him know that she loved him.

"I'm sorry, Cord. It just wouldn't work. I can't marry you."

"Not even for the baby's sake?"

She shook her head, afraid to trust her voice.

He lifted his hands in a gesture of despair. "Well, if you won't marry me, at least go back home to your kin. Let them help you take care of the child. At least then I'd know he was being looked after."

That stung...too much to pretend it didn't. She couldn't take it anymore. Not from him. "Dammit, Cord, I'm quite capable of taking care of a baby. And of myself. I don't need my family. I'm grateful for everything you've done for me, but the truth is, I don't need you anymore, either. If that sounds harsh, I'm sorry. But I need to run my own life, without any interference from anyone else. So from now on, will you please...just...stay out of my life."

"Wait a minute...that's my baby, too—"

"So get a lawyer. I will, as well. We'll let them work out how this is to be handled. I just don't want to discuss it with you anymore." She turned, the tears blinding her so that she fumbled with the key in the lock.

With a muttered oath he took the key from her and twisted it in the lock. "Sure you can take care of yourself," he said bitterly. "You can't even open a freaking door."

He strode off, without a backward glance, and disappeared behind the neighboring trailers.

Lori stumbled to her bed and threw herself down on it. She cried until she was exhausted, then she sat up and dried her face with several tissues. That was the last time, she promised herself, that she would ever cry over Cord McVane. From now on she was on her own, and she needed to be strong, for her baby's sake as well as her own. No more weak moments. No more crying bouts, and no more dwelling on what might have been. It was over.

Chapter 11

Something had to be done about Lori Ashford, Cord fumed, as he headed for the trailer. She was too damn hard-headed to be reasonable, and too damn independent to see beyond her own little world. She was thinking only about herself, instead of the baby. His baby.

Every time those words formed in his head he got a warm flutter of excitement in his stomach. His kid. Really his kid this time. He hadn't felt like this since the boy he still thought of as his son had been born. He didn't think he'd ever feel like that again. Not after the way the baby had been so cruelly snatched away from him and out of his life. But now he had a chance to do all the things he could never do for the child who hadn't belonged to him. This time his name would belong to his child for the rest of his life.

The problem was convincing Lori to agree to that. Nothing he could say or do seemed to make any difference. She had to see that it was the best thing for the child. Somehow he had to get her to see.

In front of him and several yards away, the trailers carrying the livestock rumbled into the parking lot. Stock handlers scattered around them, ready to unload the impatient animals and lead them to their pens, where they would be fed, watered and bedded down for the night.

Cord watched Kristi's slim figure darting in and out among the trucks, issuing orders and controlling the entire operation. Her daddy would be proud of her, Cord thought, momentarily distracted from his problem. The sad thing was, Paul Ramsett was hardly ever around to watch his daughter handle the stock. Even when he was, he was usually yelling at her for some fool thing or other. Nothing Kristi did ever pleased her father.

As for Lori, she was just the opposite. All her life she'd done everything to suit her family. She'd sacrificed her own needs and wishes to be what they wanted her to be. She'd followed their direction and hadn't been allowed to take a wrong step. Now that she was on her own, she wouldn't accept the fact that she was making a mistake by refusing to marry him.

Cord paused to let a truck roll by, and dug his thumbs into the pockets of his jeans. Damn Lori. How in the hell was he going to make her see sense? Maybe he could get someone else to talk to her. Kristi?

He shook his head. Women always stuck together. Knowing Kristi, she'd just tell him to deal with it himself. No, he needed someone with more influence. Someone who would make Lori listen to reason.

He hissed through his teeth when the idea hit him. At first he rejected it, knowing how angry Lori would be with him. But the more he thought about it, the more certain he felt that it was the only answer. He was a desperate man and forced to take desperate measures.

His mind made up, he hurried to the trailer. Jed wasn't there when he arrived, much to Cord's relief. This was one time when he really needed a little privacy. He took the cell phone out of his jacket and carried it over to the window, where he could see if there was likely to be an interruption. Then, with an uneasy sense that he was burning his bridges, he made the call.

The first day of a rodeo was always a busy one, and Lori's head ached with weariness by the time she was through for the day. The doctor had assured her that the tired feeling would pass after the first few weeks, but to Lori it seemed as if she had permanently lost her vitality.

She was due for a check-up with a doctor at the next stop, and she planned on discussing the problem with him. Maybe there was something she could take, she thought, that would give her more energy. She was certainly going to need it when she started job and apartment hunting.

As always, fear rippled through her when she considered her immediate future. Sometimes the problems seemed insurmountable, yet she knew she was capable of handling them. If only she had more strength.

Absorbed in her worries, she didn't recognize the three men who confronted her as she left the arena. People milled about the entire parking lot, either arriving or leaving, while others scurried around, intent on the last-minute preparations for the night's show.

The first thing she noticed were the visitors' legs. The fact that none of the men was wearing jeans and Western boots struck her as odd. She flicked a curious glance at the face of the nearest man, and the blood seemed to drain from every vein in her body.

"Hello, Lori," Richard murmured. "Remember me?"

Words evaporated, leaving her mind blank as she stared at his familiar face. He seemed different somehow—younger than she remembered. The features that she had once thought attractive now looked weak, lacking character and conviction. "What are you doing here?" she asked faintly.

"What the hell do you think we're doing here?" her brother, Dennis, put in roughly. "You should be damn well ashamed of yourself."

Lori stared miserably at her two brothers. "How did you find me?"

"Your boyfriend told us where you were," Mike said, running a hand through his sun-bleached, sandy hair. "Looks as if you've got yourself into a real mess, Lori. Mom's so distraught by all this she's taken to her bed. As for Dad, we were really worried about him. His heart isn't as strong as it should be, you know."

Lori's fury at Cord gave way to guilt. "I'm sorry," she mumbled. "I hope he's all right."

"He'll live. It's Mom we're worried about," said Dennis.

Lori sent him an anxious glance. Right then he looked exactly like her father, right down to the thinning hair and widening paunch. "I talked to Mom on the phone and told her I was all right."

"You didn't tell her you were having some degenerate drifter's baby," Mike said coldly.

"Really, Lori," Richard said in a disgusted voice, "how could you?"

Shaken beyond belief at Cord's betrayal, she felt compelled nevertheless to defend him. "He's not degenerate," she said wearily, "and he's not a drifter."

"No?" Mike curled his lip. "Then you tell us what he is."

She made a supreme effort to collect her scattered wits. "Look, I've had a long day and I'm exhausted. I really don't want to have this discussion at all, but if you all insist, as I'm sure you will, I suggest we go back to the trailer, where I can sit down with a cup of tea, and I'll answer your questions as best I can."

"Trailer?" Dennis was horrified. "You mean you're living in a trailer?"

"With that derelict bum?" Mike exchanged a grim smile with Dennis. "Oh, we're really looking forward to meeting him. We just can't wait to get our hands on him."

"Sorry to disappoint you," Lori said dryly, "but he won't be there. I share the trailer with a woman, who won't be there, either, right now. So, are we going to be civilized about this or do I have to call security to throw you all out?"

To her immense satisfaction she saw amazement mirrored in all three faces. Without waiting to give the three men a chance to answer, she brushed between her two brothers and marched resolutely over to the trailer.

All three men waited in silence while she fitted the key in the lock and opened the door. She led the way in, throwing her purse down on the armchair as she passed it on her way to the tiny kitchen.

What she really needed was a drink, she thought, sending a longing look at the fridge, which she knew contained at least a couple of bottles of decent chardonnay. Since that was out of the question, however, tea would have to do. She filled the small kettle with water and set it on the stove, then turned on the gas ring. The comforting pop seemed to steady her nerves, and she turned to face the three men, who were standing close together, looking for all the world as though they needed one another's protection.

The thought strengthened her resolve. She saw Mike give a disparaging glance around the place she now called home, and she tightened her lips. "All right," she said quietly, "you can sit down. You won't find any bugs on the furniture, if that's what you're concerned about."

Richard sat first, on the edge of the bench seat. After a moment's hesitation, Dennis sat next to him, while Mike took one of the armchairs.

"You look terrible," Mike said, as she slipped out of her jacket. "You've lost weight and your hair is a mess."

"Mom would never recognize you," Dennis agreed.

"I hardly recognized you," Richard added.

His whining voice made Lori wonder how she could have not noticed it before.

"I'm not surprised," Mike said, leaning back in the chair with his hands crossed over his chest. "What else can you expect, working in a dump like this?"

"How could you do this, Lori?" Richard chimed in. "In a rodeo of all places. It's so horribly degrading."

"It's no wonder one of those damn drifters took advantage of you," Dennis said, giving her a disgusted look. "I'm just surprised he had the nerve to call and tell us. He probably wants to get rid of you and figured that was about the only way he could do it."

"I'm amazed that you lasted this long." Mike gave another disapproving glance around the room. "Living in a hovel like this, surrounded by degenerates, sleeping with bums…you must be afraid to close your eyes at night. What the hell were you thinking of, Lori?"

"That's enough!" Lori's voice rang out, making all three men jump. Seething with anger, she stepped into the middle of the room. "Exactly why are you all here?" she demanded.

"I should think that's obvious." Mike sent her one of his lofty smiles. "We've come to rescue you from the bastard who did this to you. We're going to take you home, where you belong."

"Dad has talked to a physician who's willing to…help out with your little problem," Dennis said delicately.

"And I'm prepared to forgive you," Richard announced.

Lori swung on him. "And what does that mean?"

Richard seemed taken aback. "Well…er…" He fumbled with his tie. "I'm still willing to marry you. As long as you get rid of the baby, of course."

Of course. Lori felt sick as she stared at the insipid face of the man she almost married. "Well," she said icily, "I'm not getting rid of my *little problem,* and I'm not going to marry you. In fact, much as this might shock you, Richard, I wouldn't marry you if my life depended on it. I don't love you. I know now that I've never loved you. And I would never marry a man I didn't love."

While Richard sat watching her, his mouth opening and shutting like a starving goldfish, she turned on Dennis. "As for Dad, you can tell him where to stuff his physician. I'm keeping this baby. This is a living human being inside me, not some petty little nuisance that can be swept away with a wink and a generous check. I'm appalled and disgusted that any of you even considered such a thing. Especially you, Michael. You have children of your own. How can you condone murdering a member of your own family?"

"Now, wait a minute—" Mike began angrily.

But she cut him off with a gesture of her raised hand. "You can tell Mom that I don't need rescuing, as you put it, and I'm not coming home with you. This is my home now, and this is where I'll stay. I'm old enough to have a life of my own and I'm damn well going to live it without any help from any of you.''

"Now, hold on," Dennis said hotly. "You're our sister. We care about what happens to you. We all do."

"If you really care, you'll let me live my own life." She moved to the door and opened it. "I'll contact you when the baby is born, just so that Mom and Dad know they have a grandchild. Apart from that, I don't need your help, I don't need your advice and, most of all, I don't need your interference. I hope I've made myself perfectly clear."

Mike's mouth tightened, and he shoved himself to his feet. "Does that mean you're going to marry this drifter?"

She lifted her chin. "I've told you, he's not a drifter. He's a good man and would do a far better job of taking care of me and the baby than any of you. And what I plan to do is none of your business anyway. If I want to marry Cord McVane, I'll marry him without asking your permission."

"I suppose you know this will break Mom's heart," Mike said quietly.

Lori did her best to ignore the pang of guilt. "I'm sorry. I really am, Mike. But I can't live their lives anymore. I did that for too long already. Now I have to live mine."

"Just don't change your mind later on," Richard said stiffly as he got to his feet. "I'm not going to wait around for the rest of my life."

"I don't expect you to." She managed a weak smile. "Find a nice girl and settle down, Richard. Someone who'll really appreciate you."

"What about you?" Dennis demanded, as he followed the other two to the door. "Who's going to take care of you and the baby?"

"I am." For the first time since she'd discovered she was pregnant, she was sure of that. "I'll do just fine, Dennis. I've come a long way in the past few weeks. I'm finally standing on my own two feet, and I'm going to be just fine.''

She knew by the expression on his face that he didn't believe her. None of them did. She closed the door behind them, feeling an immense satisfaction at the way she'd stood up to them. That part of her life was over. She'd fought them all and she'd won.

It was a hollow victory at best, she admitted, as her momentary triumph faded. Her child would not have the benefit of a family to grow up with. No grandparents, no aunts and uncles. It was sad that they would all miss so much. But at least her baby would have the freedom to choose what he wanted to do with his life. There would be no one but her to tell him what to do, and she would be the last person on earth to dominate him.

She poured boiling water onto the tea bag she'd dropped into a cup, then sat with the steaming cup in her hands, trying to put some warmth back in her body. She felt frozen inside. Numb with shock and pain. Cord had broken his promise to her. He'd not only told them where to find her, he'd told them she was pregnant with his baby. The ultimate betrayal.

When she thought about what her father wanted her to do, she shuddered. If Cord knew what her father had in mind, would he still insist on her going back? She sincerely doubted it. Cord had done this because of the baby. He was willing to let her go out of his life if it meant security for the baby. He was still telling her what to do, still trying to control her life.

As long as she was around he'd go on doing that, she thought dismally. He felt he had a right to dictate to her because she was carrying his child. How long would it be until he wore her down and persuaded her to marry him? It would be so easy to give in, loving him as she did.

She had no doubt in her mind that it would be the biggest mistake of them all. For both of them. She couldn't let him manipulate her like that, and she couldn't let him sacrifice his own happiness because of something that was ultimately her mistake. She had to get out of his life. Now.

She jumped to her feet and dropped the empty cup on the counter. He'd be upset at first, but eventually he'd realize she'd done him a favor. He could go on with his life as if she'd never existed. He wouldn't have to feel responsible for her anymore. She'd let him know when the baby was born, and somehow they'd work things out with a lawyer. But right now, she had to put as much distance between them as she could manage.

Feverishly she stuffed clothes into the garment bag she'd bought with her first paycheck. When it was full she left the rest, figuring that Kristi could send them on to her when she was settled. She put a note for her friend on the counter, telling her only that she had decided to quit the circuit and find a steadier job. She would get in touch with her later. Then she let herself out of the trailer and crossed the street to the steak house, where she used the phone to call a cab.

The twenty minutes she waited for the cab to arrive seemed the longest of her life. More than once the urge to run back to the safety of the arena became almost unbearable.

She had to force herself to consider what her life would be like living with a man who didn't love her. A man who would one day resent the fact that he'd been obliged to give up his freedom and the life he loved because of her mistake. She would have to suffer her heartbreak a day at a time, watching their relationship gradually wear away until nothing was left.

Then what? Could she bear to leave him then, knowing his child would share her heartbreak? Or would she have the strength to stay, knowing that every day she was making all their lives more miserable? Either way, the prospects were unacceptable.

She would rather the break came now, happening all at once, swiftly and mercifully. It was going to hurt pretty badly, she had no illusions about that. But she would survive. And so would her child. And that was what was important.

At last the cab pulled up at the door, and she stepped inside, feeling as if she were leaving everything she loved in the world behind. Everything except one thing—the tiny life growing inside her. For her baby's sake she could do this, she told herself. For everyone's sake.

Cord sat on the fence with the rest of the cowboys waiting for their ride and tried to focus his concentration. He was next up, and he felt about as ready to ride as he was to walk in quicksand over hell. His body just wouldn't obey his mind anymore, and no matter what he did, nothing would shut out the look he'd seen on Lori's face that first day at the cabin when she'd talked about her family coming to look for her.

The second he'd made that call he'd regretted it. He had to be plumb crazy to do such a fool thing. He'd thought about going to Lori and warning her about what he'd done. But then he'd been scared she would run off and he'd never know where to find her. When he'd called her father and told him he wanted to marry his daughter, Mr. Ashford hadn't committed himself either way. He'd been shocked to hear about the baby, but when Cord had explained that he needed help in convincing Lori to marry him, all her father said was that he'd send her brothers to talk to her.

Cord glanced up at the clock, his stomach churning. They'd told him they'd be there by early evening at the latest. They could well be talking to her right now. All he could hope for was that they'd make her see sense. He'd take his ride, he decided, then he'd go right over to the trailer and face the music. He had no doubt in his mind that she'd be madder than a wet rooster, but once she calmed down she had to see that it was the right thing to do.

"You gonna sit there all night, McVane, or are you planning on taking that ride?"

Cord started at the sound of Jed's voice behind his back. He swung his legs around and jumped to the ground, avoiding his partner's probing gaze. "So what's your all-fired hurry?" he muttered, before ambling over to the chutes where two laborers waited to help him mount his ride.

His bones ached as he climbed up on the fence. He'd lost the heart to do this night after night, he told himself. His body wouldn't take much more. It was well-known around the circuit that bareback riders suffered more punishment, were injured more often and ended up with more permanent damage than all the other rodeo cowboys combined.

The ride was always pure torture, putting an immense strain on muscles and joints, pulling and twisting ligaments mercilessly. The trick was to look good while taking all that punishment. That was the part that Cord was finding harder and harder to achieve.

He stared down moodily at the shifting, restless back of the horse while the laborers placed the rigging over the animal's withers and secured it with a winch. They pulled back out of the way and he took a deep breath, then dropped onto the horse. The animal lurched beneath him, and he grabbed the rigging, tightening his fingers into a hard fist.

He thrust his feet forward, concentrating on raising them above the break of the horse's shoulders. If his feet were in the wrong position when the horse hit the ground out of the chute, he'd be disqualified before he'd begun the ride for not marking out his horse properly.

Raising his free hand, he gave a sharp nod. The gate opened and he was through. The bronc bucked, and Cord drew his knees up to spur the horse's shoulders, then thrust his feet forward again as the animal plunged back to earth. His spine lay along the entire back of the horse for a split second, then he was into the next jump.

His timing was off. He knew it the second the horse's rear end rose sharply behind him, throwing him forward. Out of the corner of his eye he saw the pickup man thundering toward him, but by then the ground was coming up to meet him.

He landed on his side, and the deadly hooves came down inches from his head. His shoulder hurt like hell…the same shoulder that had sent him to the cabin and into the life of a rebellious, independent, tantalizing young woman by the name of Lori Ashford.

He had to see her. He had to tell her why he'd called her family. He looked up at the face of the pickup man and smiled. He knew what he wanted. All he had to do was convince Lori.

"You okay, buddy?"

He nodded, wincing as pain shot through his head. He saw Jed peering anxiously over the pickup man's shoulder. "Sorry, J.C.," he muttered, "but you're not getting rid of me just yet." He blinked, wondering why the lights were growing dim. His stomach heaved, and he struggled to sit up, afraid he was going to puke in front of the crowd. The world tilted, and he closed his eyes.

Vaguely he heard Jed's voice, sharply demanding an ambulance. He tried to tell him he was okay, but the words wouldn't come. His tongue seemed to be sticking to the roof of his mouth. The roar of the crowd above the music seemed to ebb and flow like the sound of Pacific rollers on an empty beach. He smiled to himself, wondering when he'd become so poetic. Then the sound slipped away altogether, and the world went still.

When he opened his eyes again he was lying on a hospital bed in a small, darkened room. Someone moved at his side, and Jed's tanned face swam into view.

"Hey, buddy," he said softly, "how's the headache?"

Cord blinked, trying to get his mind working again. "What happened?"

"You passed out in the ring. Concussion. Doc says you're going to be fine in a day or two."

Cord lifted his arm out from the under covers and winced. "My shoulder?"

"You didn't break it, but it's going to give you some pain for a while." Jed reached out and stabbed at the button above Cord's head. "That should bring someone."

"Good," Cord mumbled. "I've got to get out of here. Where are my clothes?"

"Hold on, pardner, you're not going anywhere. Not until the doc says you can, anyhow."

"The hell I'm not." Cord glanced around for a clock. "How long have I been in here?"

"All night."

"It's morning?"

"Getting there."

Cord narrowed his eyes. "Have you been here all night?"

Jed nodded. "Don't look like that," he said gruffly. "I've been having fun passing time with a pretty nurse down the hall."

Cord managed a grin, knowing it was a lie. "Thanks, J.C. I owe you one."

The door opened suddenly, and a nurse hurried in carrying a small tray. "Mr. McVane! How are you feeling?"

"Never felt better. Where are my clothes?"

"Now, we don't need to be in such a hurry, do we?"

Cord opened his mouth to answer, and she popped a thermometer in it. "Under your tongue," she said briskly, then kept her gaze on the monitor in her hand until it beeped. "Let's see."

Cord scowled at Jed's grinning face.

"Good." The nurse tucked the thermometer back in its pocket, then picked up the blood pressure monitor. "Now, this won't take a minute."

Cord tried to curb his impatience, knowing he'd send his blood pressure up if he didn't.

Apparently satisfied, the nurse nodded. "You're doing just fine. The doctor will be in to see you shortly."

"Before you go," Cord said pleasantly, "I need my pants."

She nodded at a small closet across the room. "Your belongings are in there. But I don't want you getting out of bed until the doctor has seen you."

Cord gave her a blank look, and she glanced at Jed, then hurried from the room.

"All right," Cord said, throwing back the covers, "help me get dressed."

"You know better than that," Jed said firmly. "Concussion can be dangerous. You need to stay put for a day or two. You're not in any shape to ride today anyway."

"I don't want to ride," Cord said, easing his legs out of the bed. "I have something else in mind."

"Will you at least wait until the doc gets here?"

"That could take all morning. I don't have all morning."

"What in tarnation is so all-fired important that you have to risk your neck to get to it?"

"You'll know before too long." Cord got to his feet, surprised to see the room swimming around him. He sat down heavily on the edge of the bed again. "I need aspirin," he muttered.

"What you need is a new head," Jed muttered. "One with brains in it, preferably. Get back in that damn bed. I'm not going to let you leave here, and you're in no shape to put up a fight."

Cord buried his head in his hands for a moment. "Maybe you're right," he mumbled. "Maybe I'd better wait for the doctor."

"Now you're finally talking sense." Jed got to his feet. "I'm going to get a cup of coffee. I'll be back in a while to check on you, then I have to get back to the trailer and take a shower."

Cord nodded. "You go ahead. I'll be okay."

Jed eyed him doubtfully. "I won't be long."

Cord waited for a minute or two after Jed had left, just to make sure his partner didn't double back and check on him. Then, moving slowly and carefully, he shuffled across to the closet and opened it.

It took him longer than normal to struggle into his clothes, but by the time he was dressed, he was beginning to feel a little steadier on his feet.

He opened the door gingerly and peered out into the corridor. Nurses were hurrying back and forth, but no one seemed to be looking in his direction. There was an exit door just a few yards away. He stepped out into the corridor and walked casually toward it, half expecting someone to call out behind his back.

The door led onto some stairs, and he took a moment to steady himself, before stepping down them one at a time. He reached the floor below, thankful to see it was the ground floor. The outside door opened onto the parking lot, and he was tempted to go right on through it. He needed to call a cab, however, and he'd have to do it from the lobby.

He opened the opposite door and stepped into another corridor. It was deserted, and he headed for the lobby. He felt slightly off balance and did his best not to appear as though he'd just swallowed an entire fifth of scotch as he walked into the busy reception area.

He found the row of telephones, two of which were being used. He had almost reached the third one when a familiar voice halted him.

"Cord! I was just coming to see you. I thought you had a concussion or something."

He turned to face Kristi, who stood self-consciously holding a couple of balloons with pictures on them of sad-looking bloodhounds. Emblazoned above the dogs' heads were the words Get Well Soon.

"I saw them in the gift shop," she said, handing them to him. "I thought they were cute."

"Real cute." He took them from her, vowing to give them to the first kid he saw.

"So they're letting you out? Jed said you'd be in here a couple of days."

"Guess my head's harder than Jed thinks."

"I guess so." Kristi glanced across the lobby, then up at the ceiling, then finally down at the floor.

Cord narrowed his eyes. "Something wrong?"

She seemed uncomfortable. "I just wanted to say I'm

sorry about Lori. I know you cared about her. If you want my opinion, I think she was crazy to walk away.''

Cord went very still. ''Walk away?''

Kristi sent another hunted look across the lobby. ''Well… I know you wanted to marry her. She told me. I can understand why she left, but—''

''Wait a minute.'' He stared hard at Kristi, the cold feeling in his stomach spreading rapidly over his body. ''What do you mean… 'left'?''

Kristi dug in her pocket and pulled out a crumpled note. ''Here. I thought you knew. I'm so sorry.'' She turned away, pretending to be interested in watching a small child argue with his mother while Cord scanned the note.

The words blurred as he read them, and once more the room began to float around him. Lori was gone. And he had no idea where to start looking for her.

Chapter 12

Cord remembered little of the next two days. Jed told him afterward that he'd collapsed on the floor of the lobby and it had taken two medics and a remarkably tough nurse to get him back to his room.

He'd drifted in and out of a drugged sleep, and when he finally woke up on the third day, his headache had disappeared and his vision was back to normal. The doctor told him that he was lucky he hadn't had a brain hemorrhage. He guardedly agreed to release Cord, but not before giving him a strong warning to take better care of himself.

Jed picked him up and took him down to Arizona, where the last rodeo of the season was being held before the finals. The first thing Cord did when he got back to the trailer was call Lori's parents. He hated to worry them, but he had to know if there was any chance she'd taken his advice and gone back to live with them.

Lori's father answered the phone, and was shocked to hear that his daughter had apparently disappeared again without a trace. "I had no idea she'd left the rodeo," he told Cord, after Cord had explained who he was. "The last thing I heard was that she planned on staying there. Her brothers were absolutely certain on that point. I understand she wasn't too happy to see them."

Cord winced as guilt stabbed at him. This was all his fault. In his anxiety to make sure that Lori and the baby would be properly taken care of, he'd messed up real good. She was probably mad as hell at him, but he hadn't for one minute figured she was steamed enough to run off without one word to anyone about where she was going.

Now she was out there somewhere alone and he was responsible. If anything happened to her or the baby, it would be entirely his fault. "I don't understand why she took off like that," he said guardedly, "unless it had something to do with her brothers showing up. Did they tell you what happened that night?"

"I can tell you one thing—she wasn't running away from her brothers. According to my sons, Lori stood up to them and told them to quit interfering in her life. She more or less threw them out. They left convinced that she'd gotten everything together and was in total charge of her life. I must say, I was impressed. It made me feel a lot better about Lori being able to take care of herself." Mr. Ashford paused. "Of course, now that she's on her own and pregnant, that will make things more difficult for her. Somehow, though, I have the feeling that she'll manage just fine."

"I don't want her to manage without me," Cord said, hoping this man he'd never met would understand. "I'm going to find her, and when I do, I'm not going to let her go again."

"I think that's up to Lori to decide," her father said quietly. "And by all accounts, she's quite capable of doing that now. I wish you luck, however, and if there's anything

I can do to help, I'll be more than happy to do what I can. I have to tell you, though, that my daughter's happiness is paramount as far as I'm concerned. If she doesn't want to marry you, then I must ask you to respect her wishes and not hound her. I have the feeling she's had more than enough of that in her life.''

Cord pushed away the fear. She had to listen to him this time. Now that he finally knew what he wanted, he couldn't bear the thought of losing it all again. ''I'm hoping she'll see things my way,'' he said. ''But if not, this time I'll walk away and she won't see me again.''

''Well, she won't be easy to find. She'd managed to hide herself very effectively before you told us where to find her. She did promise Mike that she would let us know when the baby was born. If you haven't caught up with her by then, maybe we can persuade her to come home for a visit. I'll let you know. That's really all I can do.''

Cord thanked him and hung up, feeling more depressed than ever. Lori's father had made it sound so damn hopeless. There had to be some way to track her down.

He went to Kristi's trailer, and found her packing up to leave for Las Vegas, where she planned to stay until the finals. She seemed pleased to see him but became wary when he questioned her about Lori.

''She didn't tell me where she was going,'' Kristi assured him. ''I didn't know she'd planned on leaving until I read the note.''

''You said at the hospital that day that you understood why she left. I need to know why.''

Kristi picked up a magazine and flipped through the pages before setting it down again. ''I guess I'm not really betraying a confidence,'' she said at last, ''seeing as how it concerns you.''

"I can guess. Did she, by any chance, leave because I kept bugging her to marry me?"

"That was part of it. You were asking her for all the wrong reasons."

His depression cut deeper into his soul. "All I wanted to do was make sure she and the baby were taken care of properly. I wasn't asking her for a forever kind of thing…just long enough until she could make it on her own. I wanted to give that baby my name and put a ring on her finger so her family wouldn't look down on her, that's all. Was that such a crime?"

Kristi gave him a long look. "How can you be so smart about some things and so dense about others?"

He scowled. "What the hell are you talking about?"

She shook her head. "I'm talking about love, you moron. You cowboys are all alike. Think you can own a woman without giving anything in return. That's all Lori ever wanted from you. Your love. When you couldn't give her that, she left. She didn't want to marry a man who couldn't love her the way she loved him."

Cord stared at her for a second or two, then grabbed both her arms and kissed her soundly on the cheek. "Thanks, sweetheart. I owe you one."

He let her go, and she brushed her cheek with the back of her hand. "Get out of here," she muttered, "and find her. Let me know when you do."

He started at the steak house across the street and hit it lucky on the first try. The waitress remembered Lori calling for a cab the night he had the fall. He checked with the cab service, and finally tracked down the driver who'd taken her to the bus station.

The ticket agent vaguely remembered a woman answering Lori's description boarding a bus for Los Angeles. And there the trail ended. L.A. was a big city. It was going to be near impossible to find her without a lot of luck.

He bought himself a dependable truck and said goodbye to Jed, promising to meet up at the finals in Las Vegas, which wasn't that far from L.A. Kristi gave him a boxful of Lori's clothes, saying she would need them when he finally caught up with her.

"Tell her I miss her," she told Cord, as he sat revving the engine of the pickup.

He nodded, not trusting himself to speak. He just prayed that he'd be able to deliver that message before his baby was born.

He set off on a cool, breezy November morning, heading south for L.A. He didn't know where he was going or where he would start looking. He knew only that somewhere out there was the one woman who could put any meaning in his life and he had to find her. He had to, or he would spend the rest of his life hating himself for what he'd thrown away.

Lori opened the door of her cramped apartment, longing for a cup of hot tea. The busy holiday season was in full swing, and the temporary job she'd taken at the large department store exhausted her. She had no idea that working behind the counter in men's clothing could be so tiring.

A good deal of her weariness came from depression, she knew. She was facing the holidays alone for the first time in her life. In spite of everything, she missed her family, and wished a thousand times that things could have been different and she could have gone home for Christmas.

She wouldn't let herself think about Cord and her friends on the rodeo circuit. Every day she passed a huge display of Western-style clothes in the men's department. Above the jeans hung an enormous poster of a cowboy in a black hat riding a bucking bronc. The first time she saw it she felt as if her heart were tearing apart, and she had refused to look at it since.

She spent Thanksgiving alone in her apartment in front of the tiny TV she'd bought with her discount. Her frozen dinner had stuck in her throat, and she'd thrown most of it away. That was her worst moment, and she had finally broken down and called her parents.

Her mother had cried and her father had started to say something about Cord, but she'd hung up before he could finish the sentence. She didn't want to hear about anything that had to do with Cord McVane. When the baby was born, she fully intended to hire a lawyer so they could work out the visitation rights. Much as she knew it would hurt, she could not deny him his child. Not after what had happened in his marriage.

Until then, however, she wanted to be left in peace. She needed time to forget how much she cared for him. By the time the baby arrived, she hoped to be able to face him without the searing agony of loving him.

The warm California sunshine helped a little, even though it felt strange to have summer weather at holiday time. Lori opened the window to let in the cool breeze and tried not to think about Seattle winds chilled by the snow from the mountains. She put the kettle on the gas ring and closed her mind to the memory of a broken-down old stove in a primitive cabin hundreds of miles to the north.

A calendar hung on the wall, left there by the previous tenant. Lori had let it hang there, oddly comforted by the cute pictures of teddy bears. She planned to buy a bear for the baby, for Christmas. She'd seen one in the store, and as soon as she got her next paycheck, she was going to bring it home. It would help to remind her why she was doing this—why she was living in this tiny apartment in Santa Monica, alone for the holidays.

She tore November off the calendar, and realized with a start that the finals in Las Vegas were just over a week off. Despite her best efforts to prevent it, the thought that Cord would probably be there cut off her breath. Less than three hundred miles away. A four-hour trip in the car. That's if her broken-down old clunker could make it.

In the next instant she cursed herself for even considering it. There was no way she could go to the finals. The wounds were still too fresh. It would just be too painful. She busied herself fixing the chicken salad she'd planned for her dinner. Her feet ached. She couldn't wait to sit down in front of the TV and relax for a while. Maybe she could forget that she'd have to start the whole dreary procedure all over again tomorrow.

At least she had the day off after that, she thought, as she settled herself on the rented couch. She had a little shopping to do, then she could sit down and write out the few cards she planned to send. Just to her family. With no return address.

She had barely finished her tea when the knocking on her door brought her to her feet. She'd been plagued lately with all kinds of people selling Christmas gifts door-to-door. Most of them were kids, and usually she enjoyed talking to them. Tonight, however, her weariness and depression made her reluctant to answer.

The pounding was renewed. More urgent this time. Lori frowned. As a rule, if she didn't answer right away, her caller left, figuring that she was out. Warily she went to the door and opened it carefully, ready to slam it again if the visitor was unwelcome.

At first she didn't recognize him. The sun was low in the sky, shining directly into her eyes through the sparse branches of the palm tree in the courtyard. All she saw was the silhouette of a tall figure in a black cowboy hat. When she realized who he was, she might have slammed the door anyway, if it hadn't been for the sudden, quick movement of his hand.

"Don't send me away, Lori. Not until you've heard what I've come to say."

Her hands felt cold, in spite of the warmth from the setting sun. She had to force her frozen lips to move. "How did you find me?"

"Let me in and I'll explain everything."

The last thing she wanted was to let him into her home. She didn't want to hear what Cord McVane had to say. She didn't want to know all the logical reasons she should marry him. How could she possibly be logical about loving him?

She didn't want to look at his face, hear his voice or see the fierce determination in his black gaze. If she did, she wasn't sure she could stay strong any longer. "Go away," she whispered. "I don't want to talk to you." She tried to close the door, but the pressure of his hand held it open.

"Just ten minutes, Lori. That's all I ask. After that, if you want me to leave, I'll walk out and I'll never come back. I promise."

She blinked, torn with indecision. He was asking. Not ordering, commanding or telling her what to do. He was asking. Her resolve crumbled. "All right," she muttered. "Ten minutes, that's all."

The second he was inside the apartment she regretted giving in. Her first good look at him triggered waves of pain that almost made her cry out. Judging from his appearance, he hadn't slept in a week. He badly needed a shave, and the shadows under his eyes were dark and ominous. She wanted to walk into his arms so desperately she could hardly stand it. "Have you been sick?" she blurted out, then wished she hadn't when his hard gaze softened.

"Are you telling me I look bad?"

She could take anything but his teasing. She turned away, not trusting herself any longer. "No. You look...tired."

He nodded. "I haven't slept good lately."

Neither had she, but she wasn't about to admit it. "How did you find me?" she asked again.

He glanced around her small but neat living room. "Can we sit down?"

She eyed him warily. She wasn't used to this new attitude. The Cord she knew did what he wanted without asking permission from anyone. She waved at her one and only armchair. "Would you like a soda? I don't have any beer."

"Nothing. Thanks." He took off his hat, dropped it on the coffee table, then sat down with his hands pushed between his knees.

Only then did she realize how tense he was. She longed to massage his hunched shoulders. She sat down on the very end of the couch in an effort to put some space between them. She waited, though she wasn't sure for what. She wished he hadn't come. How could she forget her feelings for him if he insisted on popping back in her life?

For a moment her resentment bolstered her resolve, but all her convictions melted rapidly away again when he said quietly, "Your father told me where to find you."

She looked at him then, shocked to the core. "My *father?* How did he know where I was? Why would he tell you?"

Cord stared down at his hands for a moment, his lips pursed. "I called him when I got out of the hospital. I got a concussion the night you left and was in the hospital for three days."

She hadn't been able to stop the tiny cry of dismay at his words. She struggled to hold on to what little composure she had left. "I'm sorry. What happened?"

He shrugged. "I came off my ride and hit my head. I don't remember a whole lot. I tried to leave the hospital that first day. I met Kristi in the lobby and she told me you'd gone. That was right before I passed out. The next couple of days are not much more than a blur."

"I'm sorry" she said again.

"No big deal. Getting bruised up is part of the business. I'm used to it."

She didn't say so, but she couldn't help wondering if the shock of hearing she'd left had aggravated his injury. The thought increased her misery. "I still don't understand what my father has to do with this."

Cord sighed. "I called him to see if you'd gone back home. He told me your brothers came to see you."

She tightened her mouth. "Richard, too, thanks to you."

His gaze flicked to meet hers, then he looked back at his hands. "I'm sorry. I thought at the time I was doing the right thing. I guess I didn't think things through very well."

"Nobody ever does," she said bitterly.

"Your father says you threw them out."

"My father said that?" She almost smiled. "I'm surprised they told him."

"I reckon you did a little surprising of your own."

"I guess I've grown up," she said quietly. "I finally learned to stand up for myself and what I believe in. It's a good feeling."

He nodded. "That's a good thing. As long as you don't take it too far."

Immediately she was on the defensive. "What does that mean?"

"It means that sometimes you're so damn stubborn you can't see what's right in front of you. Just like me."

"No one could possibly be as ornery as Cord McVane."

He looked up then, and the expression in his dark eyes made her treacherous heart race. "I've been looking for you, Lori. Ever since I got out of the hospital. I tracked you down to L.A., but for a while I was stuck in front of a blank wall. I called your folks again to see if they'd heard from you, and I left my number with them. When you phoned them last week, your father had the call traced. He got the area but not the address. He told me where to start looking. I've been checking at every apartment building in five square miles of this place. There are a hell of a lot of apartments."

"I know." She dragged her gaze away from his mesmerizing eyes. "I'm surprised my father told you anything. When I talked to my brothers they were all set to rescue me from you and take me home."

"I reckon you said something to change their minds." He paused, then added quietly, "I'd really like to know what that was."

She wasn't about to tell him. Most of it had been bravado anyway. There was no need to tell him she'd deliberately left her brothers and Richard with the impression she was going to marry him. She would have told her brothers anything to get rid of them. "I don't remember what I said, and I'm sorry you went to all that trouble. I'm not going to change my mind, Cord. I'm not going to marry you."

She sat through the long silence that followed, squeezing her hands together so hard her fingers were numb. *Please go,* she silently begged. *Just go away now and let me cry in peace.*

"Lori."

His voice was husky with emotion and her breath stopped.

"Please," she whispered. "Please don't."

"Oh, God, Lori, I've missed you."

"Cord—"

"No, wait." He slid off the chair and knelt in front of her, his hands reaching for hers. She tried to pull them away, but he held on tight. "Lori, look at me."

Reluctantly she met his steady gaze.

"I'm sorry I called your folks. I reckon I broke my promise to you, but I was afraid that if they didn't persuade you to marry me I'd end up losing you. I was afraid you'd just take off without letting me know where you were. Then you did it anyway."

"I had to leave, Cord. I couldn't let you go on controlling my life."

He sighed. "I'm not trying to control your life, Lori. The problem is you're so damn scared I'll put chains on you the way your family did you won't let me take care of you. Everyone needs someone to care about them."

Again she tried to pull her hands free, but he would not let her go. "You're not worried about me," she said fiercely. "You're scared to death I'll take the baby away from me, just like your wife did. You don't have to worry. I told you that we'll work out the visitation rights. I plan to do that, but it will have to be enough."

"It's not enough." He drew closer to her, holding her fast. "You're wrong, Lori. This isn't about the baby. It's about you and me. The baby just makes it all the more special. I don't want visitation rights. I want to be a permanent part of your life. I want to grow old with you. I want a house to live in, instead of a trailer on an empty road. I want dogs, and kids, and a wife who'll love me and be happy to see me. I want someone who needs me, the way I need you. Most of all, I want to take care of you. Give me a chance and I'll prove I don't need chains to make you happy. I just need your love.''

She tried to say something, but he stopped her with a finger on her lips. ''Let me finish. You don't have to marry me. I'll understand if you don't want to. Just let me love you and take care of you. I do love you, Lori. You have to believe that. Without you I've got nothing. I'm sorry I took so long to realize that, but for the longest time I figured you couldn't possibly be interested in a broken-down, has-been cowboy like me. I was afraid to admit I loved you.''

She'd started crying right about the time he'd said he wanted to grow old with her. By the time he was finished she was beyond words. She leaned forward, instead, and pressed her lips to his.

With a muttered exclamation he closed his arms around her and claimed her mouth with the same fierce, demanding passion that had swept her away that night in the cabin so long ago. This was the Cord she knew and loved—the conqueror, the master, the lord of her heart. This was the man who knew how to make her body throb with desire and her mind explode with excitement. This was the man, the only man, she could ever love. And now, at last, he was hers.

The kiss lengthened, became more insistent, more demanding. Her body caught fire, and she searched for the buttons of his shirt, and, finding them, dragged them open in a feverish haste to get to his bare skin.

He pulled back, breathing hard, and imprisoned her hands in his own. ''Dammit, Lori, you're making it real difficult to keep my hands off you.''

''You made me that way.''

''Yeah.'' He grinned. ''I remember.''

''So what's keeping you?''

He looked uncertain. "I guess I don't want to hurt you."

She pressed another kiss on his mouth. "You won't hurt me this time."

"No, I mean...the baby."

"Oh." She smiled. "It's all right. The doctor told me it would be okay."

Cord frowned. "Why would he tell you that?"

"He was a she, and she didn't know I wasn't married."

"Oh." He nodded seriously. "That's something we gotta talk about. I know I said you don't have to marry me, but I gotta tell you, I'd really like for the baby to have my name. Though I reckon we could do that without getting married."

She pretended to think about it, while her heart and soul soared with happiness. "Well, you know," she said finally, "since you're going to be in Las Vegas for the finals, I guess we could get married there without too much fuss."

For a moment she could swear she saw tears in his eyes.

"I swear I'll make you happy. I won't hold you back on anything, because I figure you can handle whatever comes along." Once more he gathered her into his arms and spun her senses with his kisses.

When she could wait no longer, she pushed him down to the floor.

"What are you doing to me?" he muttered, when she reached for the buckle at his waist.

"Seducing you," she whispered back. "I want to make sure I haven't forgotten anything since the last time."

He looked up at her, a grin tugging at his mouth. "Wouldn't a bed be more comfortable?"

"Maybe." She tugged his jeans down over his hips. "But I can't wait that long. I've waited much too long as it is."

"I reckon I can oblige you on that score. Come here."

He pulled her down on top of him. "If I recall, the last time we tried this you were underneath me."

She rested her weight on him while she wriggled out of her pants. "I'm ready to try something new." She spread her knees and straddled him. "I'm a fast learner."

His soft groan as she settled herself onto him echoed in sizzling excitement throughout her body. "Yeah?" he muttered. "Well, I just happen to be one hell of a teacher."

She lowered her mouth to his, barely touching his lips. "Well, Teach, bring on the next lesson. We might just learn something from each other." She began moving on him, slowly and deeply, matching his rhythm with her own. Within seconds her advantage was lost as his passion exploded, and once again he took over, rolling her under him with a swift, fierce urgency that captured her senses.

She gave herself up to him, willing to go wherever he chose to take her. As long as she had his love, she could trust herself in his hands. She could accept all that he had to offer, knowing that he wanted what she wanted—to love and be loved. It was as simple as that.

Much later, as they sat together on the couch in the darkened room, he brought up the subject she'd avoided thinking about. "What about your folks? I reckon they'll want to be at the wedding."

She leaned against him, her back against his chest. "I don't know if I want them there. Especially after the things Mike called you. Did you know my father wanted me to get rid of the baby?"

His voice sounded strangled when he answered. "I'm sure glad you didn't listen to him."

"So am I." She patted her belly. "The old Lori would have blindly obeyed him."

He kissed the top of her head. "The old Lori wouldn't be pregnant with my son."

She smiled. "It could be a girl, you know."

"Yeah. I'd like that."

"Me, too."

"I still think you should invite your folks to the wedding. Your father did help me find you. I got the feeling he has a whole lot more respect for you now."

She twisted her head to give him a hard look.

"I'm not telling you what to do," he added dryly. "I'm just telling you what I'm thinking."

"My mother will want to run the whole thing. She'll probably insist that we wait and get married properly in Seattle."

"Then I reckon you'll tell her you're getting married next week in Las Vegas, with or without her blessing. Right?"

She grinned. "I have a better idea. Let's get married the day after tomorrow. It's my day off. We can be there by the afternoon. That should give us time to pick up the license and get to the chapel. I'll tell my parents that if they want to see me married, they'll have to be at the chapel when we are. Then they can decide if they want to come."

He nodded. "Sounds like a good plan. Except for one thing. What about your job? I'd have to stay on in Las Vegas for the finals and I sure as hell don't want to stay there without my wife."

She tilted her head to one side. "I guess I'll have to quit."

"I reckon that's up to you."

"I didn't like it anyway." She looked at him anxiously. "Will you be disappointed if my family don't come to the wedding?"

"Will you?"

"Yes," she said honestly. "I think I will. But I won't let it spoil our day."

"I guess I'll ask Jed to be my best man. He's already in Las Vegas. Been there about a week or so."

"So has Kristi. Do you think she'd be my bridesmaid?" She sat up, caught up in the excitement. "This is going to be so much fun."

"Not half as much fun as the honeymoon."

She looked at him in delight. "We get to have a honeymoon?"

"If you don't mind waiting until after the finals."

"Where will we go?"

"Anywhere in the world you want."

She thought about it, awed by such an impressive choice. "You know, I think I'd like to spend our honeymoon in the cabin," she announced at last.

He let out a roar of laughter. "I offer her Hawaii, China, Europe, the Caribbean, and she chooses a broken-down old shack in the mountains."

She waited for his laughter to subside, then said quietly, "I wanted so much to be the kind of woman you'd want when we were there. I'd like to go back now, knowing that I am that woman."

His eyes softened, and he brushed her lips with his. "It's snowing up there."

She returned the kiss. "All the more cozy."

"You got it, ma'am. We'll leave right after the finals." He stretched an arm above his head and yawned. "If I'm going to quit, I'd like to go out in style. I reckon that if I can win the bareback finals, I'll just have enough to squeeze into the all-around."

"Of course we'll wait until after the finals." She studied his face anxiously. "Will you miss the rodeo?"

"Well, as a matter of fact, that's something I wanted to talk to you about."

She felt a small leap of anticipation. She hadn't admitted

it to herself until now, but she knew she'd miss the excitement, the travel and the unpredictable life on the circuit. On the other hand, she didn't like the idea of watching him risk life and limb on the back of a horse too much longer. "You've decided not to give it up?"

"Oh, I'm giving up riding rodeo, all right." His dark eyes crinkled at the edges. "This old body of mine won't take much more of that punishment."

"Well, that's a relief."

"I thought you liked watching the show."

"I do, but not if it's my husband being trampled by a bad-tempered horse."

"Well, you won't have to worry on that score. I've been talking to Kristi. Her father's thinking of retiring from the producing side of the business and concentrating on raising stock. I did think I might try my hand at producing. Maybe you could help me out when you're not attending to the kids. We wouldn't have to travel that much, unless you wanted to—"

He broke off when she gave him a meaningful look. "It's just a suggestion," he added hurriedly. "We don't have to do it unless you want. There're lots of other things I can do...."

"I think it's a great idea," she said evenly. "And I'd love to help you when I'm not taking care of the kids."

He looked at her uncertainly. "Well, that's great, but why are you glaring at me like that?"

"Who said we were going to have more babies? Aren't you taking a whole lot for granted?"

His face cleared, and a gleam appeared in his eyes as he drew her close. "Well, I reckon if you're going to make a habit of seducing me, we're likely to end up with a whole brood of little 'uns."

"Hmm, I'll have to think about that." She placed her

hands on either side of his head and kissed him hard on his mouth. "I'm not sure how I like the idea of raising a whole team of rodeo men."

"Like you pointed out, they could be rodeo women."

She grinned happily at him. "Well, now, that's a whole different thing."

"I had a feeling it would be." He sighed in resignation. "I'll be fighting off a bunch of cowboys if they all turn out as gorgeous as my wife."

"No, you won't," Lori said softly. "You'll be a wonderful father to them, and you'll teach them to be independent and strong. You'll be there if they need you to guide and advise them, but you'll let them make their own choices and learn by their mistakes."

"I hope they'll understand that now and then a man needs to protect the woman he loves."

"I'll make sure they do."

"Then I reckon it's a deal." He pulled her close to him and wrapped his arms around her. "So how about seducing me some more."

She went willingly, secure in his love. There would be times, she knew, when they'd butt heads, but they'd both learned from their mistakes in the past, and together they'd make a good life. She was sure of that now.

Epilogue

Lori stared at herself in the mirror of the tiny dressing room. Had it been only two days since she'd found her new life? In the whirl of phone calls, shopping for clothes and making wedding arrangements, she'd barely had time to consider how her life was about to be changed forever.

In a few minutes, she would be walking down the aisle to join the man she loved. It all felt so unreal. Even the woman staring back at her in the mirror seemed like an image in a painting.

She wore her dark hair piled on top of her head, with tiny white pearls and baby's breath threaded through it. Her dress, bought the day before, was simple white satin, its short skirt swirling above her knees and the low, scooped neckline edged with embroidery and pearls. The wedding package had included a bouquet of red and white roses and a filmy white veil that reached her shoulder blades.

She didn't look like the Lori who'd lived in jeans and shirts for the past few weeks. Nor, she was thankful to note, did she look like the Lori who had stood like this in front of another mirror, worrying about another wedding that now seemed a lifetime away. The woman in the mirror gazing back at her was so much more serene, more confident, with a glow that radiated into every corner of the room.

The door opened abruptly, and she swung around, hardly recognizing the pretty young woman who entered. It was the first time she'd seen Kristi in a dress. The pale-blue silk made her appear feminine, and startlingly attractive. "You look fabulous," she told Lori, grinning at her. "Cord's going to fall apart when he sees you."

"You look pretty good yourself." Lori grinned back.

"Oh, by the way. Your family have arrived. Cord told me to let you know."

Lori felt a jump of apprehension. "I wasn't sure if they'd make it. Did my brothers come?"

"He didn't say."

Lori turned anxiously back to the mirror. "You're sure I look all right?"

"You look positively gorgeous."

A rap on the door made Lori's pulse skip. "I guess it's time," she said nervously.

She heard the opening strains of the music as she followed Kristi into the dimly lit chapel. Huge vases of flowers sat at the altar, where a single white candle flickered between two unlit ones at the side of the smiling priest.

Cord waited for her at the end of the aisle, impressive in his black tux, while Jed fidgeted at his side. Lori sent a glance to where her family sat, their heads turned to watch her walk down the aisle. They were all there...her mother and father, her three brothers and Mike's wife. She felt tears prick at her eyes and blinked them back. She would not cry at her wedding.

Cord's face lit up when he saw her, and his smile was the most beautiful sight she had ever seen. The service was short but meaningful, and as she and Cord each took a candle and lit them from a third, the significance of the ceremony almost overwhelmed her. She and this man were now joined as one. Together they would travel through life, raise their children and grow old together.

She turned to him as the priest announced they were man and wife, and his kiss sealed their union. "Hi, Mrs. McVane," he whispered. "I love you."

Again the tears threatened to fall. "I love you, too."

Together they turned to meet her family, who spilled out into the aisle as the music joyfully proclaimed the end of the service. Proud of her new husband, Lori couldn't wait to introduce him.

Her brothers shook his hand, though they all seemed somewhat distant, and her mother looked as if she were terrified of getting too close to Cord. Her father, however, clasped his hand and patted his shoulder. "Take care of her," he said gruffly.

"I intend to," Cord promised him.

Lori's mother offered her a polite hug, then sniffed and dabbed her nose. "I hope you'll visit us," she said, giving Lori a reproachful look.

"Of course we will." Lori turned to her father. "Thank you for coming."

"I wouldn't have missed my daughter's wedding for anything."

He held out his arms and she welcomed his hug. "Don't worry about the rest of them," he whispered in her ear. "Cord seems like a nice fellow. Just be happy. They'll come around."

She moved out of his arms and smiled at him. "Thanks, Dad."

She glanced up at her handsome husband, who held out his arm. "Shall we lead the way, Mrs. McVane?"

He led her out into the hallway, where there were a flurry of goodbyes, as everyone left in cars to head for the hotel where the reception was being held. Alone in the car at last with the man she loved so much, Lori snuggled up to his side. "Oh, Cord…we're going to have such a good life."

He gave her one of his rare, beautiful smiles. "You bet we are, sweetheart. A forever kind of life." He pulled her to him and kissed her, once more lighting the fires that always consumed her at his touch.

He was right, she thought dreamily. A forever kind of life and a forever kind of love. What more could she ask?

* * * * *

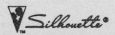

If you enjoyed what you just read,
then we've got an offer you can't resist!

Take 2 bestselling love stories FREE!

Plus get a FREE surprise gift!

Clip this page and mail it to Silhouette Reader Service™

IN U.S.A.	IN CANADA
3010 Walden Ave.	P.O. Box 609
P.O. Box 1867	Fort Erie, Ontario
Buffalo, N.Y. 14240-1867	L2A 5X3

YES! Please send me 2 free Silhouette Intimate Moments® novels and my free surprise gift. Then send me 6 brand-new novels every month, which I will receive months before they're available in stores. In the U.S.A., bill me at the bargain price of $3.57 plus 25¢ delivery per book and applicable sales tax, if any*. In Canada, bill me at the bargain price of $3.96 plus 25¢ delivery per book and applicable taxes**. That's the complete price and a savings of over 10% off the cover prices—what a great deal! I understand that accepting the 2 free books and gift places me under no obligation ever to buy any books. I can always return a shipment and cancel at any time. Even if I never buy another book from Silhouette, the 2 free books and gift are mine to keep forever. So why not take us up on our invitation. You'll be glad you did!

245 SEN CNFF
345 SEN CNFG

Name	(PLEASE PRINT)	
Address	Apt.#	
City	State/Prov.	Zip/Postal Code

* Terms and prices subject to change without notice. Sales tax applicable in N.Y.
** Canadian residents will be charged applicable provincial taxes and GST.
All orders subject to approval. Offer limited to one per household.
® are registered trademarks of Harlequin Enterprises Limited.

INMOM99   ©1998 Harlequin Enterprises Limited

COMING NEXT MONTH